"PERHAPS, STAR COMMANDER, YOU MISUNDERSTOOD THE QUESTION?"

Bast stood up. "You are a freeborn, after all. I forget that things must be spelled out. What I said, honored warrior, was that the Clan eugenics program produced superior warriors. Which, of course, means that it produces superior human beings. Therefore, *we* praise the eugenics program here, *quiaff?*"

Aidan knew that he must respond, but he could not say it. Why did a simple *aff* lodge in his throat?

Bast leaned toward Aidan, the stink of his breath rushing forward. "We praise the eugenics program here, *quiaff? QUIAFF*, you rotten freebirth!"

All restraint left Aidan in a rush. He grabbed Bast and roughly pulled him forward. Bast staggered backward. His eyes showed terrible pain. Aidan got Bast's neck between his forearm and squeezed it with a steady pressure. Then something in Bast's neck snapped and vision left his eyes forever. The man's body quickly slumped and Aidan threw him to the floor the way he would toss away litter.

BATTLETECH®

LEGEND OF THE JADE PHOENIX
VOLUME 2

BLOOD-NAME

ROBERT THURSTON

A ROC BOOK

ROC
Published by the Penguin Group
Penguin Books USA Inc., 375 Hudson Street,
New York, New York 10014, U.S.A.
Penguin Books Ltd, 27 Wrights Lane,
London W8 5TZ, England
Penguin Books Australia Ltd, Ringwood,
Victoria, Australia
Penguin Books Canada Ltd, 10 Alcorn Avenue,
Toronto, Ontario, Canada M4V 3B2
Penguin Books (N.Z.) Ltd, 182–190 Wairau Road,
Auckland 10, New Zealand

Penguin Books Ltd, Registered Offices:
Harmondsworth, Middlesex, England

First published by Roc, an imprint of Dutton Signet,
a division of Penguin Books USA Inc.

First Printing, October, 1991
10 9 8 7 6 5 4 3

Series Editor: Donna Ippolito
Cover: Bruce Jensen
Interior illustrations: Jeff Laubenstein
Mechanical drawings: Steve Venters

 REGISTERED TRADEMARK—MARCA REGISTRADA

Prologue

Some years previously, when Diana was still a child, she had learned many things about her father.

"He is of the Clan and yet not of the Clan," said her mother, whose name was Peri.

"I do not understand Clan," Diana piped, her voice clear and precise even at the age of four years. Though she often heard other children or lower-caste adults use contractions in their speech, Diana never did, nor even slurred her words so that childish sounds might be mistaken for contractions.

"Clan is what we are, what we belong to, what we are loyal to. The Clan provides for us, for all castes within it. It is the Clan that makes sure all have useful work, work that contributes to the common goals. Someday we of the Clans will return to take our rightful place in the Inner Sphere, restoring the Star League that once ruled all the stars in that vast space."

"What is the Inner Sphere? What is the Star League?"

"In time, Diana, you will learn about both, but in the proper places."

"What is wrong with this place?"

They were in a corner of a large laboratory, the largest at the science station on Tokasha, where Peri had worked as a lab tech for more than five years. Even though their quarters provided for child care, Diana considered the lab her real nursery, the place where she loved to come and sometimes play, but mostly inhabit just to be with Peri. She was at the stage of not wishing to be parted from her mother.

Freeborns were like that, said a portly man named Watson, the project leader on Tokasha. In a sibko, on the other hand, the children could only depend on one another; their alliances were intersib. Because freeborns usually had at least one known parent to care for them, their tendency was to stay close out of fear that the parent might be taken away—by death or by the Clan. Children learned very early that the Clan did not respect freeborn parentage and did not hesitate to separate parents from children. Even at age four, Diana feared that more than she feared monsters or shadows in the night.

It was a legitimate fear, as events turned out. When Diana was nine, Peri was assigned to the Main Science Center on Circe, where her work would not permit taking the child with her. Now a full-fledged scientist, Peri sent fewer and fewer communications to her daughter. Her specialty was the study of how sibko members went from childhood to warrior training to the Trial of Decision, where they got their one chance to become members of the warrior caste. For each stage Peri compiled data on how many sibko members did not succeed in the Trial and into what other roles in Clan life they were channeled. She was particularly concerned with how many cadets made it to the Trial (damn few, as it *always* turned out) and how many of those actually tested out to become warriors.

Diana's father had been a cadet who failed in the Trial, and one of Peri's goals was to establish for her own knowledge why that had happened. And, for that matter, Peri wanted to know why she herself had flushed out during one of the later stages of warrior training. (During this period, she often recalled the afternoon she had to leave the sibko barracks forever after flushing out, and the talk she had with the boy who would one day become Diana's father. As a result of that long-ago conversation Peri had conceived the ambition to do exactly the research that was now her work.) As her work began to absorb her more and more, the writing of reports superseded the writing of letters to her daughter. Her findings were, Peri was informed, an important contribution to a much larger project whose purpose was to discover methods to graduate more warriors from the sibko/cadet groups into the warrior caste.

Then Diana received her own assignment, and mother and daughter lost touch completely. But when Diana was four, they were still very close.

"There is nothing wrong with the laboratory," Peri said, smiling down at her daughter. "It is just the wrong place for you to learn about the Clan. There will be schoolrooms and training sessions and memory drills. You will know enough soon enough. Now is the time to be young."

"Tell me again the name of our Clan."

"We are the Jade Falcons."

"And what is a jade falcon?"

"A bird that may be mythical, although some claim to have sighted them and even trained them for the hunt. They fly high, it is said, and do not easily come down to ground level."

"Like my father."

Peri laughed. "Like your father. He wanted to be a great warrior, your father, but he tried a trick during what is called a Trial, a test by which warriors are chosen, and he lost his chance. Not long after, other warriors came here, to Tokasha, and took him away. I do not know what has happened to him since."

"And my father's name?"

Peri hesitated for a moment, but the child Diana could not have guessed that it was because her mother was uncertain about whether the child should know his name. In that brief instant, she must have decided it would do no harm, given the size of the Clan sector and all the possible planets where Aidan might eventually have gone.

"Aidan. His name is Aidan."

"I wish he would return to us."

"No, that would not be Clanlike. Whatever task he is fulfilling right now, he is a warrior at heart. He is from a sibko, which means that he did not have a mother and father, but was formed from what are called genes—and do not ask me to explain them. Warriors, even those reassigned to another caste, do not oversee their children, especially freeborn children.''

Peri had never told Diana that she had once belonged to the same sibko as Aidan, a fact that should have prevented her from ever giving birth to a child in the conventional manner. Being a scientist, however, Peri had been able to alter her own body chemistry so that she might know the freeborn privilege (she thought of it as a privilege, even if most trueborns would not) of childbirth. She had never fully understood why this had become so necessary. Having failed as a warrior, she had known almost immediately that if she would not be seeing life through the viewscreen of a BattleMech cockpit, then she would never be able to go it alone. Diana had been the solution to her loneliness.

Later, after Peri had more or less abandoned Diana, similar thinking had guided her. Seeing Diana's potential, Peri had reasoned that it was best to cut the cord of parentage and leave Diana to find her own way. Otherwise Peri's own need might someday make her do something that would hold the child back. It was not an easy decision, but she had made it with the coolness of one bred and trained to become a trueborn warrior.

''Mother?'' Diana asked after a long pause during which her brow was furrowed in what Peri knew was complicated thought. Diana was a specialist at complicated thought, very complicated for her age.

''Yes?''

''I do not think I want to be a scientist when I grow up.'' For the past year Diana had told Peri every day that she intended to be a scientist.

''Oh? And you would like to choose your caste? That is not like a freeborn, you know.''

''No, it is not. But I know what I want to be. I want to be a warrior.''

Peri's heart seemed to stop beating. These were not

words she wanted to hear. It had nothing to do with wanting less than the best for her daughter, and more to do with the kind of treatment suffered by the few freeborns who qualified for warrior training. Sometimes they had to become cannon fodder for sibko cadets, while the few who made it to the Trial of Decision would face even worse odds than trueborn cadets. Peri did not like the idea of Diana going into that kind of life. Warriors were the most honored members of the Clan, and even menials from the lowest castes dreamed of becoming warriors, but some maternal instinct made Peri want an easy life for her daughter. In the warrior caste, life was never easy, whether you were free- or trueborn.

"You have plenty of time to plan your life, Diana. Be four years old for now."

"I *am* four years old, mother."

"I know that. I mean—well, it does not matter what I mean. I see your father in your eyes. You will seek whatever you decide to seek. I cannot stop you."

Diana liked the last thing Peri said, and she would not let go of it for days. "You cannot stop me, mother. You cannot stop me."

Peri knew then how true that was, and she knew it later, when she had stopped communicating with Diana so that the girl could go on to warrior training without any complications. Yet Peri could not sever the bond completely. Though Diana would never know it, Peri maintained close observation of her daughter's career as she persevered through cadet training and became the warrior she had vowed to become at the age of four.

1

He was the picture of frustration, and his name was Kael Pershaw. For two years, for too long, he had been base commander of Glory Station, the Clan Jade Falcon encampment on the planet Glory. To his mind, the assignment might just as well have been to an asteroid in the farthest reaches of the universe. Though Glory was within each of the five original Clan worlds, it was still at the outer edge of the globular cluster, all those worlds that had become part of the Clan Empire. The Jade Falcons had only recently won half of Glory, the other half still awaiting challenge.

Even the planet's name seemed absurd to Pershaw. In this dreary place, the only glorious thing about Glory was its air. It was breathable, without need for adaptive mechanisms or uncomfortable implants to filter dangerous gases into air fit for humans. Pershaw had already done enough unpleasant time on the less atmospherically pleasant places during the peripatetic phases of his military career.

How Glory had earned its name was a mystery. Its mountains did not rise high, its lakes rarely shimmered, and its vegetation was often runty and sparse. The one distinctive geographical feature was a major jungle area near Glory Station, but even it was repellent and dangerous. Pershaw rarely left the main encampment, preferring to send others, preferably members of the freeborn Trinaries, out to such dangerous areas. It was not cowardice, but rather the certainty that his talents did not require him to risk his life except in major arenas. Was that not what it meant to be commander of a base?

Perhaps even more absurd were the forces Kael Pershaw could muster if another Clan demanded a Trial of Possession. Though his Cluster consisted of the usual four Trinaries, with three Stars each, only Striker Trinary was of any worth. Its complement of 15 trueborn warriors and 75 of the genetically bred infantry known as Elementals was too small a force to undertake any Trial of Possession. The other three Trinaries had BattleMechs only, and were barely fit for garrison duty. Piloting those 'Mechs were older trueborn warriors (who had settled for demotion rather than volunteering to get themselves killed in honorable fashion) and freebirths. Pershaw did not know which was worse. To top it off, the 'Mechs were so outdated that these Trinaries would be more hindrance than help in battle.

"Could you stop working for at least a few minutes?" came a voice behind him. It was Lanja, the warrior who served as his coregn, or aide. He had chosen her from the ranks, where Lanja was, in fact, a skilled warrior in line to be a Trinary commander. Besides being Pershaw's personal aide, Star Commander Lanja commanded Striker Trinary's Elementals. In selecting her as aide, Pershaw had chosen well. In the field, she commanded her armor-suited infantry in perfect consort with Pershaw's BattleMechs. In garrison, her administrative skills were equally complementary. Lanja was shrewd, efficient, and—as he had discovered—sexually skillful. A sexual liaison was not so unusual between two people in such a close working relationship, but it was not always so delightful. He would regret her forced departure at the end of the current contract. Pershaw could not form a new contract with her until another coregn had served a minimum period of time.

Though Lanja towered at least two heads over her commander, she was shorter than most of the Elementals she commanded. Pershaw sometimes teased her about having freeborn genes.

"I will always stop working for you," he said now, standing up to gather her in his arms. Even through her stiffly starched warrior uniform, Pershaw thought he could feel the soft curves of Lanja's body underneath.

He knew that he and Lanja were unusually passionate for Clan lovers. Had he not chanced upon a disk of some old Terran romances in a Brian Cache, Pershaw might never have known that human love could be intense and romantic. As a Clansman, he could barely grasp the idea of romance, but his liaison with Lanja was probably deeper than any he had ever known before—in casual sibko alliances, in previous relationships with warrior women, and in other coregns. In its way, their relation was as fathomless as any in those fanciful tales of love.

But Kael Pershaw was a warrior above all, and he did not relish the idea of someone stumbling into his office to find him and Lanja locked in an embrace. Perhaps that was why he let her out of his arms sooner than he wanted to.

Lanja brushed back some of her dark hair, which looked even blacker against her emerald green Jade Falcon headband. "Something is bothering you," she said, and her brow furrowed with worry. "The usual things?"

"In a way. The stagnation, I suppose you would call it."

"Stagnation is a good word, especially with Blood Swamp so near the camp." Perhaps it was the mere thought of the swamp that made her brush away an imaginary insect. Blood Swamp was not its real name, which was long-forgotten. From the first days of Glory Station, warriors stationed there had been struck by the reddish glint, almost like long, bloody streaks, cast by the reflection of Glory's moon shining over the swamp.

"You will be transferred someday," Lanja said. "I am sure of it."

"I know. Relocation and redeployment are Clan ideals, but I am not due for a while. I wish to go now.

I want to be in a place where there is reason to be a warrior. I am tired of prodding troops with fake conflicts, just to keep their skills honed. They need real combat, and so do I.''

"I had a dream that you were in combat. No, do not say it. My dreams. You do not believe in them. Even when you have seen them come true. Let us retire to the bedchamber. No, I do not mean to tempt you that way. It is just that your eyes look so very tired, like pools surrounded by dark earth."

"And are they stagnant, too?"

The remark made Lanja smile. "No, that they are not."

"Soon," Pershaw whispered. "We will go there soon. Just let me finish writing up some reports."

"They cannot wait?"

"It is only that I wanted to get this one about the brawl out of the way."

"The two Star Commanders? Bast and Jorge?"

"Exactly. What a blot on my command. That a freebirth could so easily defeat a trueborn in a foolish squabble."

"Foolish? As I recall Bast insulted Jorge."

"True. And if they were both trueborns that might not be a matter of shame. But Jorge soundly beat Bast—nearly broke his neck—while all those freebirths stood cheering Jorge on. It was disgusting." Though Pershaw's face rarely registered emotion, this time the revulsion was obvious in his eyes and in the downturned corners of his mouth.

"Jorge is a fine warrior, freebirth or not," Lanja said softly. "I was not there, but I understand that he beat Bast rather convincingly."

"Nevertheless, Jorge should be intelligent enough to stay out of such a battle. I depend on freeborns understanding that I do not wish to have true/free conflicts in my command, and it is up to them to . . . to . . ."

"To stay in their place? To let themselves be trampled on by us trueborns? Not, in fact, to act like warriors at all?"

Pershaw smiled, a rare event that Lanja realized she

would have to treasure for a long while until it occurred again.

"I accept the criticism, Lanja. The truth is that I despise having any freeborns in my command. If I could, I would ship the lot of them somewhere else, and deal only with trueborns."

"I understand. But so long as you command even one freeborn, you must expect trouble, especially if he is as independent as this Jorge. Did you punish him this time?"

"I tried. But the *surkai* exonerated him."

Lanja's eyebrows raised. "Oh? I would not have expected Jorge to perform the rite of forgiveness successfully. His arrogance would—"

"I did not say that he performed the rite well. He was arrogant as ever. But I accepted it. I had to, *quiaff?*"

"Aff. And now you should forget it all."

"I cannot. Jorge is like a land mine. Step on him again and he will explode. There will be more trouble."

Lanja nodded. "Well, purge yourself for the moment with the report. Incidents like this will not look well on Jorge's codex."

Pershaw shrugged. "A freeborn's codex means next to nothing. Freeborns cannot become part of the gene pool, so it affects them little."

She touched his forehead. "You are thinking too much, Kael Pershaw. You need to rest. Join me soon."

She left the office. Pershaw labored over the report for a few minutes, but found it difficult to concentrate. Something had to change, he kept thinking.

But when the change did come, less than half a day later, he was surprised by it.

"How is a freebirth Star Commander different from a rock swine in a Clan uniform?"

"I do not know, Bast. How?"

"The rock swine can qualify for front-line duty."

Bast and the others laughed, a blend of brutish noises that only those who knew them would have interpreted as amusement. Aidan knew he was the Star Commander who was the intended butt of the joke, but he wondered if Bast realized that he had just entered the room and stood only a few steps behind him. How could the man be so stupid? He still wore a neck brace from the last time he had taunted Aidan and wound up with Aidan's elbow contracting his larynx. Aidan had an urge to sneak up behind Bast and crush the neck brace into what was left of the trueborn warrior's neck.

But there was an invisible leash around his own neck and he could not act. Not revealing the least sign that he had heard Bast, Aidan went to the bar of the officer's lounge and ordered a fusionnaire, the drink currently popular among freeborns, a blend so volatile that only warriors as defiant as freeborns would place it near their lips. Aidan not only drank it down quickly, he let it linger in his mouth, where it felt like it was melting the enamel off his teeth.

The lounge was as plain as all the other facilities on this outpost. Every interior was done in drab grays, mud browns, sickly greens. At times Aidan was actually happier to be in the jungle, even though it was said to contain lizards with tongues so poisonous they could immobilize a 'Mech's leg. That was only barracks exaggeration, of course, but Aidan had no inclination to test its truth. Unfortunately, his unit, freeborns all and therefore lowest in the command structure, were generally the ones chosen for any mission into that jungle. All they had seen so far were nightmarish twisted trees whose bark dripped with thick, noxious-smelling sap and with animals whose shapes were almost indiscernible because they vanished so quickly. Yet, in an off-duty moment he had discovered some flowers whose beautiful blood-red petals were speckled with bright yellow streaks. He had turned some over to the station lab, which had reported back that these flowers, now named blood-petals, had already been identified for certain medicinal applications. A serum drawn from them had been tested on some warriors and techs afflicted with a strange disease that sapped their energies and made them drowsy. Though the blood petal serum was not a cure, it did give the patients a few hours of vigor and alertness.

Aidan could use a bit of alertness right now, he thought, as the sudden impact of the fusionnaire momentarily clouded his vision. It was said that enough fusionnaires over a short period of time might make a person blind, but so far only these brief dizzy spells had impaired his sight. He did not mind the danger, for the drink provided the only escape from the dreariness of his present duty.

He had spent much time on such backwater assignments, one Glory Station after another, where his unit always suffered the worst assignments, not to mention the desultory and often rude treatment that freeborns always got from the trueborn warriors, whose status, regardless of time in service or rank, generally gave them the advantage in any situation. In any dispute between freeborn and trueborn, the officers tended to vote in council for the trueborn's side, unless the freeborn's evidence was so overwhelming it could not be ignored.

Even when treated fairly, a freeborn always heard the resentful cadences in the voice of a trueborn superior officer. Aidan had been through so many Trials of Refusal, the challenge that any Clan warrior or military unit could make to protest a decision, that he now planned his reaction even before a single judge had heard his voice. The last time, after he had nearly broken Bast's neck, Star Colonel Kael Pershaw had obviously wanted to punish him severely, but Aidan had used the rite of *surkai* against Pershaw. Although the commander had not revealed his reaction, Aidan left the office happy, believing he had left the man incensed by his tactic.

As he finished his second fusionnaire and listened to Bast begin a joke about two freebirths encountering one another in a war-torn village, Aidan wondered if he should just stand up now and yell out to all the trueborns in the room that he, too, was a product of the union of genetic materials in a laboratory, then raised in a sibko. Like them, he was trueborn. He would like to see their faces, all their sneering, overbearing faces, when they realized that this Star Commander, whom they continually reviled in their humor and conversations, was not, after all, a freebirth. That this warrior, known to them as Jorge, had assumed a freeborn's identity when the real cadet by that name, along with all the freebirth members of his training unit and their training officer, had been killed in a training exercise. At least that was the official version.

Aidan knew that Jorge's death had been a murder, arranged by Falconer Commander Ter Roshak to give Aidan an unprecedented second chance at the Trial of Position. In his first Trial, Aidan had failed because he had been over-eager in his strategy. Although cadets did not usually have a second chance at a Trial, Aidan got one, though the reason was known only to Ter Roshak. At first Aidan had been angry that so many others had to die so that he could climb into a BattleMech and prove that he did have the makings of a warrior, but the satisfaction he took from warrior status dimmed his anger over time. Worse than any doubts about how he had achieved reinstatement was having to keep the freeborn identity in order to be a warrior. He hated that, had hated it every day of every year of his life as a warrior. There had been so many times when, like now, he had wanted to shout to others that he was a trueborn.

But Ter Roshak had insisted that the switch be kept a secret. The second chance was so antithetical to the way of the Clan that Roshak could be executed if the truth were known. Any of his genetic legacy stored in any lab, any chance he had of being honored through gene transmission to a sibko, would be removed and destroyed. As Aidan later learned, the Roshak genes had been combined with another's for only one sibko, which had turned out to be undistinguished. None of its members had become warriors.

Aidan was signaling for another fusionnaire when

he felt a hand on his shoulder. He knew without looking whose it was.

"You are not my protector, Horse," he said. "I do not need you to tell me when to quit drinking fusionnaires."

It had been a matter of honor for Aidan to return to the warrior style of speech, even if everyone else believed he was a freeborn. He had not used a contraction in years. Warriors sneered at anyone who did so, and Aidan had no intention of giving them that satisfaction.

Horse had a deep, rumbling voice that suited his imposing appearance, but it was his piercing gaze that now communicated disapproval. The two men had been together so long that Aidan could read Horse's thoughts by just such a look in his eyes or the way he held his body.

"You told me to stop you after the second fusionnaire," Horse said calmly, his hand remaining on Aidan's shoulder.

"Oh? Did I? I do not remember that."

"You never do, Commander."

"I am going to have that third fusionnaire. Look, the man already has it poured."

The bartender, a stocky tech with an expressionless face, placed the drink on the bar in front of Aidan.

"See, Horse? I have to drink it now. The way of the Clan and all that."

As he reached for the drink, Horse's hand seemed to leap off Aidan's shoulder and onto the bar. He grabbed the glass, seizing its edge in his fingers, just before Aidan's hand would have closed around it. Still holding it delicately by its upper rim, Horse tilted the liquid quickly into his own mouth, downing it in one smooth swallow. Then he placed the glass in Aidan's curved fingers, which had remained in place on the bar.

"Now it is drunk," Horse said.

"And I am not," Aidan said bitterly.

"You are on duty."

"All the more reason to—"

"You are trying to be ironic, *quiaff?*"

"Aff. As you well know, Horse."

Aidan squinted at Horse. His hand closed around the fusionnaire glass, as though it still contained something to consume.

"You like irony, I can see. It is because of your secret cache of books."

Turning toward Horse, Aidan raised a finger to his lips. "I thought you knew better," he hissed. "You must never mention the, the—you know—here. The, uh, you know are a violation, remember?"

"Of course I remember. But I am a freebirth. In social matters we slip up easily."

Aidan laughed abruptly. "Horse, you are trying to feed me raw coolant."

Behind Horse, Bast's voice had risen. "Then the freebirth says, 'No, but if you want to, please use a socket wrench.' "

The other warriors roared with laughter. Aidan had not heard the lead-in to the punchline, nor did he recall hearing this particular joke before. Bast seemed to come up with new ones regularly from his vast store of anti-freeborn humor.

Aidan noted the tenseness in Horse's body. He could see that his comrade was about to wheel around and hurl an insult back at Bast. He did not blame Horse, but Kael Pershaw had sent out a directive that specifically ordered Aidan's unit to stop fighting with the regular warriors. Aidan suspected that his freeborns had wrought too much havoc on the trues in most of their brawls, and that Pershaw was merely exercising command privilege to prevent any more damage. Ever since Aidan had arrived on Glory, Pershaw had regularly overruled Aidan's orders and generally encouraged the trues to insult him. It was only after a few trues wound up injured that Pershaw also set stiff penalties for brawling. No matter who started a fight, the Commander always sided with the trueborns over the frees. He, in fact, gleefully trumpeted his own inequitable judgments as a device to keep both sides stirred up.

Standing up, Aidan shook his head at Horse, who seethed at the cautionary gesture.

"We agreed to stay out of trouble," Aidan said softly.

"You agreed."

"And my word holds for the whole Star, *quiaff?*"

Horse seemed reluctant to reply. "Aff. But we look like fools and—"

"Time will pass. We will find our edge."

Horse's eyes narrowed. "What has happened to you, Jorge? Once no base commander could have prevented you from avenging an insult. Once you would've been the first one to wade into a fight. You would have had five enemies on the floor before anyone else could throw a single—"

Aidan smiled. "I appreciate your faith in me, Horse. You make me sound like a hero in one of those Clan folk myths. But I have to protect the Star from—"

"We need protection from nothing, and no need to become poltroons because of—"

"Poltroons?" Aidan said, still smiling. "Where did you get that word?"

"I can read, too. You keep leaving books around and—"

Aidan's smile turned into a glare. "I told you not to mention them in here."

Horse's face reddened. "Sorry. At any rate, I pick up information here and there. And, anyway, why didn't you get mad when I called you that name?"

"First of all, the word is too funny when you hear someone actually speak it. Second, I understand why you said it. And, it might seem strange that I say this, but I agree with you. Even I do not know why I remain passive. No matter what we do, Kael Pershaw will find a way to throw even more discredit on me and the Star. Let me put it this way: Our bid is a loser, no matter how good it is, no matter who is bidding against us, no matter how much we flaunt the odds—what amuses you, Horse?"

"Flaunt. Another of your words. Maybe it's the—the, well, you know—that's keeping us down."

"No, it is the old biases against us. There sometimes seems no way we can—you are smiling again. Another word?"

"No. In a way, yes. You said us. You continually include yourself as one of us, even though you were actually born a—"

This time Aidan gave Horse a slight kick to the shin. He had never known his comrade to make so many slips of the tongue in so short a period. Perhaps Horse had downed his own equivalent of a triple-fusionnaire before coming to the officer's lounge.

"I am one of you now," Aidan said. "My, well, origins do not matter. We have served together, fought together, brawled together for too long. I could never return to—"he peered around the room, saw that no one was eavesdropping—"never return to my old, well, status again. Do you understand, Horse?" Horse nodded. "Good. Now, let us get out of this place, while the stink of these trues is still mild in the air."

With Horse leading the way, they headed away from the bar. Aidan, who knew better, decided to walk past Bast and his rude friends. There was just so much passivity he could take.

"Star Commander Jorge," Bast said with mock formality.

"Star Commander Bast."

"I hope our little jokes did not offend you."

Aidan was tempted to rise to the bait, but he said instead, "I heard nothing that would offend me."

Bast glanced toward his cohorts. "See? They understand caste, too."

"I understand I am a warrior, yes."

The amusement drained out of Bast's face. "I did not mean that. I meant you are a freebirth and therefore genetically unsound, made from the materials of chance. Do you not agree?"

"All life is chance, opportunities to be bid for."

"That is not what I meant. I meant that the finest warriors are created by scientific design, the genes of superior warriors brought together to form a line of children. One mating creates many of a preeminent order, therefore trueborns. The other mating is the result of sheer accident and creates no more than, say, a small litter of genetically unpredictable freeborns. The superiority of trueborns is logically proven, *quiaff?''*

Aidan felt pulled in two. As a genuine trueborn, he saw the point of Bast's crude logic. But having fought side by side, lived side by side, with freeborns, he knew also that genetic chance could, and often did, supply military forces with warriors every bit the equal of those who had graduated to the role from sibkos. At the same time that his mind weighed the argument, the sheer repulsiveness of Bast made him think of murder.

"Genetic hegemony has been argued at length," he finally said to Bast.

"Ah, and the scholars have almost unanimously decided that the Clan eugenics system produces superior beings."

"Yes, but—" Aidan wanted to say that there had been times in history when scholars had been wrong. But then he would have had to reveal his sources, and it was vital to him to keep his personal library a secret. Kael Pershaw would seize it in a minute.

"But what?"

"You said almost unanimously. There have been dissenters."

"Traitors, yes."

"Not traitors. Scientists, researchers, theorists."

"Traitors. All traitors. We praise the eugenics program here, Star Commander Jorge, *quiaff? QUIAFF?''*

"Aff. You praise the eugenics program here."

"You? I said we. You do agree, *quiaff?''*

Aidan, although he was in an open area of the room, felt his back against a wall. He remembered the scene in Pershaw's office, after Aidan had mockingly performed *surkai*, when the base commander had insisted on a promise that Aidan and his freeborn warriors would stop brawling with the trues. Kael Pershaw had vowed that any aggression from one would result in the punishment of several and that any aggression from Aidan himself would bring down punishment on the entire unit.

"Perhaps, Star Commander Jorge, you misunderstood the question?" Bast stood up. "You are a freeborn, after all. I forget that things must be spelled out. What I said, honored warrior, was that the Clan eugenics program produced superior warriors. Which, of course, means that it produces superior beings. Therefore, we praise the eugenics program here, *quiaff?*"

Aidan knew what he must respond, and he did not know why he could not say it. Why did a simple "aff" lodge in his throat? Why could he not say it? Beside him, he could sense Horse bristling.

Bast leaned toward Aidan, the stink of his alcohol-saturated breath rushing forward as he spoke. "We praise the eugenics program here, *quiaff? QUIAFF,* you rotten freebirth!"

All restraint left Aidan in a rush. Anger, fueled by a triple dose of fusionnaires, took over. It no longer mattered what he had vowed to Pershaw. There was no freeborn in his unit who would have wanted him to capitulate to this overbearing enemy. "Freebirth" was the epithet most insulting to all warriors, regardless of their birth status. Trueborns offended other trueborns with it, used it almost casually against freeborns. Aidan had been called a freebirth many times since he had assumed the identity of Jorge, but this time, coming from Bast, it made him furious.

Grabbing Bast by the neck brace, he pulled him forward roughly. Then he butted the trueborn warrior's head, letting go of the neck brace and pushing him back. Bast staggered backward, knocking over the chair on which he had been sitting, and his hands went to his neck. His eyes showed terrible pain. Aidan hoped he had reinjured the man's neck, that the injury was even worse than before. He relaxed, the anger out of him now. The other trueborns, clearly enraged but prevented by Clan warrior law to act as long as the fight was only between Aidan and Bast, muttered encouragement to their still-reeling companion. Aidan laughed scornfully. Bast reversed his backward motion and took a pair of stumbling steps forward, his hands still clutching the neck brace.

Aidan was caught off guard. He should have seen

that some of Bast's pain was fakery. Bast drew a knife from some hiding place in the neck brace and quickly flung it at Aidan. The knife, aimed at Aidan's left eye, nearly hit its target. Jerking his head to one side, Aidan seemed to feel a light, glancing touch from the weapon as it passed by without being diverted from its path. Then Bast charged at him like some mad animal.

There was no moment when Aidan considered choice. He knew he could take Bast, he had done so already, and he merely wanted to finish him forever. After a few moments of scuffling, Aidan grabbed at the neck brace and tore it away from Bast's neck, exposing bruised and reddened skin. Slapping Bast across the eyes with the edge of the brace, he took advantage of his enemy's obvious dizziness by going for the man's weak spot. Throwing his forearm around Bast's neck, he squeezed with a steady pressure. Clarity came back into Bast's eyes for a moment, then something in the man's neck snapped and vision left his eyes forever. His body slumped heavily, and Aidan threw it to the floor as though it were only so much litter.

Bast's companions, now shaking with anger, rushed at Aidan. Horse intervened. Soon the whole room was in a free-for-all. Aidan personally, and with some satisfaction, seriously disabled two warriors from Bast's Star.

When a group of Elementals from Lanja's Point came into the lounge to break up the battle, Aidan volunteered responsibility and was taken to command headquarters.

Before he left, he stood over Bast's corpse and muttered, "What's the difference between a truebirth and a rock swine in a Clan uniform?" He paused for a moment, as though the dead man would respond, then he said, "No difference, Bast. No difference."

2

"**A** Jade Falcon JumpShip has been detected arriving in Glory Sector. A DropShip has detached and is heading for Glory," Star Commander Craig Ward reported to his superior, Star Captain Dwillt Radick. They were officers in the Wolf Clan's Sixteenth Battle Cluster, and they despised each other.

Radick, who had been pretending to examine a star map of the Glory Sector, merely nodded to Ward, the slight shift of his head seeming to indicate that the news was of little interest. It was, in truth, fascinating information.

"Perhaps the Jade Falcons had advance information about our attack," Ward commented. He could not have said anything that Radick liked more, because it set him up for his superior.

"They could not have advance information, as you say, Star Commander. It is obvious that the Jade Falcons do not value Kael Pershaw's genetic legacy. They have given him a backwater command on a planet the Clan does not value highly. His Cluster's equipment is obsolescent and his command is full of freebirths. Clan Jade Falcon would never even imagine that Clan Wolf desires the spawn of Kael Pershaw for mixture with one of our own, *quiaff?*"

"Aff."

"And you will use any excuse to express disapproval of our operation?"

"That is not true, sir. My—"

"Come now. Your pacifistic views are well-known.

Am I to understand that you believe our coming challenge and the acquisition of Pershaw's genetic legacy is to be praised? You would praise them, Star Commander Craig Ward, *quiaff?*"

Ward knew that it was futile to argue with Radick, and he had devised several slippery ways of escaping the man's verbal clutches. This time, however, he was stopped cold. If anything flustered him, it was being challenged when merely performing the duties of a messenger.

"*Quiaff,* Star Commander?"

"You know where my sentiments lie. But I will also do my duty."

"You will certainly do your duty."

Radick continually sent Ward out on the most difficult and risky missions.

"Well," Radick said, "what do you make of the JumpShip's sudden appearance?"

"If it is not the result of intelligence data, then perhaps it is a normal cargo delivery or a troop rotation."

Radick looked thoughtful, the effort making his face look pinched. "All right then," he said. "I think we should make a contingency plan for the bidding. If new warriors and 'Mechs will be arriving on Glory, which the presence of the DropShip does indeed suggest, then our bid must include some aerofighters."

"Why aerofighters?"

"To help us win the bid against Star Captain Zoll, for the honor of leading the attack."

"I still do not understand."

"Star Colonel Mikel Furey intends to issue the challenge for the Trial of Possession within a few hours. It will take the Jade Falcon DropShip at least five hours to land. Nevertheless, I believe that Kael Pershaw will include the DropShip and its 'Mechs as part of his defensive forces.

"Star Captain Zoll is not very imaginative. He will simply adjust his bid to lead the assault by a Trinary of BattleMechs. I, on the other hand, will bid three Points of aerofighters, along with two Trinaries. The aerofighters will eliminate the DropShip and its load of 'Mechs before it lands. I will win the bid and defeat Kael Pershaw.''

Star Captain Joanna, of the Falcon Guards, fought the severe nausea that always overcame her traveling in a starship making its jump across hyperspace. This time the waves of nausea were more like fierce tidal blasts that crushed cliffs and made beaches disappear. She did not vomit, however, having carefully avoided food the day before and having taken every known anti-nausea remedy. She coughed up some bile, but that was about it.

In contrast to the severity of the nausea, the dizziness that usually followed it was not so bad this time. The room spun only about ten or twelve times before settling back to normal. She could, like the other passengers, have spent the arrival time in med bay, but that would have been an admission of weakness, something Joanna never did. Knowledge of one's weakness could give another warrior an extra edge. Besides, too many warriors considered any sign of vulnerability to be proof of old age. Among the Clans nothing was worse than being considered too old. She could not allow *that*.

Joanna knew, of course, that she *was* getting older and still going nowhere as a warrior. If she had not won her Bloodname by now, it was not for lack of trying. Several times she had even made it to the final stages. But there was always someone better, someone else with the skills to win the Bloodname, leaving Joanna behind, with battle scars and great courage but only a single name.

Gripping the stumble-bar, the long railings on at least three sides of any compartment and both sides of all JumpShip corridors, she waited to make sure she could walk without stumbling. Unfortunately, before she felt steady enough to move, her chief tech, Nomad, entered the compartment. What bad luck! The last person she wanted to see while in this condition was Nomad. Though he was of a caste famous for deference and politeness, Nomad never lost a chance to remind Joanna of a weakness or a failure.

"A bit of a hyperspace spell?" he said immediately. "Or were you just doing an exercise series on the bar?"

"No spell, and how many times have I already reported you for rudeness?"

"Lately? Or over the years?"

"Lately."

"Five, I think."

"Only a third as much as you deserved. I do not see why you stay. You could have transferred long ago."

"I like it here."

"Are you some kind of curse that has been put on me?"

"What makes you say that?"

"Never mind."

There was the usual sarcastic twinkle in Nomad's eyes, their color so pale they almost disappeared into the dark skin around them. He was bald now, had been for some time. When they had first worked together, Nomad's skull had been decorated with a full head of light brown hair. They had gone on a mission to locate Cadet Aidan, who had become an astech and then escaped the training planet on Ironhold. He had been thinner, too.

When Joanna had finished her tour as a training instructor on Ironhold, Nomad had also been reassigned, coincidentally, to her command as its chief tech. She had no doubt that it was thanks to his efficient supervision of the maintenance and repair crews that the unit lost so few 'Mechs. In the early days, she had blocked any move on his part for transfer. But then came a time when, in spite of his invaluable abilities, she could no longer endure his continual sarcasm. She had told him he could have any transfer for which he might apply. He had not applied since.

She had even considered killing him. But how? He was not easily ruffled, so he could not be provoked to a fight. Besides, a fight with one's chief tech, even if condoned in the Circle of Equals, had an element of dishonor attached to it. Deliberately putting him in jeopardy under fire was possible, but against her sense of ethics. And murder was out of the question. So she had to let him live. Worse, Joanna knew that if ever she were to see him in danger during a battle, she would rescue him. How often had she pondered what good it was being a Star Captain if you could not get rid of your chief tech?

On the other hand, her own success as an officer was partly due to Nomad's efficiency. She could think of a number of close skirmishes where the makeshift battlefield repairs by Nomad and his crew had made the difference. An inept or indifferent chief tech could send his or her Star down the crater to oblivion.

"I am stuck with you, Nomad, *quiaff?*"

"Aff. We might as well be lovers."

"Do not blaspheme. I would not bed a tech, you know that."

"Yes. Warriors do not have sex below their caste?"

"Is that sarcasm? You know they do. I do not."

"A sense of ethics?"

"A sense of disgust. You are not appealing, Nomad."

The ironic look did not leave his eyes, but the remark silenced him. Joanna would have liked to continue the silence, but there was the ritual of duty to be performed.

She and her Trinary of fifteen MechWarriors were being rotated to Glory Station to replace the MechWarriors of Trinary Striker. Nomad made a daily check of the cocoons where their unit's 'Mechs were stored before reporting to her. Nothing, of course, would be wrong. It was routine duty, the kind that made Joanna's nerves edgy with boredom.

There were rumors that the invasion of the Inner Sphere would come soon. She hoped so. Clan warriors did plenty of fighting, it was true, but it was mere skirmishing, trivial battles over geographical territory or fights over genetic materials. It was a way to keep one's combat skills sharp, but had never been enough for her. She wanted the landscape of a major battle, the prodding to heroism. That was what being a warrior was all about. By the sacred name of Nicholas Kerensky, she vowed that she would not die in some minor battle or become cannon fodder like so many old warriors whose skills had diminished. She did not fear dying; she only feared dying for an inconsequential cause.

Joanna had initially tried to protest her assignment to Glory Station. If a significant war broke out or the Inner Sphere invasion began while she was on this remote outpost of the Clan empire, she could end up either out of the invasion altogether or summoned too late, when the really good fighting was over. It would take all her considerable manipulative powers to find a way out of Glory Station, but she was certain she could accomplish it.

She was about to give Nomad his orders for the day when the DropShip captain's voice came over the private intercom, the one that fed only into officer's quarters. "This is an All Officer Alert. Ensure that all troops are in combat readiness, then report to the bridge." The message was repeated, then the intercom went silent again.

"Down to the 'Mech bay," Joanna told Nomad. "It is time to prepare our 'Mechs."

The tech needed hear no more. He knew the meaning of an Officer Alert.

"Make sure the 'Mechs are secure," she shouted after him as he rushed down the corridor. Then she turned in the other direction, heading for the bridge. Coming to the corridor leading to it, she was not surprised to find it already crowded with other officers.

The DropShip captain, a sharp young warrior named Essel, informed the assemblage that a JumpShip from Clan Wolf had just appeared in the region and was sending out DropShips, all of them headed in the general direction of the planet Glory.

"No communication has come from the Clan Wolf ships, but we suspect that combat is imminent. Star Colonel Kael Pershaw has informed me that he intends to include this ship and the Trinary it carries in his defense. Please prepare your troops and await a General Alert. Return to your stations.''

The adrenaline always came early for Joanna at the slightest prospect of a fight. She needed a good one to rid herself of her current frustrations. Taking it out on someone like Nomad, no matter how insubordinate the man became, did her no honor. She was a warrior, and only happy when functioning as one.

What luck that Kael Pershaw intended to use this ship and her Trinary. Joanna could not be sure whether this was genius or desperation on the Star Colonel's part because this DropShip was only a troop transport never intended for orbital assault. The move surprised her, but she could not help but admire the man's determination.

I hope we can get off this ship before combat begins, she thought. I would hate to sit this one out as an onlooker in orbit around Glory. I surely would.

3

Kael Pershaw indeed had no advance intelligence network to warn him of the Wolf Clan's intrusion into his sector. Clan Jade Falcon was not expecting any attacks, for what enemy would seek to invade Glory Station?

When the commtech brought him word that some anomalies at the outer rim of the sector might be ships, Pershaw was not much concerned. Perhaps these were only merchant ships arriving a month or so early, or even some pirates looking for a place to hide. If the ships were merchant, their captains would bring their deals planetside soon enough. If pirate, Pershaw would let them hide here, provided it was not in his hemisphere of Glory.

What really was on his mind was standing before him right now, looking calm. Star Commander Jorge's uniform was not even marked from his recent fracas. It was as if the clothing had smoothed itself down around his body even after having been severely rumpled. Jorge was the type who survived anything. A good trait in a warrior, Pershaw thought, but this particular warrior, skilled as he was, was only a repulsive freebirth.

"It seems we have just had this same encounter, Jorge," Pershaw said. "The last time you fought with Star Commander Bast, was it not?"

Jorge nodded. Pershaw glowered. This Jorge was a block, a statue, a grisly piece of work. He would have to crush him.

To Aidan, Kael Pershaw's face appeared calm, almost serene. That was a clue, he knew, to the man's actual wrath. The angrier Pershaw became, the less it showed on his face or body. Warriors said that when Kael Pershaw became insane with rage, he looked nearly comatose. At this point, Aidan realized, the base commander was nearing the comatose state.

He had stood up to greet Aidan. When their eyes met, Pershaw smiled hugely. Another bad sign. If the man laughed, Aidan would consider making out his last will and testament.

"This time, however, Bast is dead," Pershaw said, his smile and voice not losing even an ounce of good cheer.

"So it appeared when last I saw him," Aidan replied.

"You choose to be insolent even at such a moment?"

"No, sir. I merely stated a fact, sir."

"I know you, Jorge. You have a way of stating facts that is not a way of stating facts."

"I do not understand, sir."

"You do not understand, but you do. You are not ironic, but you are. You do not lie, but you do. Yes, you do understand. You certainly do."

There was something like a twinkle in Pershaw's eyes as he studied Aidan, looking him up and down as if measuring him for a burial cloth.

"Bast was not a bright man, as warriors go. But he had learned how to make his 'Mech think for him, something you, Jorge, will never do. He was a valuable warrior, and—however much he may have provoked your assault—Bast is a greater loss to me than your worthless freebirth self will ever be."

"I have served the commander well, I believe."

"And you are arrogant enough to point that out. Well, arrogance is a good trait in a warrior, and I will not fault you for it. There are times when you are almost like a trueborn in your manner, speech, and abilities."

"What if I were a trueborn?"

When Pershaw let out a loud laugh of true mirth, fear seemed to prod at Aidan's spine. "Do not blaspheme," the commander said softly. "Some freebirths make competent warriors, and you are one of them, I must reluctantly admit. But a freeborn can never be a trueborn and you befoul the eugenics ideal by even suggesting an equality between frees and trues. Saying such is just another black mark on your already well-blotted record, Star Commander Jorge."

"Sir, am I to assume that you hold me to blame for the death of Bast?"

Kael Pershaw's grin got wider, more mysterious. "Hold you to blame? How do you even ask the question? Of course I hold you to blame! You killed a fine warrior, one already injured from a previous brawl with your worthless freebirth self. We do not waste our personnel in inconsequential spats. We have a duty here, and that duty means conserving warriors, just as we conserve our weapons and supplies. That is the way of the Clan. Bast's death was wasteful, especially as it merely satisfied the petty feelings of a worthless freebirth warrior."

With each insult, Aidan bristled inwardly. He wanted to challenge his commander to a battle in the Circle of Equals, the one place where a warrior could legitimately fight a superior officer, but Kael Pershaw had banished the Circle. It had become debased, he claimed, by its use for trivial quarrels.

Kael Pershaw no doubt sensed Aidan's uneasiness, but Aidan had vowed to show no emotion before him. That oath was becoming more difficult to honor, with the Star Colonel's broad smile indicating clear and present danger.

"It is economy, Star Commander Jorge, that saves you from the punishment you deserve. If I could, I would deny you the rite of *surkai* and have you shot on the spot, but there is no one in your Star to take your place. I trust you will not be insulted when I say that your unit is the most motley, unskilled, and worthless group of warriors it has ever been my misfortune to have in my command. You are undoubtedly the right commander for them, and unfortunately, the only one I can spare for the job. So, let us initiate the rite of forgiveness, then return to duty.''

Pershaw came around the desk, ready to accept Aidan's *surkai,* and was startled when Aidan said, ''No. I refuse to initiate *surkai* this time. I was justified in killing Bast, and I need no forgiveness for it.''

Pershaw was clearly enraged. If not, why did his voice drop almost to a whisper?

''I demand that you perform *surkai,* Star Commander Jorge.''

''No. I will not.''

''I order you.''

''No officer may order *surkai.* Shall I quote you from *The Remembrance* on this subject, sir?''

''No, you will not.'' He walked away from Aidan, toward the only window in the room. It was so blackened from the gritty mists that came from Blood Swamp that only a few small areas still offered any possibility of a view. He stood for a moment, hands clasped behind his back, then abruptly turned.

''All right, then, we can only resort to symbology. Lanja!''

Lanja appeared immediately. Aidan knew she had been standing by the doorway, awaiting her commander's order. With Pershaw, all contingencies were anticipated. From the first moment he awoke after he had ordered himself to sleep, his day was firmly scheduled. He no doubt always had a plan ready for the rare occasion when a warrior might refuse *surkai.*

Lanja carried a slim case, holding it as if it were part of a ritual.

''Lanja, set the case on my desk.''

''Yes, sir.''

''Now open it.''

Lanja slowly opened the case, with the same public precision she always used in response to an order from her commander. Aidan knew what was coming. If Clan loyalty had not restrained him, he could have strangled both Lanja and Pershaw at that moment.

Lanja held the black ribbon delicately in both hands. She extended it toward Kael Pershaw, who took it from her carefully, as if the ribbon were precious.

"Star Commander Jorge, you have brought discredit to your Star. There is nothing more shameful than an unnecessary death. For the period of the next month, you must wear the Memorial Ribbon and this picture across your chest. Lanja?"

Lanja displayed a holographic photograph of Bast, balancing it on the tips of her fingers to keep from damaging it in any way. The photo depicted Bast in a surly mood, the kind of tough-looking portrait of which warriors were so fond. One might find hundreds of nearly identical ones in any Clan file.

"Before I place the dark band on you, you are allowed by law to make a defense of your dishonorable action. Go ahead, Jorge. Respond."

"Would there be any point?"

"Yes. I am not unfair. Respond."

"Bast insulted me."

"If you were a trueborn warrior, that might be a legitimate defense. But you are a freebirth. Bast was allowed to insult you. Anything more?"

"No."

"Good. Fit him with the dark band, Lanja."

Lanja, her eyes peculiarly somber, placed the ribbon across Aidan's chest and waist, then spent moments smoothing out the band's wrinkles, fussing over the placement of Bast's photograph. Then she stepped back, still looking quite critical of her accomplishment.

The smile faded from Pershaw's face as he gave the proper orders in the proper voice. He told Aidan that during the time he would wear the Memorial Ribbon all would shun him and he could speak to no one unless given express permission. Further, Aidan must not venture out in public without wearing the dark band, that should anyone speak to him about the band, Aidan must respond with neither word nor deed, that he must always remember that the Memorial Ribbon was to remind him—as it reminded others—of the unnecessary death he had caused.

When Kael Pershaw was done, Aidan saluted him, then passed by the somber Lanja, realizing he could kill them both. But especially Pershaw. Just as he had with Bast, Aidan would take great pleasure in standing over the corpse of his commanding officer.

Lanja watched Jorge walk out the door, then turned to Pershaw and said, "He is a proud young man. And clever. He may turn the wearing of the dark band into a virtue."

Pershaw sighed. Uncharacteristic of him to sigh, Lanja thought. "We are Clan. We can only follow the rituals as prescribed. I would rather hang him by his thumbs from a yardarm or stick his head through stocks or even burn him at the stake."

Lanja laughed suddenly. "Just what are you talking about?"

"Those were old forms of punishment, of humiliating the chastised. You do not think Jorge deserves this punishment?"

"I did not say that. I merely said he was proud."

"But was that not admiration in your voice?"

"Was it? Perhaps so. There is something admirable in being able to wear the dark band proudly."

"Then the punishment has failed, has it not?"

"I did not say that. You are merely expressing your own worries, *quiaff?*"

"Aff. I think the man possesses some strange core that is unpunishable, that cannot be humiliated."

"And you do not admire that?"

"No, I do not. I do not."

They might have continued this conversation, and perhaps found themselves wading in dangerous waters, if a messenger had not delivered the communiqué from the Wolf Clan invaders.

Aidan's walk back to the barracks where his Star was housed was agonizing. One after another, as if the call had gone out to form a gauntlet for Aidan, trues stared at the dark band when he passed. Sneers, anger, taunts, crude joking remarks rained down on him. Aidan shut off his mind as best he could and strode with his eyes fixed straight ahead. He knew that if he looked even once into the eyes of any of the trues who were insulting him, the anguish of his shame would drive him once more into the kind of fight that Pershaw and the law of the dark band expressly forbade. Rebellious as he was, even he must accept any ritual that symbolized the way of the Clans.

Horse stood at the door of the barracks, watching the final steps of Aidan's proud walk. A few trues were now stalking his every step, hurling new taunts at him. Horse came out to join him.

Though they could speak no words, Aidan knew his friend was silently saying, "Ignore them," as he came close.

"I will," he said fiercely to himself.

Horse joined him and the two walked together into the barracks. The taunters stayed for a while, making the gesture of the coward in the direction of the barracks. The gesture involved placing one's hands in succession over the face, the throat, the chest, and the genitals. The trues eventually tired of the game, and began to drift away. Their raucous laughter drifted back on the wind for a long while after they were out of sight.

Aidan remained silent for even longer, staring straight ahead, unwilling to look down at the dark band. Horse reclined on a bunk, also keeping quiet. Finally, Aidan spoke:

"I think I must kill Kael Pershaw."

Horse shrugged. "That may be so. But I think this is not the right time."

Aidan smiled. Horse's laconic comments often amused him. "You mean, while wearing the dark band? Just after killing another true?"

"Something like that."

"Perhaps a time will come . . ."

"You're not a murderer."

"I was not one. Perhaps I am now."

"There is a book among your books about a man who plans and carries out a murder, and then cannot live with himself."

"Yes, I know. There is a moral to it, but I never much believe in the morals from books. They do not seem to apply to our lives."

Horse shrugged again. "Maybe so."

"But maybe not?"

"Whatever you say."

"Sometimes, friend Horse, you seem to speak in codes."

"Maybe."

Horse's half-smile made Aidan laugh. He kept laughing until his hand accidentally found the dark band and its silken texture. Was it his imagination or did it deliberately press against his chest, constricting his breath?

"We have to get away from here," Aidan said. "Get to some duty that—"

"You told me that the next time you started bemoaning our lives on this backwater planet I should remind you that you had vowed to stop."

"Horse, you always—"

He was cut off by the strident blare of an alarm klaxon. It was sounding off in long, steady tones, a signal that the base was under imminent attack. Reacting instinctively, Aidan and Horse grabbed their battle gear from their lockers as the rest of the Star assembled.

"Horse," Aidan said, "I think we may finally be getting some action."

"Don't bet on it."

Sometimes Horse could be irritating, and no more so than when events proved him correct, as they were about to now.

4

Aidan was convinced that even the furniture selected for freeborns was carefully, and cruelly, chosen by the trues. As he stared at the video monitor, watching the start of the formal declarations of the Trial of Possession, he could not sit still. His body sought some comfortable position in this yellow plastic deformity but found only resistant bumps and a curvature that could only have been meant for some upright lizard species. Each bump and curve was yet another reminder of all the ways trueborns treated frees as inferior.

"How do *you* manage it? Sitting in these things?" he asked Horse, who seemed quite comfortably ensconced in his chair.

"I beat the system by convincing myself that all discomfort is comfort, for discomfort is all that a freeborn is ever allowed. It's a kind of perverse utilitarianism."

"Util—"

Horse put his finger to his lips, a signal that he had learned the word from one of Aidan's secret books. Aidan smiled. He knew there was probably no reason to keep the books a secret. Most trueborns would find Aidan's penchant for literature a curiosity and do nothing about it, but some were ornery enough to search out some law somewhere that would let them confiscate the material. It was better to hide the books. They had, after all, been hidden in the first place. Most warriors were not casual readers, anyway. Technical manuals, military strategy treatises, and endless quoting of *The Remembrance* were about their speed. Aidan was a great admirer of the latter, the Clans' major epic poem, but it could sound grotesque when recited by some of the trueborn warriors whose rough voices and indifference often diminished the poetry.

Aidan had discovered the books in the hideaway of a Brian Cache, one of many underground shelters for BattleMechs and war materiel. One section was devoted to a vast supply of computers and data banks. These must have been from the days when the great and noble General Kerensky had ordained that his people must preserve the knowledge and data they had brought with them from the Inner Sphere. Each skilled person, whether warrior or technician, then recorded what he or she knew into the computers of the Brian Cache.

One day Aidan had been on duty in a Brian Cache, attempting to relieve his boredom by studying the boxed disk-files of information. Behind a shelf, in what appeared to be a temporary wall, he noticed a rectangular section that seemed lighter in color, as if a picture had once hung there. There was no interior decoration in the entire Cache, so Aidan reckoned the rectangle served some other purpose. When he gave one corner a push, it slid open. Inside were several boxes, filled with real paper-and-ink books. Not disks, not print-outs, not manuals, but the kind of books that, according to legend, might be found only in the quarters of the highest-echelon personnel. With the help of Horse and others in his command, he had discreetly moved them to his own cache, a narrow false wall in the freeborn barracks. Since then he and Horse had been devoting their rare free time to reading them. The books had certainly helped him endure the painful duties of Glory Station and the antagonism of its commander.

Aidan squirmed more in the chair. The snakelike movements seemed to amuse Horse. "It's not the chair, is it?" he said. "It's that you're not in there with the rest, making your own bids. Instead, we have to sit out here, with other frees, separated from the trues."

Horse was right. Aidan resented that only trues could enter the command chamber for the bidding procedures. He sighed. "I suppose it does not matter. We will be bid away and left to view the battle from the barracks monitors. Or, worse, detached to supervise logistics so that the trueborns there can be sent to more *important* strategic areas.''

He glanced down at the beeper on his belt. It was partially obscured by the dark band fitting over part of it, but the light in the center was still visible. When that light went out, it would indicate that Aidan's unit had been eliminated from the bid—the forces Kael Pershaw would use to defend against the Wolf attack. It would probably happen immediately after the Wolf *batchall*. Not only did Pershaw resent having freeborns under his command, but he was now furious with Aidan because of the Bast incident.

The Wolf Clan commander now came onto the screen. Dressed in full Clan regalia, the Star Colonel made an imposing figure.

''I am Star Colonel Mikel Furey of Clan Wolf's Six-teenth Battle Cluster. What forces defend the spawn of Kael Pershaw?''

An almost imperceptible shudder went through Kael Pershaw's body, and an eruption of shocked reactions flowed from the assembled trueborns. The Wolves were not here for Glory Station but for the genetic legacy of the base commander!

''What're they doing now?'' Horse asked.

''Probably trying to absorb the impact of the Wolf Clan *batchall*. I do not know if Kael Pershaw expected that the prize of the battle would be the gene heritage of his own bloodline. It is an insult of the highest or-der.''

''Insult? I thought trues regarded their blood heritage as something sacred. I think I'd like it if an enemy wanted to fight over my bloodline. Quite an honor. Of course, my blood heritage is a seamstress and a comm-tech. Not much to fight over there, and of course, it's difficult to obtain the genetic materials from them now.''

''Do not be obscene.''

''Is it obscene? I'm only referring to my own par-ents.''

Aidan felt a twinge at hearing the word *parents*.

Some of his old trueborn legacies, feelings about freeborns and reactions to words referring to procreation, were so ingrained that they still rose up as instinctive responses. He hated the casual way frees tossed around words relating to the birth process and parental matters. Motherhood, womb, fathering—words like that. He, like all trueborns, knew no parents. Truebirths were born out of metal containers that they often liked to refer to as canisters or iron wombs. Any talk of lower-caste birthing and parental matters was disturbing, not only to Aidan but to all trues. Freeborns were often beaten for the mere mention of their so-called natural births.

For warriors, it was the canister that was natural, not the repellent and even dangerous procedures that produced freeborns. At any rate, warriors knew the theoretical advantages of their caste. Genetically engineered humans, it was said by the experts, represented the most perfect beings in the evolution of the race. Natural births, with their random genetics and casual DNA factors, could not possibly compete with the union of the genes from successful warriors that were "mated" scientifically in laboratory vessels.

Kael Pershaw regained his composure and responded.

"I am Star Colonel Kael Pershaw of Clan Jade Falcon, commanding the Glory Station Garrison Cluster. I will meet any foe on Glory Plain or in the skies above with the forces that I now designate."

Pershaw's hand moved to the console in front of him, swiftly slapping one button, then another, and then, after a second's hesitation, a third.

"Seyla," intoned Pershaw as his hand hit the transmit switch that would send the Clan Wolf Colonel a history of his forces.

"Seyla," intoned Star Colonel Mikel Furey as the Wolf Clan leader broke communications.

The *batchall* had ended. Aidan glanced down at his beeper. The light had not gone out.

The *batchall* had ended, and Kael Pershaw, as was his right, had submitted his bid. Aidan's beeper light had not gone out, which meant his Star was still part of the forces being bid to defend Glory Station.

At his own bidding place in the bridge of his DropShip, Dwillt Radick evaluated the forces Clan Jade Falcon had committed.

"I see he is using the new troops in the incoming DropShip," Radick said.

"Yes. You knew he would."

Radick nodded with some pleasure. He liked to hear Craig Ward give him due credit.

"Very well. As junior, Zoll must bid first. He is timid, so I expect him to use all three of the Cluster's Supernovas. That will give him thirty first-line BattleMechs to Kael Pershaw's thirty and a two-to-one advantage in Elementals. I will counter by bidding Bravo Supernova, Command Supernova, and a Star of fighters. That should be enough to destroy the DropShip. If Zoll is overly aggressive, I can eliminate four Points of Elementals and three Points of fighters."

"What of Clan Jade Falcon's Garrison Trinary?"

"Freebirths and has-beens. Nothing of any account. In fact, I am glad Kael Pershaw did not eliminate all of his freebirth units from the defense. There is nothing like a few of those damned frees to stir up our troops to a fighting frenzy, *quiaff?*"

"Aff."

The comm screen in front of Radick split in half. On the top was the face of Star Colonel Mikel Furey, on the bottom that of Star Captain Zoll.

"Star Captain Dwillt Radick, Star Captain Zoll. You have heard the response of Star Colonel Kael Pershaw of Clan Jade Falcon. Star Captain Zoll, what forces do you bid to take the spawn of Kael Pershaw?"

Zoll pressed a series of buttons that made the icons for three Supernovas appear.

"I bid Supernova Third, Supernova Second, and Supernova Command."

"Star Captain Dwillt Radick, what is your counter?"

A smile appeared on Radick's face. As his fingers

touched the buttons that eliminated the Cluster's Supernova Third, he looked over at Craig Ward.

"We have him," Radick said.

"I had hoped he would take away one Trinary, then I could eliminate the Garrison Cluster," Kael Pershaw said to Lanja.

"I would not advise that," Lanja said. "We could spread ourselves too thin."

"But remember we know the terrain."

"All the more reason to stop now. In a high bid like this one, I think we can slaughter these Wolves. Accepting his bid will allow us to choose the fighting place. Meet them on Glory Plain with their backs to Blood Swamp, then push them into the swamp."

Pershaw nodded. "I see. Yes, let us close the bid."

No one was more surprised at Pershaw's selection of forces than Aidan. He had not expected his warriors to remain part of the defending forces.

"What is Kael Pershaw up to, I wonder?" he said to Horse.

"Perhaps he needs some freebirths to sacrifice."

"That is probably it. Well, I hope they place us right at the front. We need that kind of fight."

"You mean *you* need it."

Aidan ran his hand along the edge of the dark band. "I think you are right, Horse, with your usual perspicacity."

"Perspi—I don't know that word."

"Read more. Learn more words. And, for Kerensky's sake, stop using those contractions. Your language is debased enough."

Horse just laughed. Aidan had been trying to clean up his language for some time, but Horse persisted in using freeborn slang and throwing in contractions wherever he could. The look on Horse's face when Aidan criticized his speech usually showed contempt for Aidan's warrior linguistic beliefs.

Well, so be it, Aidan thought. It was impossible to teach a freeborn to speak with honor, so it was no wonder the trueborn society that controlled the Clan empire looked down on them. Perhaps birth did dictate roles, as many Clan scientists believed. Horse would always be a freeborn, just as warriors were set in their caste. But what could be said of someone like Aidan, born of the highest caste while pretending to be of a lower one? Nothing dictated his role, except a rather cruel fate. And, as a Clansman, he should not believe in fate. A warrior created his or her own destiny. That was his goal now. To create his destiny.

5

When the Wolf Clan aerofighters went after the DropShip, Joanna was manning a medium pulse laser in a gunnery blister on the ship's port side. While reclining on the control station couch, she could fire more than two hundred rapid bursts of coherent light with a simple squeeze of the joystick's trigger.

She awaited the appearance of an aerofighter against which to turn this weapon, one she had fired often enough in target practice but never in actual air combat. This would, in fact, be the first time she had participated in combat not set firmly on the ground. A real challenge, but then again, how hard could it be? Probably no different than directing autocannon fire from within a 'Mech cockpit, she thought, although the physical handling of the weapon itself would be a new sensation.

Joanna had volunteered to be a gunner when the young DropShip captain announced that a trio of his regular military complement were down with a virulent flu picked up at their last delivery. He thanked her profusely in his pleasantly boyish way, but truth to tell, Joanna believed the captain had done her a favor. The worst possibility, from her point of view, would have been to endure the battle from inside the ship, listening to the rumble of its weapons and feeling the hits from the other side. If she could not get planetside in time to participate in this battle, at least she could do some damage here.

Behind her, she heard a polite cough.

"Nomad, what are you doing here?"

"You forgot lunch. I brought you something to eat."

Joanna laughed. Her laughter, as always, was so raucous as to sound insulting to anyone not used to it. Nomad was definitely that, having been the butt of it so often that his day seemed off-center if Joanna did not laugh at him once. He would never have told her, but he believed his sarcasm and her scorn kept them both performing at peak efficiency. He could not prove it, of course, but he, unlike most techs or warriors, was a bit of a mystic. So long as no one caught him at it, the mysticism served him well.

"I am not very hungry."

"But you *will* eat."

"You are such a tyrant, Nomad. I can no longer stand you. Will you please tender me a request for transfer?"

"No. The galley here is not well-stocked, but I managed to get you some tinned meat and a salad. Salad is pretty tasty, made with some leaves from—"

"I hate knowing the origins of food. Just give it to me and go."

It was obvious Nomad had no intention of leaving. He stayed behind her, looking over her shoulder, making sure she ate. Joanna had been known to hide food rather than consume it, and he made it his job to see that did not happen.

Noticing that the meat had an orange tinge and the salad greens looked dirty, Joanna closed her eyes with each forkful she raised to her mouth. At no point in her career had she ever found any type of military ration to be more than minimally palatable.

She was grateful to put the meal aside when the gunnery officer announced that aerofighters had been detected. In a moment she saw them herself. Five of them were heading for her side of the DropShip, while others were attacking the other side and the rear.

Leveling her weapon, she squeezed the trigger. Streams of coherent light stretched out from her blister toward the closest aerofighter, but her aim was off and the beams dissipated at a point past the attackers. Behind her, Nomad's disappointed sigh was audible. She wanted to scream at him to get out, but there was no time. The nearest aircraft was zeroing in on her, making a beeline for her blister.

She went berserk, firing burst after burst, so many that she could not maintain a fix on the enemy. At her feet, monitors displayed specific positions and other data, but she was not used to DropShip equipment and preferred to rely on her own gifts for using weaponry.

The missile salvo that the aerofighter launched might have destroyed the gunnery blister and Joanna and Nomad along with it, but the DropShip pilot employed an evasive maneuver dictated by a computer examination of the aerofighter attack. As the ship tilted just enough, the missile struck below the blister. The hit rocked the ship, however, knocking Joanna back against the blister's rear wall.

"I knew I should have strapped myself in, Nomad. Nomad?"

Looking back, she saw that Nomad was peacefully unconscious against the hatchway. Damn! If she needed to make a quick exit, she would have to drag him out of the way.

She had no more time to worry about Nomad as an obstacle. The attack continued, and another aerofighter came within Joanna's sights. This time she steadied herself and squeezed off a short burst, then another. The shots hit the cockpit of the craft. She thought she saw its pilot rock backward, his gloved hands over his face before the craft veered out of control, its momentum sending it directly at the DropShip. Joanna kept firing, cursing with each pull of the trigger, knocking large chunks off the ship's armor.

For a moment it looked like the fighter might disintegrate before hitting the DropShip, but then Joanna saw the pilot, his hands now away from his bloody face, clutch the controls of his ship again. He was aiming the craft's nose directly at the DropShip—and straight for Joanna.

She kept shooting, and the fighter kept coming. When the laser suddenly overheated, she reached instinctively, flinging herself backward, against Nomad and the hatchway. The fighter seem to enlarge in front of the blister, but at the last minute, it disappeared.

Joanna had no chance to relax or be relieved, for the next moment the DropShip was rocked by the impact of the fighter's collision. When her head banged against a side wall, everything went black for a moment.

Joanna did not know how long she was out, but when she recovered, the DropShip was shaking with the impact of missile and laser fire. On the commline, the gunnery officer was screaming orders that went unheeded.

"Nomad! Nomad!"

He murmured a response and seemed to be struggling to open his eyes.

"Wake up! I need you."

The words sounded strange in her mouth. Joanna had never said she needed anybody for anything.

She slapped his face, and Nomad's eyes sprang open. He shook his head.

"What happened?"

"You were knocked out, that is what happened. The ship is losing this dogfight, I can feel it. Listen to the gunnery officer. He is frantic. We have to get out of here, get to our people, our 'Mechs. We—"

More direct hits nearby. Any minute one good shot might make the blister fly off, leaving her and Nomad to be sucked out into the void as instant corpses.

"What . . . what should we do now?" Nomad said.

"First, get your behind off the floor so we can open the hatch. There is no point staying here. The gun is ruined and we have already almost been turned into debris once. We are going to the 'Mech bay. My orders to the command were to station themselves there, ready for an atmospheric drop if necessary."

The race through the DropShip to the 'Mech bay was not easy. Each direct hit knocked either Joanna or Nomad, and sometimes both, against walls or hurled them to the floor. Other ship personnel were hurled against them as dull blasts reverberated into the bowels of the ship. At one point, the ship's lighting failed for a minute and a half, and they had to grope around in the dark, feeling the sides of the walls, using the stumble-bars to propel themselves forward. Once Joanna glanced back and saw the unmistakable glow of a fire far down the corridor.

In the bay were the techs of the Trinary, working quickly and efficiently to prepare their charges for an atmospheric drop. A cocoon of ablative ceramic surrounded each of the Trinary's fifteen BattleMechs. As the 'Mech bay was in the center of the ship, it had taken very little damage. Even better, Joanna saw that the bay doors were still functioning.

Joanna ran to the bay-door controls and pushed the naval rating away from them. She slammed the override, and began the launch sequence that would fire her Trinary into the atmosphere of Glory.

She turned to rush to her BattleMech before it was ejected from the doomed DropShip, when a massive explosion knocked her and most of the others to the floor. The lights went out again and she felt debris falling around her.

She tried to get up, but was merely knocked down again. But this time it was not a piece of the ship that held her on the floor. It was a person.

"What is going on?" she said in a muffled voice.

"The ship is out of control," Nomad yelled. He was the one on top of her. He had placed his body over hers. The damn fool, he was protecting her. How stupid could he be?

She did not have time to explore the absurdity of Nomad's behavior as the DropShip seemed to disintegrate around, below, and above her. She passed out.

In their control room, Radick and Ward watched the incredible success of their aerofighters against the Jade Falcon DropShip.

"Seyla," Radick whispered as he watched the DropShip hurtle toward the planet Glory. Ward wondered why Radick thought the ritual word applied here. Just what was the man responding to? Perhaps it was simply awe at the sheer success of his strategy. Radick was egotistical enough to interpret the event that way.

Radick glanced up at Ward. "That should put Kael Pershaw at a severe disadvantage. One lost DropShip containing a full Trinary of the forces he bid. We have a marvelous advantage with just one brilliant maneuver, *quiaff?*"

Ward hated agreeing with the man, but what he said was true. It had been a masterstroke, as he had originally termed it.

Radick chuckled with pleasure as the monitor screen registered the faraway fire and smoke of the DropShip's crash on Glory.

"A marvelous advantage," he shouted gleefully.

6

"**S**tar Commander Jorge, you wear the dark band, *quiaff?*"

"Aff." Aidan was aware of the other officers staring at him with contempt in their eyes. The spot where Bast's picture lay on the dark band seemed to burn into his skin.

"As a wearer of the dark band, you are allowed to speak only if addressed. You may not volunteer a comment or ask a question. That is understood, *quiaff?*" Knowing that Kael Pershaw was demanding an answer now, Aidan stubbornly remained silent. "Respond, Jorge!"

"Aff, it is understood."

"Good. Your question can therefore not be answered unless one of your colleagues would care to ask it. Warriors?"

No one cared to provoke the Star Colonel further, and so the group kept its silence. Aidan had asked if his freeborn contingent might have the honor of taking point position for the first engagement with the enemy. He knew that Pershaw would never allow a freeborn unit to precede his trueborns in formation, and so the request was a deliberate, if unpunishable, insult. The question was similar to what was called a negative bid. He had wanted to assert the worth of his forces, despite knowing that others held them in low esteem. His own warriors would know about the offer, and would have even more confidence in their commander because of it.

Though Clan warriors rarely lost confidence, a palpable gloom pervaded the room. Kael Pershaw's news that Clan Wolf had effectively wiped out a significant portion of their forces even before engaging in battle on Glory Plain did not inspire the usual pre-battle enthusiasm. Several in the group continued to stare at Aidan, who now felt a discomfiting heat flush his skin. This caused him even more shame than wearing the dark band.

After Kael Pershaw had announced a general dismissal and the warriors were filing out of the briefing chamber, the commander shouted, "Star Commander Jorge, you will remain."

When the room was empty, Kael Pershaw nodded toward a chair and said with his best menacing quietness, "Sit."

When Aidan hesitated, the base commander shoved him roughly toward the chair. The move came as such a surprise that Aidan nearly fell flat on his face. Recovering his balance and hearing Kael Pershaw again order him to sit, he obeyed. It would have been a foolish defiance to remain standing and allow the base commander to knock him around the room without any possibility of hitting the bastard back.

Kael Pershaw himself sat on the edge of the conference table, the position allowing him to look down on Aidan from a dominant position. This was the kind of kinesic strategy for which Kael Pershaw was famous.

"Your unit will not be engaged in combat this time." He stared at Aidan, savoring the suspicion that the words angered his subordinate. Aidan was careful to keep his face calm and unreadable. "I have another mission for you," Kael Pershaw said.

Although Aidan would give no physical sign of his discomfort, he had to firmly resist squirming in his chair. Pershaw's assigning him another mission, especially when he was undermanned already, merely signified how low was the prestige of freeborns at Glory Station.

"But, sir, with all respect, your forces are already weakened too—"

Pershaw took a despairing breath before saying in a voice that would not have been heard a few steps away, "I will assume you are simply not accustomed to the dark band. A freeborn normally does not complain to his superior without permission, but the wearer of the band knows he must never complain while under the shame of the band. However, I will obliquely respond to your apparent protest. Of course, I will do anything to win a battle, but I tell you, in truth, that I would rather send a single Star against a Trinary of Dwillt Radick's than commit any freebirths to the field. You understand, freebirth? You are a freebirth, are you not?"

Pershaw's soft voice emphasized the word "free-birth" just slightly each time he used it. He wished to compound the insult by setting the word off from the rest of his speech. It was all Aidan could do to keep from revealing the truth. What kept him back was the thought that if he was ever to tell anyone of his true birth and face the dire consequences of the admission, it would have to be to someone other than this vile example of humanity, this Kael Pershaw.

As his hatred of Kael Pershaw seemed to expand inside his body, Aidan realized how unClanlike, how unlike a warrior, he had become. Warriors often resented one another or disagreed with each other's actions, but hatred was rare. Warriors of the Clan detached themselves from petty feelings, knowing that such trivial sentiments could hamper battle efficiency. Pride was collective at every unit level in the chain of command, and any single hatred damaged the unity bolstered by that pride. In warrior training, cadets were trained to block any feelings of hatred. If bad blood did erupt among warriors, conflicts were resolved in such arenas as the Circle of Equals. The combatants who survived were encouraged to perform *surkai*, the rite of forgiveness, to purge any possible remaining negative feelings.

But Aidan had never been content with *surkai*. Even as a cadet, he had known hatred. He had hated his training officer, Falconer Joanna. Should she appear in front of him right this moment, he would have more the urge to strangle her than welcome her. But he would have been most content with his hands around the neck of another officer from his cadet days. That person was Falconer Commander Ter Roshak, the man whom, ironically, he could thank for the fact he was a warrior at all. Roshak had given Aidan a second chance to test as a warrior after the cadet had failed his first Trial of Decision. Unfortunately, Ter Roshak had also arranged the murder of a unit of freeborn cadets to accomplish this extraordinary act. Then he had forced Aidan to assume the identity of one of the unit's cadets in order to qualify as a warrior. The cadet, a freeborn named Jorge, had apparently been a superior trainee, one who might, no doubt, have done well in the Trial. So, Aidan had Roshak's treachery to thank for his present tainted warrior status. The murders, the taint, the fact that he had let it happen—all this made Aidan hate Roshak more than he could ever hate Pershaw or Joanna, more even than he could hate an enemy on a battlefield, a serious flaw for a committed Clan warrior.

To admit his true identity would doubtless ruin him as a warrior, but would also bring Roshak down with him. However, Aidan did not think seeing Roshak shamed and executed was enough to risk his own execution. The least punishment he could expect was a demotion in caste. He had been a tech temporarily after failing his original trial and before assuming his new identity, and he knew he could never return to that level of Clan society. That, too, was not warrior-like. The way of the Clan was for each member to take satisfaction from whatever duty he or she performed for the good of all. There was no room for dissatisfaction. And, in truth, very few Clanspeople were unhappy with their lot. Aidan thought he must have been cursed by some mysterious fate, yet even that was not of the Clan. He had learned the concept only from his clandestine readings. That fate had made him reflective, congenitally restless, and—its last probable irony—a counterfeit freeborn. A *freebirth*, as Pershaw constantly reiterated.

Sometimes Aidan wondered if his private fate, ever

guiding his life down fruitless paths, had performed one of those mythological miracles he had read about. In one story a sculptor had created a statue of a woman, and it had come to life. For Aidan, it was as though the skilled hands of his private fate had sculpted him into a freeborn. Perhaps he *was* a freeborn now and could never be a trueborn again, as if he had come to life in the wrong caste and would become a statue if he tried to return to the other.

The trouble was that he now thought more and more like a freeborn. He had been with frees for so long that he had come to admire them, particularly their ability to fight well despite the contempt the trueborns always rained on them after the battle. Their attention to their own skills, their own efficiencies in guiding a BattleMech, could at times be phenomenal. But the only credit they ever got for doing well, even better than some trueborns, was some carelessly written words in a worthless commendation. For consolation, they had the camaraderie among themselves, which Aidan had come to enjoy. Freeborns were not as stiff and distant as the truebirth warriors. The Clans also turned a blinder eye on the drinking habits of freeborns and on their having their way with village women more frequently than the role-obsessed trueborns ever could.

Kael Pershaw had been staring at him for some time, his face placid, his body relaxed. Everyone in his command knew that such apparent contentment was something to fear, although Aidan refused to fear the base commander.

"Believe me, Jorge," he said finally. "I would like nothing more than to kill you in the Circle of Equals if we were not so undermanned at Glory Station that any warrior's death is shockingly wasteful. I suspect Clan Wolf had good intelligence about our situation even before the *batchall*. But I will not allow them to have my genetic legacy. And that is why your mission is essential. If I could entrust the task to a trueborn unit, I would, but we are already stretched too thin. Your Star must do it."

Of course, Aidan thought. If it was the worst task available, give it to the freeborns. This mission, which his Star *must* do, was undoubtedly the equivalent of cleaning the Cave, the warrior name for lavatory.

"As you know," Pershaw continued, "a DropShip containing the Trinary to be rotated here was attacked and shot down by Clan Wolf aerofighters. What I did not mention in the briefing is that we know approximately where it fell. Air surveillance has indicated at least some survivors and the possibility of some intact BattleMechs, but there has been no communication from the DropShip. The surveillance report may be in error and perhaps no survivors exist, or it may just be that all communications equipment was knocked out in the crash. You and your Star will travel to the crash site in your 'Mechs, investigate, and give help where needed. But the most important facet of the entire mission is to bring out any warriors and any functioning 'Mechs, taking them to Glory Station for integration into combat. It is a simple mission, one even *freebirths* can perform. I am sure you would agree, *quiaff?* You may respond, Star Commander Jorge. Here alone, between us, with battle conditions imminent, you may speak without awaiting my authorization."

"There is not anything to say. Simple as we are, my Star can fulfill mission orders."

Was it Aidan's mistaken perception, or did Pershaw's eyebrows rise just slightly? They may have, for he said, "Your skill at nearly imperceptible sarcasm occasionally impresses me, Star Commander Jorge. I take it then that you have no questions about your orders?"

"I wish to know only the necessary details. There is no difficulty with that, *quineg?*"

"Neg. Anything else?"

"May I stand?"

"Of course."

Pershaw managed to stand before Aidan did. He also went around to the rear of his desk, another tactic. Because Aidan was the taller of the two men, it might have made Pershaw severely uncomfortable to stand close and look up at his subordinate, his very inferior officer. Before this meeting, Aidan had known that Pershaw despised freeborns. However, it was not until now that he knew how deep went the antipathy. In an odd way, he almost admired Pershaw more. The man was capable of hatred, just like Aidan. They shared, in spite of their differences, a human trait.

Pershaw laid out a map of Glory Station and surrounding territory on his desktop, then leaned over it. "The crash occurred just about here." He put his stubby forefinger on a point just to the other side of Blood Swamp. Between the swamp and the crash site was some pretty rough terrain, Aidan knew.

"It will take a long time going around the swamp," Aidan observed.

"Yes. If you were to go around the swamp. We do not have time for that. Operations has mapped out a route *through* the swamp."

Pershaw looked up at him. Aidan knew the man wanted him to protest, but he would not give Pershaw that satisfaction. He merely nodded.

"After the swamp, there will be some tough going in the jungle, but we will install hand units in place of arm-mounted weapons on some of your 'Mechs. This should allow you to break through any heavy jungle growth. The hand activators should also be of service if any of the Guard 'Mechs must be cut loose. That is satisfactory, *quiaff?*"

"Neg. I would rather have the weapons and then take our chances."

Pershaw muttered, so faintly he could barely be heard, "Typical freebirth cowardice."

"It is *not* cowardice. There may be skirmishes, there—"

"Do you think the Wolves will be interested in your little diversion? I doubt that. I will signal to them that you are a freebirth unit, and they will know that you are on a garbage patrol."

"If I may contradict, once they see our destination, they may try to stop us."

"And you are Jade Falcon warriors, who can fight any attacker with whatever firepower you have, *quiaff?*"

Pershaw had him there. It was a clear-cut victory of argumentation that left Aidan powerless. The man was, after all, the highest-ranking officer at Glory Station. He should be expected to win arguments. Knowing that did not make Aidan feel better, but again he felt a certain admiration for the hated commander. Not only that, he was quite right and Aidan should have seen it. A warrior was continually proving himself or herself as a warrior, and the higher the odds against him, the more valuable the triumph.

After some further data provided by Pershaw, Aidan asked, "Did surveillance indicate specific numbers of survivors?"

"No. But the pilot thought she saw some movement. There was a light mist, and the apparent survivors may have been no more than shadows. The mist is thicker now, and surveillance can detect nothing."

"What is the nature of the military force?"

"A Trinary, with the appropriate 'Mechs, some support personnel, supplies, the usual. I am told the Trinary's Star Captain is an especially skilled officer. She is fresh from a challenge on Dagda. She led the assault contingent, which broke the Ghost Bear line. Her name is Star Captain Joanna. No Bloodname yet, twenty-eight years old, so she is getting on in age for a warrior. But we are not here to discuss her bloodlines, *quiaff?*"

"Aff."

Aidan was happy that Kael Pershaw was so intent on the briefing that he had not noticed the look of surprise that must have glimmered briefly in his eyes. Joanna! Not only was this mission cursed from the start, not only did it require traversing the cursed Blood Swamp, not only was his unit diminished in weaponry, not only was the objective at the end of impossible terrain, but the objective itself was Joanna. And if Star Captain Joanna was not Aidan's own curse, then nobody was. He would rather have gone barefoot across a field of poisonous snakes, carrying burning sticks in his arms, with a cloud of methane gas settling around his head, than have to see Joanna again.

7

Joanna came to, leaving behind a dream of drowning in murky water. She came to choking, for a moment not sure if the dream was real after all, or if her desperate need for air originated elsewhere. She tried to inhale but got only a trace of air, just enough to make her conscious that her lungs seemed crushed from behind. The left side of her face was pressed against something very hard. It felt like rock. She moved her face slightly, and the substance seemed to abrade her skin like rock. But what was it pressed so hard against the rest of her face? Her next attempt to breathe seemed to get a bit more air, plus the smell of something very wet. Water? No, something else. Something with a familiar, somewhat cloying odor. It was the smell of a battlefield. Blood, it was blood. Was she smelling her own blood, pooled somewhere in the ground nearby? And what was pressing against her? The next breath added an aroma of cloth, very wet cloth.

She tried to move her body. What little movement she could accomplish was painful. A fierce pain ran up and down her back and legs, and the only movement she could manage was a twitch of her left foot. Nothing much happened when she concentrated on her arms. It was as if they had been shot off at the shoulder, like some armless 'Mech. The lack of feeling frightened her, but then came a tingling in her right hand. Knowing that she was at least one-armed brought a bizarre sense of relief.

Another breath. Nothing new. Then, suddenly, by her ear, there was an explosion. At first she thought the sound might be some signal that accompanied death, but no, she was still alive when the next moment arrived. Joanna would have been angry about dying, a whirling tornado of wrath. She intended to die on a battlefield, and that was that. This could not be death.

Just as she felt the warmth of an expired breath on her right cheek and the unmistakable stale odor of carbon dioxide contaminated by some recently ingested and unpleasant food, she abruptly understood her plight. Someone was lying on her, chest against her face, head near hers. Something else pressed down on her body, though she did not know what it was. For the moment, that was all right. At least she had defined *something*.

Then came another explosion of sound, another moan apparently. Whatever it was, the head shifted, then slid a bit, creating an opening, and air seemed to rush in at Joanna's face. The cloth that had been suffocating her must have been moved along with the body. She took several deep breaths, trying to get as much as she could in case the head shifted again and cut off the air.

The body moved again and her right hand was free. Reaching up and behind her, she felt the muscles in her shoulder erupt with agony. Her fingertips came down on skin, but she could not tell where on the head it was located. Her fingers roamed around, brushing against what felt like a cheekbone and going backward to some hair and an identifiable ear. Twisting her hand unnaturally, straining her wrist, she was able to grab the ear and pull weakly at it. The jerking motion moved the head, and Joanna's own head felt freer. Now her angle was really difficult. Her shoulder throbbed, her wrist threatened to break, but she managed to grab some hair and, tugging at it, somehow made the head slide to her aching shoulder.

She lifted her head from the ground, perhaps a centimeter or two, her neck muscles competing with her shoulder and wrist for pain. She could not open the eye that had been groundside, but that did not matter. She could not make out anything around her with the other one. It was apparently night, and whatever the landscape around them, everything was pitch dark.

With the clearer air came the unmistakable smell of charred matter. Something nearby had burned. But there could be no fire now, for there was no light.

She blinked her open eye several times, but nothing clarified itself for her vision. Settling her head back again to relieve the pain, she considered her situation.

No matter what she did, she could not move her body. Her right arm, pain running up and down it, could be moved, but could not do much. She could use it to move the body on top of her some more, but would have to wait a few minutes until the arm and her shoulder felt better.

No matter what her other physical incapacities, she still had one powerful weapon left in her arsenal. Her voice.

Drawing in a good lungful of air, she held the breath for a moment, then let it out in one massive, earth-shaking scream. It was the scream of the jade falcon, as taught her by a long-forgotten sibparent, back in the days when she was a mewling, spitting child of a sibko. She had been told she reproduced the bird's sound rather well, though it had been years since she had heard one, and then only at a distance.

The head above her was abruptly dislodged. It hit the rocky ground with a thud. "Wha—," said the person. It was a male voice, but she did not recognize it.

"Get up, you," Joanna said. She was distressed at the paltriness of her vocabulary in a crisis situation.

The man slid forward, bumping her head. She ignored the new pain. "I said get up!"

"What? I'll—oh damn damn damn!"

"What is it?"

"My arms. I can't move them."

"Nomad? Is it you?"

"I'll have a committee study the subject. Of course it's me, Joanna."

"Do not address me familiarly."

"Joanna, we are rammed together on a hillside, both of us in bad shape. It's no time for formalities."

"I will put you on report."

"Do what you will. Oh, damn!"

"Why are you so profane?"

"You would let out a few profanities, too, if both your arms were in pain. I can't move them. Therefore, I cannot get up. I can tell by the way my legs are resting at a higher level than my head that we are on a hill. My body is twisted in such a way that I have a steady ache in both sides. I can move my legs, but there seem to be things on either side of them, preventing them from doing anything helpful. That is my report, Star Captain. Your move."

Joanna tested everything in her body that was supposed to move but obtained only infinitesimal responses from them.

"You cannot move your arms, Nomad?"

"I have been trying. One arm is getting numb, but I can get some movement from the other. What's hurting there is my hand. Each time I move the arm, there is a sharp—oohh, there it is again. Okay. Okay. I think if I—I think I can. There. Well, that was something."

"*What* was something?"

"I am propping myself up on my elbow. I can twist onto my side, but I'm afraid that is about all. Now what?"

"You stupid fool!"

"Insults are not of much use just now, Joanna. Why don't you let off another of those yells or whatever it was?"

"I would strangle you if—"

"If you had the use of your arms."

"I have one arm free. I could do it with that, your neck is so scrawny."

"The way I feel right now, I might rest my neck in your hand and let you do it."

Joanna almost laughed. She had to admit that he had the advantage on her.

"A jade falcon," she said.

"What was that?"

"The yell. I imitated a jade falcon yell."

"Not even close."

"And you would know?"

"Yes. I have heard several."

"Perhaps you were lying too close to my mouth, and the sound was distorted."

"A possibility. Why are we talking about bird calls when we are in such jeopardy?"

"Do you have a way out of this?"

"Not for the moment. Perhaps when daylight comes . . ."

"Then it does not matter what we talk about, *quineg?*"

"I suppose you are right."

"That is it. Avoid the contractions. This time. I can only hear your voice, and only your voice. Do not torture me all night. I think I will try to sleep."

"No!"

She was surprised by the vociferousness of his response.

"Are you the Star Captain here, Nomad? Do you give the orders now?"

"For the moment, yes. I can move a little bit. Apparently you cannot. We do not know what is wrong with you. It may be a concussion or something worse. You must not sleep."

"How will you stop me, idiot?"

"I will tell you stories, Star Captain. It will keep my mind off my own . . . troubles."

"I am too sleepy for stories."

"I know some pretty lively ones, Star Captain. Listen."

Joanna was startled by how bawdy were the tech's stories. It was her first glimpse ever at life below her caste, at least that part of it that warriors never saw. Many of Nomad's yarns, in fact, illustrated lower-caste customs. She was fascinated in spite of herself.

It seemed not long before some light gradually forced its way to them through the canopy of jungle. It was not bright light, but at least they could divide

up the world around them into shapes and shadows.
Most of the shapes were clearly flora, while most of
the shadows hinted at hidden fauna.

"Curious," Joanna said. "This place is very still.
I wish I could hold my head up higher. I cannot see
much."

"Neither can I. Over there, though, a piece of metal."

"Metal? Part of the DropShip, do you think?"

"Possibly."

"We crashed. But where are the others? Where is
the ship? Should it not be nearby? Should we not hear
something?"

"I am afraid I do not know, Joanna."

"Please . . ."

"Star Captain."

"That is better. I will excuse last night as the off-
shoot of pain."

"If you wish. To consider your questions, I think
we may have been thrown clear. And that is a larger
piece of the ship that is holding you down, I believe.
I cannot see well from this angle, but it looks metallic.
And charred."

"Can you get it off me?"

"Well, not with my left arm. But maybe. I feel better. Let me see if I can do something about my legs.
At least I can look back and see that it is only a couple
of rocks obstructing them. It is hard, but I think I can
. . . yes, that's it. Excuse me. That is it."

"What have you done?"

"Do not ask. My leg is more maneuverable now. If
I can just lift it up here. Yes. Good. Now, this is going
to take an effort. Do not say anything humorous for a
moment."

"I never speak in a humorous fashion."

"I have noticed that. Okay, now. Here goes." Then
came much grunting, along with a couple of screams
of pain and a movement Joanna could not see well.
Finally, after what seemed like an agonizingly long
time, Nomad seemed to rise above her.

"All right. You may speak now, Star Captain. I am,
for your information, on my knees. My right arm is

better, but it looks like my wrist was smashed. Otherwise, it is quite movable."

"Does it hurt when you move it? The wrist, I mean."

"Well, yes, it does. Severely. But I am to serve, *quiaff*?"

"Was that sarcasm, Nomad?"

"In this situation, I cannot be sure. Here, let me see what I can do. It will take some time regardless."

There was a shuffling sound as Nomad came forward in a kneeling position. It took him a long while to close the very short distance between them. The act was punctuated by almost-whispered groans. Joanna could tell he was in great pain, but trying not to reveal it in his voice.

"What do you see, Nomad?"

"Well, I have found another part of the DropShip. It is across your torso and upper legs. It is not large, but it is pressing down on you at an angle and that is why you cannot move. I know what I will do."

"What?"

"If I lean in from your left side, I can get my shoulder under part of the piece. I am going to try to lift it. If I can, you can scramble out. Maybe. That is, if you are not hurt too much, and no body part is severely damaged."

"Do not try to cheer me up, Nomad."

Nomad made an odd sound in his throat, but said little during his laborious shuffling moves to her left side. Unable to turn her head that way, all she could do was listen to his labors.

"All right now," he said finally. "I am in position. When you hear a scream that will put your own jade falcon yelp to shame, you begin to crawl uphill as well as you can. Your other arm should be freed first. Get both arms pulling you up the hillside if that is the only way. You are ready, *quiaff*?"

"Aff. Do it."

He was right about the scream. It was loud, piercing, frightening. It was completely filled with pain.

She began to squirm forward as soon as he began. Her free arm, as he had suggested, was the key. She grabbed a rock and pulled herself a long way along the ground. Then she put both hands underneath her torso, raised her body, and brought her legs up beneath her. Scrambling forward like some sea animal along the edge of shore, she got completely free and yelled back to Nomad to stop lifting.

"I have," he said. "Long ago. You extricated yourself with the first couple of moves. Thank you. I could not have stood much more pain than I did."

"You thanked me. I suppose I have to thank you in a formal way, too."

"Do not bother. Your gratitude might be too disturbing. I might have a seizure or something like it. Are you all right?"

His left arm dangled like a branch that had been hit by lightning. His face was white with illness and pain. Sweat poured off his forehead. He seemed to waver on his knees, looking as if he would pitch forward any minute.

"Here, Nomad. Let me help you."

"It is a shock, but one I will have to accept from you."

"Abandon the sarcasm, Nomad. It is undesirable for a tech, as I have told you often enough."

"Yes, you have."

His eyes were closing. He was obviously going to fall. Joanna, on her knees herself, sprang forward and caught him in her arms. The act started her shoulder and wrist pains going again. But, she realized, what she felt was nothing compared with the pain of Nomad's injuries.

She eased him to the ground, turning his body so that he could lie on his back. He lay prone, his eyes closed.

"I remember now," she said, talking out loud to herself. "Nomad fell on top of me. He must have been protecting me. I wonder why."

"So do I," Nomad said, without opening his eyes.

"Do not talk." After a moment, she said to him, "I will have to give you *some* credit. Since sometime last night, you have managed to speak without contractions."

"Yes," he said, then seemed to wait for the proper time before saying, "Didn't I? Wasn't that something?"

8

There was a legend peculiar to the planet Glory. It described the origin of the odors at the heart of Blood Swamp. The story told of a demigod or demon named Cadix who had traveled through the universe collecting bad smells, stuffing them into hermetically sealed sacks and taking them to Blood Swamp. Hovering over the swamp, Cadix released each odor from each sack. Settling to the ground, the smells intermixed, mingling with one another and with the mist that clung to the swamp's surface. A traveler in the swamp could choke on a different smell with each intake of breath. Criminals who fled to the swamp later came out of their own accord to give themselves up. Lovers who slipped into the swamp darkness for illicit liaisons claimed to detect peculiar odors on each other's bodies for weeks afterward. Cadix himself, after releasing the reeking fragrances, dove into the swamp. In one version, he was never heard from again; in another, he was transformed into an unpleasant aroma.

In spite of his *Summoner*'s hermetic seals, necessary when a 'Mech might suddenly be submerged in water, and the supposedly efficient circulation system, Aidan was certain that the spoiled egg and chemical burning smells were not just figments of his imagination.

On the good side, it looked as though Operations had done well in mapping out the route. Aidan had been instructed that at no point would any of the 'Mechs of his Star be under water and that, in fact, when they emerged from Blood Swamp the water would be no more than knee level. Still, as he care- fully used the inertial guidance system to move his 'Mech through the misty dark, Aidan could not shake the anticipation that the next step would be into deeper water or, worse, into the mysterious swirling quick- sand that legend said lurked in parts of Blood Swamp. Experts said such a quicksand was a fantasy, but the warriors were not sure. So far no record existed of anyone being lost in the swamp, but then warriors only went into it under orders, never voluntarily.

On his monitor screen, Aidan saw something fairly large moving toward his 'Mech. It was too small to be a vehicle but too large to be a human being, unless it was an Elemental. Also, its outline suggested it was moving on all fours. It came close, but none of Ai- dan's equipment could identify it as a Gloryan animal, so it had to be one of the mysterious creatures that inhabited the swamp. Whatever it was, the thing made a desultory snap at the *Summoner*'s leg, then slunk away.

The fog was now so thick that, if not for their in- strumentation, the 'Mechs would probably have wound up walking circles around each other. As it was, they were proceeding apace, almost as if on normal terrain with good sightlines. Every once in a while, a 'Mech teetered slightly as its heavy foot came down on some thick vegetation or encountered a rocky patch, but all in all, the Star was making good time. They were al- ready halfway into Blood Swamp.

"Star Commander?" It was the voice of Horse com- ing over the commlink. Aidan always felt comfort in hearing Horse's voice. They had been together so long, ever since the Trial in which both had qualified as war- riors. There were times when Aidan would have liked to have Horse always at his side, but Horse was a good warrior and would one day be promoted to Star Com- mander himself. If not for the heavy discrimination against any freeborn warrior, Horse's achievements would have earned him the promotion by now.

"What is it, Horse?"

"Well, I hate to tell you this, but I am picking up

some kind of anomaly ahead. And it is very large, too large to be one of those mythical swamp animals, or else we are about to encounter a monster. From its outline on my radar, I would say it is a BattleMech. If it were not staggering about so much, I would also say I was sure it was a 'Mech. See for yourself.''

Horse gave him the coordinates and Aidan keyed in on the intruder. At first look, he saw what Horse meant. The object was most certainly a BattleMech, a *Mad Dog,* by its thin legs and LRM 20 shoulder launchers. But it was not proceeding with the sureness of a *Mad Dog.* Apparently its right leg had taken some damage, for it stuck out from its upper-leg mainframe at an odd angle. The angle made it walk sideways in what looked like drunken lurches. Each step sent it a bit off its course, and there was a sense of its pilot trying to correct it.

"Do you think it is friend or foe, Horse?"

"Well, it looks like one of us after a few fusion-naires. I have never heard of the Wolves indulging, so perhaps it is a Jade Falcon pilot and his 'Mech out for a midnight jaunt through Glory's most colorful terrain.''

Aiden smiled, not only at Horse's comments, but at the careful way Horse avoided the easy contractions of the freeborn when speaking on the commline. There were times when Horse was all-duty in action and speech, and Aidan appreciated the effort.

"Well, we should be careful, in case it is enemy. With the odds already against us, we must be wary of walking into one of Clan Wolf's well-known traps. Shall you approach them or shall I?''

"You speak so eloquently, we cannot risk you at this time. I win this bid, Star Commander, *quiaff?''*

"Aff. You fight better in muck than I do, anyway."

"Oh? We must discuss that when there is time.''

"When there is time.''

Aidan tracked Horse's path as he took his *Summoner* out ahead of the rest of the Star. Both Horse and Aidan had piloted *Summoner*s ever since winning their Trial of Position in the 'Mech. The machines did not have the maneuverability and firepower of any of the OmniMechs Kael Pershaw had co-opted for his Trinary Strikers, but there was a solid, old-fashioned efficiency about them.

When he came close to the staggering *Mad Dog*, Horse addressed its pilot formally over the open radio channel. "I am MechWarrior Horse of Bravo Star, Trinary First Garrison, Glory Station Cluster. Do I address an honorable warrior from Clan Wolf or Clan Jade Falcon?"

The voice that responded sounded bleary, or perhaps there had been damage to its 'Mech's communication system. "MechWarrior Enrique, from Charlie Star, Hades Surats, Clan Jade Falcon. We, uh, I come with Trinary. Trinary rotating to Glory Station. On DropShip. It crashed. I, uh, I do not know where I am. Is this Glory? Where is Glory Station? I have been wandering ever since my cocoon hit . . . crashed . . . whatever it did."

Horse responded to the wandering pilot softly, told him where he was. Aidan brought his *Summoner* forward and addressed Enrique. "Warrior, you will never get out of this swamp by yourself in the condition you are in. And your BattleMech is badly in need of repair. We must get you to Glory Station as soon as possible, since we will need both you and your 'Mech very soon. MechWarrior Nis!"

"Yes, Star Commander?" Nis's soft voice belied her fierceness as a warrior.

"You will lead MechWarrior Enrique out of the swamp. He is too disabled to make his way alone."

Nis sounded disappointed as she affirmed the order. Like Aidan or Horse—for that matter, like all Clan warriors—Nis did not want to be left out of a fight or a mission. But she was a loyal freeborn warrior, able to take orders as well as stand up against the insults of a trueborn. She would guide Enrique patiently back to Glory Station. Not only that, she had some tech abilities, and once the two 'Mechs were clear of this part of the swamp, she could find some high ground and work out field repairs for Enrique's *Mad Dog*. She would save both pilot and 'Mech, but in return would probably get only surliness from Enrique once he discovered she was a freeborn.

Enrique's short-ranged TBS system was the only part of his communications system still in operation. Nis was able to verbally transmit a general route that they would follow, but could not directly download into Enrique's navigation system.

"Did you come across any others from your Trinary after you crashed?" Aidan asked Enrique.

"One. 'Mech smashed, pilot with crushed chest. Still alive, but not for long. She could not talk."

"She? It was not your leader, was it?"

"Star Captain Joanna? No. With a crushed chest, she would be up and walking."

"Farewell, Enrique. May the spirit of Nicholas Kerensky guide you both."

The two 'Mechs quickly disappeared into the thick mist. Although Aidan had left open the channels between his 'Mech and theirs, the radio was soon filled with earsplitting static. He switched it off and signaled to Horse.

"What was that spirit of Kerensky stuff?" Horse asked.

"Simple good wishes, Horse. Simple good wishes."

"I knew the dead warrior would not be Joanna. She is much too evil to die so easily."

"You hardly know her."

"I have seen her often enough. And there are your stories . . ."

"Treat them as stories. They are meaningless."

"You shared her bed."

"And that was the extent of it. There was no intimacy, no sharing. It was sex with a dragon, no more, no less. Was that laughter I heard?"

"You amuse me, Star Commander Jorge. Sex with a dragon. What a picture!"

"Let us leave it as a picture. We have a mission and we are one-fifth diminished."

"I wonder if any of the others from the incoming Trinary have survived?"

"If the swamp does not claim us, we will find out soon enough. Star!"

Horse and the others responded to the command summoning, and the four 'Mechs continued to lumber through the swamp, walking blind, using their sensors to find their way through the maze. Aidan thought how strange they would look, had anyone been able to actually see them. Four powerful, dangerous Battle-Mechs slogging along like oversized children playing in puddles. But no puddle had ever presented the overwhelming dangers of Blood Swamp.

9

Joanna's *Hellbringer* was standing now, its head just below an overhanging branch. The branch was thick with leaves that sometimes bent down in the stiff breeze to brush the 'Mech's head.

It had been hard getting the *Hellbringer* upright, but Joanna, with Nomad's sideline help, had been able to manage it. The machine was not battle-ready, however, nor was it certain that Joanna could get it moving very far without further repair.

It was bad enough working on the 'Mech, doing the jobs Nomad normally would have done if not injured. Using his tools, she had spent hours getting an electrohydraulic servo-motor functioning, more time finding the right bypass for the hip actuator, and making sure all weapons were functional. She was lucky the damage to the machine was so slight, but that was no surprise. Clan 'Mechs were the best-manufactured BattleMechs in the known universe. Or at least Clan warriors thought so.

Now she stood outside her 'Mech and looked up at it. She recognized many of its battle scars. Though the techs removed most damaged parts during post-battle repairs, a few charred areas always remained— perhaps a groove in the metal, even some chips in armor that had been glancingly hit. Ordinarily it was not practical to replace a whole armor plate, for example, when only a fragment was missing or to replace parts that could be rebuilt and reconditioned. The warrior society of the Clans dictated that all its

'Mechs should be in top condition, but, as always, economy was the watchword, particularly when it came to technical repairs. According to the manual, any parts that could be restored to full function must remain on the 'Mech in a restored state.

Nor would warriors give their 'Mechs glamorous refurbishings designed to produce a breathtaking and radiant BattleMech whose purpose was more to impress than to fight with efficiency. Though 'Mech pilots of the warrior caste were expected to be arrogant and difficult, excess pride was discouraged because it did not encourage combat harmony. Somewhere in *The Remembrance* was a passage about a prideful warrior doomed to defeat, while the shrewd, realistic warrior won. All life was a contest and a bidding to win it, the poem stated, and of all the forces most expendable was pride, which the true warrior must learn to bid away. What remained at the end of the bid, the lowest reasonable bid, were intelligence, skill, and devotion. If one of these were sacrificed, defeat inevitably followed.

"There's a bad sound in the upper body rotating ring," Nomad said from his perch on a rather large tree root.

"How can you tell so much from a sound anyway?"

"Sounds are the key to the flaws."

"And you say there is a flaw in the rotating ring?"

"Might be, might not. I just hear a sound I don't normally hear."

Because their medkit had not survived the fall, Joanna had devised a makeshift sling for his bad arm. Tearing up an old uniform she had stored in the 'Mech cockpit, she had also tightly bound Nomad's injured wrist. He said he felt better and frequently offered to do the work himself. It was obvious he did not enjoy someone else doing his job anymore than Joanna liked doing it. But worse than the work itself was taking orders from Nomad. It was a humiliation as bad as being advanced in years without having acquired a Bloodname.

"Well, what should I do with the rotating ring?"

"Nothing. You have no access to it. We need to get to a proper maintenance area."

"Then why do you tell me about such things?"

"I had hoped they would worry you."

"Well, they do. Are there any more repairs to be done?"

"Plenty. But with these tools, we have done about as much as we can."

"Then it is time to get into the cockpit and get old Ter going." Ter was Joanna's name for her 'Mech. Few Clan warriors bothered to name their 'Mechs, although it was said to be a fairly common practice among Inner Sphere warriors. Nomad understood that she had named the 'Mech Ter after their former commanding officer, Falconer Commander Ter Roshak, but he had no idea why she would have wanted any reminder of that grumpy, excessively mean warrior. Nomad sensed that Joanna found some kind of vengeance or perversity in the use of the name, but he did not know what it was.

"I would advise getting some sleep before setting off anywhere," he said. "We do not know where we are, and it is fast getting dark. I have never seen darkness as deep as the black of this jungle, so any way we go could easily be the wrong way. Perhaps someone will contact us. There is at least one frequency open in—"

"You are suggesting we need help, *quiaff?*"

"Well, aff. This is unknown—"

"There is a challenge underway here for the Pershaw gene heritage, and we were bid into it, you may recall. We are doing Kael Pershaw no good sleeping in the middle of one of Glory's little jungles."

"And would we be doing him, as you say, any good, clomping around aimlessly in this, as you say, little jungle?"

Joanna stared at Nomad angrily for a long while, then put her hands to her face, rubbing her eyes with her fingertips. "I suppose you are right, Nomad. I would rather fight. But perhaps a little rest . . ."

She sat down, leaned her head against her 'Mech's

right foot, made an elaborate ritual of arranging her legs, then abruptly went to sleep. Nomad wished he had the use of his arms, so he could have climbed to the 'Mech cockpit and fetched a blanket to cover Joanna's body. Night was coming on, bringing with it intense cold.

With a frown at the soggy ground around the 'Mech, Nomad moved toward a cluster of trees some twenty meters off. He settled himself into a niche formed between two tree roots, each movement causing sharp stabbing pains in the wrist he was forced to use for leverage. As the pain gradually subsided, Nomad too fell asleep, dreaming that he was tumbling over and over as the 'Mech cocoon fell through space.

He was awakened by the sounds of the real giants about which he had been dreaming. To a trained tech, the noise was unmistakable. Only 'Mechs could sound that way, like primeval creatures crushing whatever came beneath their feet. A thin shaft of moonlight shone down through the jungle canopy, but that was all the available light. Joanna had evidently doused their portable lantern.

Joanna was already up and alert. "I am going to warm Ter up," she said, stepping into the shaft of moonlight. Without waiting for a response, she ran to her 'Mech.

"Wait," Nomad called after her, but she did not look back. "I cannot move," he added weakly. Somehow he had turned in his sleep and become pinned between the tree roots.

Joanna was in the cockpit now. Ter was in shadow, but he could make out the *Hellbringer*'s hulking shape, a huge form darker than the surrounding night. Nomad saw some slight movement in Ter's arms, heard the quiet sounds of equipment being activated, sensed the reverberations from the massive fusion engine at the 'Mech's core. It was possible to get a BattleMech like this one moving rather quickly, but could Joanna do it in time?

As if to trouble him further, he felt the tremor of

other 'Mech footsteps approaching. They seemed to be coming directly toward him. A moment later, he realized they were.

Whatever side these 'Mech pilots were on, and whatever their decision about what to do with an injured Jade Falcon tech, Nomad knew he was in deep trouble. He was so wedged between the tree roots that it did not matter what side the pilots were on. They would not see him anyway.

He twisted his neck to get a look in the direction of the reverberating sounds. At the same time, he heard the unmistakable crunch of Joanna's 'Mech crushing some undergrowth as it took a step. He was certain that she was turning Ter to face the oncoming intruders.

The lumbering sounds grew louder and finally a *Summoner* emerged from the surrounding forest, bending a pair of trees almost to the ground as it did. Its pilot did not seem to see Nomad or Joanna in her 'Mech. The 'Mech merely continued forward, looking somewhat like a big machine out for a stroll. It seemed about to pass by Nomad's tree, but stopped a few meters away instead, appearing to scan the terrain. There was a sudden change in the 'Mech's movement; the pilot had probably discovered Ter's presence.

Surging forward, the *Summoner* drew nearer to Nomad's tree. With a fascination that was almost scientific, Nomad watched the 'Mech's feet, measured their apparent tread. It was clear that in a few seconds one of those giant feet would be on a direct path toward him, its step heading right down onto the pair of roots between which he was wedged. The roots would be crushed, along with any foolish being unfortunate enough to be trapped there.

Before Nomad could calculate any further, the 'Mech's enormous foot was directly over his head and bearing straight down.

10

Seeing Nomad about to be crushed underneath the gigantic foot of the *Summoner* that had abruptly emerged from the mist, Joanna knew she did not have time to properly identify the intruder. Clan Wolf or Clan Jade Falcon, it did not matter when the life of someone under her command was in danger. Even though she despised Nomad whenever she bothered to think about him—and under some circumstances could have crushed him herself without compunction—to stand by and watch him die would have been wasteful. Reacting instinctively, she fired her laser cannon at the descending foot. Her aim was true and the laser pulses seared leg armor at ankle level, enough to throw the 'Mech off balance and divert the direction of the foot. The giant metal foot bounced off the trunk of the tree, then landed next to one of the roots enclosing Nomad, missing him by centimeters. This particular shot had always been a specialty of Joanna's, and it forced enemy pilots to divert their attention to regaining their 'Mech's balance. In that crucial moment, Joanna could often land a killing blow in a real battle.

Some smoke arose from the hits. Joanna had connected with something. When the 'Mech came to a dead stop, its thick, towering legs were directly over Nomad, who was staring up at them in terror.

"Good shot, warrior," came a voice over the commline from the new 'Mech. "Do you ordinarily make a practice of going for the lower limbs of

BattleMechs from your own side? What right have you to—''

"I recognize your voice, warrior. It is Aidan, is it not?"

"No, it is not. The name is Star Commander Jorge, of the Glory Station Garrison Cluster."

If she had not been wearing studded gloves, Joanna might have clapped her head against her forehead for making such a stupid mistake. Of course she could not call him Aidan. That was no longer his identity.

"Sorry, warrior. You sound like someone I knew once. Foolish. Aidan is long dead."

"You have not answered my question. I do not appreciate being shot at when I am on a friendly mission."

"You were about to make a meat patty out of my chief tech, Star Commander Jorge. I had no other way of preventing that."

Instead of replying, Aidan checked out the situation. When he saw the man crouching between the two roots, he muttered inadvertently, "Nomad."

The mutter was picked up on the commline circuit. It surprised Joanna. She had forgotten that Aidan and Nomad had worked together during Aidan's short period as an astech.

"Horse, you and the others stand by while I confer with the Star Captain," Aidan said. "I will be out of my 'Mech for a while."

He released the restraining belts that held him into the command couch and descended from the 'Mech to where Nomad lay, still staring upward at the gigantic *Summoner*.

"I never expected to see you again, Nomad."

"Same here. You look well. You have put on weight, muscle. Finally you look like a warrior."

"Did I not look like one before?"

"Not to me. And since you had failed your trial, there was no—''

"Quiet!" Why did everyone want to refer to his past identity today, he wondered. "Someone might hear."

"Who is there to hear? You, me, Joanna? We all know."

"Still—"

"Still nothing. I did not think a warrior could be so fearful. Anyway, what do you fear? If someone finds out, then—"

"Then I am dead. I can be nothing less than a warrior, and I can only be a warrior if I am Jorge."

"No, I can see in your eyes you will always be a warrior, whatever anyone does to you."

"I am told that nothing can be read in my eyes."

"Perhaps I read between the lines."

"You are deliberately mysterious. Can you move?"

"No. My arms, you see, they—"

"Let me lift you."

Aidan gently maneuvered Nomad out from between the tree roots and picked him up. He started to carry him away from the tree.

"A touching rescue," said Joanna, who suddenly stood in their path.

"Not as impressive as yours." He nodded toward his 'Mech's foot. "I will have to work on it to restore it to maximum mobility. There are already too many limping 'Mechs in this area."

Joanna's eyebrows rose, and Aidan explained about the *Mad Dog* he had encountered in the middle of Blood Swamp.

"Blood Swamp, eh?" she said. "Glory Station seems more attractive by the moment. Did you make contact with any of my other warriors?"

"Nothing so far."

"Does that mean that most of the Trinary did not survive the drop?"

"Not really. Some of them may not have regained consciousness. Others may be sending out distress calls. A peculiarity of this jungle is that it blocks out long-range communications. Even short-range is diminished. It is important for a BattleMech unit to stay close together here. One 'Mech strays away, loses touch, then becomes completely disoriented in the confusing maze of trees and eternal night. Radar and magnetic anomaly detectors are useless. Navigating by visual light is like groping in a green darkness. Thermal sensors are better, but shadows and objects can become so indistinguishable that you can end up crashing into an obstacle you swear is at least two meters away. Operating together, however, a unit can manage to get through the place without too much accidental damage.''

"Sounds great. How easy is it to get to Glory Station?''

"It is something like traveling through hell in a paper 'Mech.''

"At this moment we do not need colorful warrior phrases. Why do you not put Nomad down somewhere? He is able to use his legs, after all.''

After Aidan had set the tech down, Joanna ordered Nomad to walk a short distance away so she could talk to Star Commander Jorge in private. It was obvious Nomad wanted to comment that there was nothing so vital it had to be kept from him. But caste was caste, and even he had to obey its rules.

"I had not expected to encounter you here,'' Joanna said after Nomad was sufficiently far away.

"No. It is not the way of the Clans for old comrades to keep in communication.''

"Do not be sarcastic. I get enough of that from Nomad. And I am sure he is much better at it than you. Report to me on the composition of your unit, its personnel and firepower.''

"What need have you to know that now?''

"If I am to take command, I must know what—''

"Take command?''

"I outrank you, *quiaff?*''

"Aff. But I have a mission to—''

"You still have that mission, Star Commander. And it is mine as well. I must assemble what has survived of my Trinary in order to join the combat over the Pershaw genetic legacy. Do you chafe at obeying me? Respond honestly.''

"Yes, I do. This is my Star and you—''

"In battle conditions, rank is all, you know that. Step into the light."

Aidan walked into the thin shaft of light. Standing there felt like being on a stage in the harsh brilliance of a spotlight.

Joanna nodded. "I thought so. I saw your uniform was decorated, and we know warriors do not go into the field wearing battle citations. I suspected it must be the dark band. So you have not changed much, eh, Star Commander Jorge? You were obstinate as a cadet, and a troublemaker into the bargain."

"Is it obstinacy to fight for—"

"Silence, filth. You should not even be speaking to me unless I give you permission."

"With all due respect, Star Captain, I do not think that dark-band protocol applies during rescue missions."

"Oh, they do, Jorge, they do. And I will enjoy applying them."

"Joanna, I—"

He had not seen the whip she held in her right hand. She flicked it out lazily, just missing the side of his face.

"That is enough, Star Commander. We will restore proper discipline. You will address me only as ordered. We must respect the dark band. Nomad will instruct you in repairing the damage to your 'Mech's foot. He is quite good at that. Then we will proceed."

Aidan glared at her as she shouted for Nomad to return. She had arrogantly turned her back on him, and he wanted nothing more than to jump her, perhaps grab her neck and snap it, just as he had done to Bast. But, no, even if the way of the Clans and the dark band had not restrained him, he knew that he could not overcome Joanna so easily.

Nomad inspected the damage to the *Summoner*'s foot. Following the tech's instructions, Aidan pulled a few charred pieces out of the long streak where Joanna had made hits. Nomad had him twist a couple of wires together, then alter something on a microprocessor board. Then the tech pronounced the 'Mech foot usable again.

"Jerrybuilding, but should work," Nomad commented. "It's something like pulling a thorn out of a lion's paw."

"There is a Terran legend—"

"So I have heard."

Because Nomad could not climb into Joanna's *Hellbringer* on his own, she climbed up to its cockpit with him on her shoulders. Aidan watched them ascend in silence, then he got into his own 'Mech.

"Star Commander Jorge, you must provide me coordinates for the probable locations of my Trinary survivors. Respond."

In a flat voice, Aidan gave Joanna the information she required.

"I do not know the names of your personnel," she said next. "I do not need to, for undoubtedly they are all freebirth filth. Like yourself." Since Joanna was one of the few who knew Aidan's true genetic identity, her insult was carefully calculated. Waves of long-forgotten but deep resentment surged through his body. Though he had not seen her in several years, the hate was fresh, unchanged. When the dark band was off, he knew now which particular warrior would be his adversary in the Circle of Equals—if Kael Pershaw ever restored the Circle.

"Star Commander, one of your warriors must travel as point, clearing the way. I will follow, then you and the other two 'Mechs behind me, *quiaff*. Respond."

Aidan felt as if he were back on Ironhold, having to do Joanna's bidding in her role as his training officer.

"Aff, Star Captain. Horse, you take the point."

"Yes, Commander."

Aidan watched on his monitor as Horse forged ahead of Joanna. On their private channel, Horse said softly, "Jorge, what is going on here? That arrogant bitch is bossing you around like a—"

"She has the rank, Horse."

"But she has never been on Glory before. Any sensible officer would defer—"

"She has the rank."

"You are capitulating too easily. That is not like you. Something is wrong. Is it the dark band? It is, isn't it?"

"Do your job, Horse."

"I did not know the dark band turned its wearer into a coward."

Aidan felt like screaming at Horse, but he kept his voice calm. "Do as you have been ordered, Horse."

Horse grumbled, but he began to lead the Star, restored temporarily to the full five Points, out of the clearing and into an area of jungle that seemed darker and more threatening than anything they had seen so far.

11

With every unit in which she had ever served, Joanna immediately became notorious for her cool indifference. No disaster, no tragedy, no death of a comrade could break through her wall of ice or rock. However, the wall broke down often enough to terrify her subordinates. She could become angry, even wrathful, in the face of incompetence and stupidity. Too many such eruptions had, in fact, kept her in rank for too long. And a certain strategic carelessness had led to her many failed attempts to win a Bloodname.

Her famed indifference was severely tested in Glory's jungle, as she and Aidan's Star came across one piece after another of crash debris. She saw Battle-Mechs so damaged they could never be repaired in time for the current struggle with Clan Wolf. She saw warriors of her command lying dead amid tangled wreckage or barely able to walk forward to greet her. She saw blood in pools and streaks, blood as dewfall from leaves. The scenes were enough to draw a tear or a sigh of regret from even a Clan warrior. She heard gasps over the commlink from the warriors in Aidan's Star, her Star now, but of course they were freebirth filth and could not be expected to maintain proper decorum. Still, even Joanna had to admit some inner pangs of revulsion. Not that she would display them physically or verbally. Even more than revulsion, she felt anger at the sheer waste of it all. Once she had had a Trinary to command. Now she was reduced—at least temporarily—to a Star of freebirth filth. And the few operable 'Mechs from the Trinary that were able to rev up and follow her Star. She nearly smiled when she thought of the phrase. Follow her star. That was an old saying, was it not, one that probably dated back to Terran history. In villages she had occasionally heard people say, "Follow your star and success will be yours." Villages were good places to hear useless conventional wisdom. Freeborns could buttress their lives with the most regrettable apothegms and catchphrases. Warriors did not need them. For a Clan warrior, the only gains were those achieved personally. One succeeded at the Trials, one was victorious in war, one achieved a Bloodname, one contributed to the sacred gene pool. There was no need to follow a star or rely on faith or trust in fate, as lower castes often did. A warrior was his or her own reason for faith, his or her own director of fate.

At any rate, her unit now numbered nine. She, the four warriors from Aidan's Star, and the four remaining Trinary warriors. Other surviving personnel—techs and warriors whose 'Mechs were inoperable—were crammed into 'Mech cockpits for transport back to Glory Station, where they might be useful as reserves or support personnel.

Aidan had wanted to suggest leaving behind the techs and the warriors without 'Mechs, to be rescued later. The unit as a whole could move faster without placing extra burdens on the 'Mechs. But Joanna did not ask his opinion, and the dark band prevented him from volunteering advice. So what? he thought. The band, after all, made little difference when dealing with Joanna. She would not listen to advice, no matter who offered it. Once she had decided what the universe was about, it could never be anything else. She had been that way on Ironhold, and seemed to have changed little since then.

Now all the 'Mechs were gathered in a clearing. The vegetation was less dense over this part of the godforsaken jungle, and the night brought some slight illumination from the few stars seen through the canopy overhead. Perhaps the animals of the place were disturbed by the strangers in their midst for there were more sounds of movement among the trees, and chatterings, screeches, and calls seemed to increase rather than settle down for the night.

"Star Commander Jorge," came Joanna's hated voice over the comm, "we have, I believe, accounted for every warrior in the Trinary. Some techs are still among the missing but, well, they are merely techs, after all."

Aidan understood her only too well. By "merely techs," she was saying that they were, most of them, freeborns. And the trueborns among them had failed to qualify as warriors. So they were all expendable, disposable.

"Can you supply me the coordinates of this location so I may plot our journey to Glory Station?" Aidan enjoyed the privilege of remaining silent, awaiting her specific permission. "All right, all right. Respond, Jorge."

"I can transfer the program to your communications system, but I recommend you allow us to guide you and your warriors out. We have traveled this way before. There are many pitfalls, dangers . . ."

Her sudden silence entertained Aidan. He pictured Joanna in her cockpit, squirming relentlessly, struggling with herself to give in *for once* on a point.

"I agree," she finally said. "And Jorge . . . From now on, I give you permission to respond without awaiting my signal in any mission or tactical situation."

How much that concession must have cost her, he thought, and the idea gave him more enjoyment than a triple fusionnaire with a native wine chaser.

His pleasure was short-lived, broken by the distant sound of explosions and the flashes of light suddenly illuminating the jungle canopy.

"Freebirth!" Joanna shouted. Even over the comm, the stridency of her tone came through. "The battle has begun. We must get started. How far is it to Glory Station?"

"About a hundred kilometers."

"And the plain is nearby?"

"The site Kael Pershaw has chosen is ten or twelve kilometers from the station."

"That is too far. Plot our course so that we come out of the swamp on Glory Plain."

"With all due respect, Captain, I think we require some downtime in the station to make repairs and—"

"We have no time to backtrack to the station. We are Clan. It does not matter if our 'Mechs need repair. Considering the many we lost in the crash, I believe destiny has awarded us our present condition."

Aidan wanted to tell Joanna that she was getting carried away, but he held his tongue.

"Kael Pershaw is undermanned," she continued. "His bid is demeaned by Clan Wolf's deceptive strategy. If we are not on the field soon, the battle will be lost. Jorge, you and your unit are bid into the battle, *quiaff*?"

"Aff."

"I thought that, as you were freeborns, you might have been withheld. You must choose our route to Glory Plain."

"Star Captain Joanna, with all due respect, you just delegated me as your guide out of here. Not only do the 'Mechs need to be checked out, but we should go out into the field fully armed. We do not even know if the weapons systems of your surviving machines are completely operable. Not only that, but—"

Even though Joanna was not speaking, Aidan could sense her busily plotting and relishing her next words. "Star Commander Jorge, you seem to have no taste for combat. I had not thought your dark band was for cowardice."

"It was not. It was for—"

"Then why do you attempt to oppose my order? I propose getting right into battle and not slinking back to Glory Station to lick our wounds. We are fighters, we are warriors. You know all the chants. They do teach the chants to freeborns, do they not? Respond, please."

"They do, Star Captain."

"I see. Perhaps the words are not understood by freebirth filth in the same way we trueborns do. Indeed, for us it is more than mere understanding. We *absorb* the words that proclaim the bravery of our warriors and the way of the Clans. They become part of our personality, our character. Listen to me, Star Commander Jorge, and do not protest like the freebirth filth you are. Plot our course out of his hellhole. Do you understand?"

"I understand. But there is one order . . . belay that word, one *request* I must make of you and your warriors."

"Yes?"

"You must power-down your weapons systems, shut them off completely wherever possible."

"Your request mystifies me, Star Commander."

"We are going to be traversing one of the most cluttered terrains in the entire Clan empire. The area we will pass through is more forest than jungle. At times you will be surrounded by trees. A blast from a laser, an idle shot at a spooky shape in the darkness, and the entire forest can be instantly aflame around you. You could be incinerated or turned into a dessicated shell before you could eject. And, if you did manage ejection, chances are you would drop into a severe conflagration. With a battle raging at the other end of our journey, and the odds against us, we cannot afford to lose any more 'Mechs through accidents."

"All right, Jorge. I will give the orders. But when we are in Blood Swamp and can smell the foul stench of the Wolves, we jack them back to full power."

"Agreed."

"What right have you to agree, freeborn filth? The proper response is a mere affirmative, *quiaff?*"

He suspected she relished his hesitation as much as she liked the sound of her own words. "Aff," he said finally.

As she instructed the contingent to phase down their weapons, Horse's voice came over their private commline. "What kind of swamp gas were you emitting there? The whole forest instantly aflame? There's about as much chance of that happening as there is of me becoming ilKhan. The leaves positively drip with moisture, the bark is like sponges.''

''I was counting on Joanna's ignorance of the terrain. Her weakness has always been impulsive action. I did not want her to endanger her . . . her *command* with a rash act, especially since a too-quick trigger finger could—''

''Wait, wait. You know I hate the trashborn and would not mind if they were all enveloped in fire. But I don't believe you are all that concerned about the safety of the *command*. This is something between you and Star Captain Joanna, isn't it? Isn't it?''

''Please, Horse, no contractions.''

''Now I know that something is going on with you. You only get upset about contractions when you go back to seeing yourself as trueborn. You're on your high horse, Jorge. This Joanna has taken over your role and you're looking for revenge. I hear it in every response you give her. And maybe this urge for vengeance goes all the way back to Ironhold, am I right?''

''I just do not want trigger-happy intruders killing wildlife native to—''

''You are reaching for straws. Since when were you so worried about wildlife? You're angry at her for pulling rank. You want to exert control, even if you have to do it secretly. Pull strings from behind the scenes.''

''Give it up, Horse. We have a mission here.''

''Just don't put the rest of us in jeopardy for your own private vendetta, Jorge. We may not have the same genetic brand as you, but we have served you well.''

''I know that, Horse. I grant you that I resent Joanna, and I would welcome the chance to get her into the Circle of Equals and crush her this time, but—''

''*This time?* It has happened before? You two have fought before?''

Aidan recalled the time Joanna had beaten him in an honor duel within the Circle. And suddenly he saw that Horse's speculation was quite accurate. He wanted to avenge that defeat, *needed* to. There was a moment when, back then, he had vowed that he would. The vow was as good as a Clan oath to him.

"There is no need to discuss this further, Horse. We have a mission."

"I hate it when you turn trashborn."

"I *am* trashborn and you know it."

"Yes, I know it."

Horse's voice was unusually bitter as he abruptly cut his link to the commline. The one person in the universe Aidan did not want angry at him was Horse. They had been together for so long that, in a skirmish, they acted in concert without communication. They had qualified in the Trial together and had served in the same units since. He would have to make it up to him.

When he thought of Horse as the single person whose approval he needed, Aidan realized that it was not quite true. There was Marthe, too. Since the last time he had seen her on Ironhold, she had, he assumed, risen quickly in the ranks. She was probably a Star Captain by now. She had, after all, entered the warrior caste with two "kills" in her Trial, which started her at a higher rank. Aidan never asked others if they had heard about her and never checked rosters of other Clusters on other worlds for her name. They had grown up together in the sibko, and until Marthe had surged ahead of him in warrior training, had been very close, closer than most sibko members ever became. Joanna would probably know where Marthe was now. But he would have gone on his knees and begged Kael Pershaw for the information before he would ever ask Joanna anything.

12

Star Captain Dwillt Radick's BattleMech, a *Viper*, surged with power and what he liked to think of as confidence, as the 'Mech's own eagerness to get into battle, an alacrity that duplicated his own. As he settled into the cockpit's command couch for another check of his instrumentation, he called up terrain maps onto his secondary screen. Kael Pershaw's choice of combat site had surprised him. It was a relative flatland, and except for a swamp into which no Mech-Warrior would take his 'Mech by choice, offered few hiding places. A lot of scrub and large clumps of shaggy bushes dotted the ugly, so-called Glory Plain. This area deserved neither the name of plain nor of Glory. Plains were meant to be magnificent, even majestic—fields of grain moving with the wind, brilliantly green grasslands, open spaces with few civilized interruptions.

From what he knew about Glory, very little of the planet reflected the honorable name given it by some mad cartographer. It was a hellhole where no sensible person would come unless he or she had a damned good reason. The Pershaw gene heritage was just such a reason. The Pershaw line was a solid one that had consistently produced the kind of warriors Clan Wolf respected. No gloryhounds, just heroes with an astonishing victory ratio. Clan Wolf scientists had sifted through Bloodnames from several Clans, and the Pershaw line had checked out as among the most superior. Because neither Radick nor even Mikel Furey was privy to the major goals of Clan Wolf, Radick could only suspect that acquiring genetic strains with a glorious tradition was part of the rumored program to make the Wolves the most powerful of the seventeen existing Clans.

Looking into the distance, Radick saw some hills to the left and Glory Station to the right, but neither landscape was any more interesting than the one before him. Behind the Clan Wolf forces, at the foot of a long slope, began the infamous Blood Swamp. Pershaw's strategy of setting the Clan Wolf forces in front of the swamp had an insidiousness to it that Radick admired. He was not especially eager to fight with a swamp at his back, but it was a drawback he could easily turn to his advantage. He had already given his Cluster a stirring speech about their having so little room behind them because Clan Jade Falcon obviously knew that Clan Wolf would never retreat. The enemy, on the other hand, had plenty of room for retreat, proof of their cowardice. But all that was mere rhetoric. Radick knew that Pershaw and the warriors of the Jade Falcon Clan were brave and famed for tenacity. Pershaw had chosen this troop deployment for some strategic purpose, perhaps related to his already-diminished manpower. Radick had already sent a couple of 'Mechs into the swamp to see what might be gained if he were forced into it. He hoped those scouts could find their way back.

"Star Commander Ward!"

"Yes, sir?"

"What do you make of the Jade Falcon deployment?"

"It is strange. It reminds me of what I have heard of ancient Terran warriors battling in front of city walls."

"Freebirth! You are improvising. City walls, indeed. Kael Pershaw would not know anything of pre-Clan military history."

"As you say, sir. It was merely an observation."

"Instead of observing, calculate. What will be the Jade Falcon's first move?"

"To wait for ours, I expect."

"No, we will wait for him. He is undermanned. It is only fair that we, out of courtesy, allow him the first move. How much time until the battle may commence?"

"Three minutes."

Radick returned his attention to the terrain, trying to find in it a clue to what Kael Pershaw might be up to.

"Lanja!"

"Yes, sir."

"Time?"

"Two minutes, sir."

"Are your Elementals ready?"

"As always."

"Yes. I need not have asked."

Kael Pershaw was performing his last prebattle checklist. He had stared at charts and screens for hours, it seemed, and no matter how he analyzed and reanalyzed, he did not have good numbers for going up against Clan Wolf. Star Captain Dwillt Radick had the extra Trinary on the field, while Pershaw's was off somewhere beyond Blood Swamp, perhaps twisted in wreckage, or disabled, or lost. And then there was Jorge's Star. Pershaw hated to admit it, but with the impressive enemy array in front of him, he would not mind having that contingent of stinking freebirths in the field right now. Lanja had told him often enough that they were good fighters—a bit unorthodox, but good. Still, he would be happier to be on a planet where there were no freebirth warriors.

"It is almost time, Colonel," Lanja said. "One of my Point says he knows of Dwillt Radick, and that the man will wait for you to make the first move."

"How civilized of him. Our first move, as you call it, must be a majestic one, *quiaff?*"

"Aff. We await your order. The time is up."

At the same moment Pershaw gave the order, the LRM-equipped 'Mechs in his command sent off a barrage that might have been compared to a similar massive flight of warrior arrows in some ancient battle. Unlike arrows, of course, these missiles were riding invisible beams to their targets. He had ordered half his 'Mechs to fire the long-range missiles at a flat trajectory, while the other half lobbed theirs in a high arc. If nothing else, this forced the Wolves to allocate their anti-missile systems to one group or the other, with the chance that some of the other missiles would hit without being engaged.

Even before any of the missiles had come close to their targets, Lanja—with the bloodcurdling scream that was her trademark—started her three Points of Elementals forward. Fifteen of the armored giants shot up on tongues of flame that would send them toward the Wolf Clan line.

Pershaw watched both tactics on separate screens, his head twisting back and forth to trace the dual actions. As he had expected, many of his LRMs were blown out of the air, sending up a curtain of smoke and debris that partially obscured their direct visuals of the Clan Wolf forces. The low-flying missiles were something else. Countered by the anti-missile systems, their explosions occurred closer to their targets, kicking up dust and boulders, many of which made contact with 'Mech legs, and sometimes higher. Pershaw was satisfied to see some leg armor flying, and he had hopes that these hits were the beginning of attacks that would disable 'Mech limbs.

Seeing one of the salvos make a direct hit without being engaged, Pershaw responded with a satisfied grunt. The Clan Wolf 'Mech had either used all its anti-missile ammunition or been the victim of a malfunction. The hit was not fatal, but large chunks of armor sailed outward, strong walls undergoing the first cracks of the assault.

Under cover of the explosions and smoke, Lanja's Elementals had already gone halfway across the intervening field before any Clan Wolf Elemental had even moved. Radick had bid away so many of his Points that the Jade Falcon infantry was the one battle factor where Pershaw had a slight edge. The Points of Elementals from each side were an awesome sight as they headed toward one another. In their battle suits of super-thick armor plate, they looked like alien beings from some distant corner of the universe. For a face, they had a dark, V-shaped viewport. Their feet were cloven and shod with steel. With no real neck to the suit, their heads looked like mere lumps rising from their shoulders. The right arm ended in the muzzle of a laser; a machine gun was slung under the left forearm. Mounted on the back of the suit was a boxy double-barrelled missile launcher. Bred for height and strength, these Clan infantry were supermen on the field. Clan Wolf's Elementals opened fire first, but the Jade Falcon Points were quick to retaliate. Soon crossfire seemed to weave both sides together, but not a single 'Mech from either side had yet moved.

Time, Kael Pershaw thought, to take the next step in the initiative.

"Charlie Assault Nova," he ordered, "take the right flank."

He had decided to send this detachment from his Trinary Striker Force because it had more than one reason to fight well. It had been Star Commander Bast's unit. Traditionally, units that had lost leaders (Bast had been replaced by MechWarrior Ersik, whom Pershaw had given a field promotion to Star Commander) fought more fiercely. No one knew whether it was to impress their new commanding officer or to honor the memory of the dead one.

As Pershaw gave further moving orders and started his own unit, Alpha Striker Nova, on the attack, he saw many holes in his line of battle. These openings might be just what the Clan Wolf warriors needed to rush through and trap the Jade Falcons in a pincer movement.

Dwillt Radick was thinking trap. He knew that Pershaw was committing virtually his entire Cluster to this engagement, while Radick was able to maintain a Nova in reserve. Perhaps he should have brought in all his troops, too. Overwhelmed Pershaw, taken the contract for the genetic package, and lifted off this hell-hole. But even with the troops he now commanded, he should be able to defeat Pershaw and his backwater warriors. The secret was to do so without losing too much of his own force.

Craig Ward, already in the thick of battle, firing off laser pulses as he guided his *Ice Ferret*'s magnificent strides forward, found himself coming under the fire of Pershaw's Charlie Nova. The *Ice Ferret* rocked as two Jade Falcon 'Mechs, a *Summoner* and a *Mist Lynx*, fired simultaneously trying to disable his left-arm laser cannon. Rotating his 'Mech's torso, he wheeled on them. Firing at them alternately, Ward sent shards of armor hurtling through the air. The *Mist Lynx*, damaged by Ward's ambuscade, wavered on its feet before it went stumbling forward. Just as Ward was ready to finish the 'Mech off, he was diverted by heavy fire from the *Summoner*. Peering out his viewport, he saw a thick hunk of armor fly past. It was a moment before he realized it was a slab from his own 'Mech.

Kael Pershaw had scored well in academics during warrior training, amassing some of the highest cadet ratings in the history of the Ironhold Training Center. He could see now, as the Clan Wolf 'Mechs surged forward, passing the Elementals who were engaged in a standoff in the center of the field, that the left-flank attack was failing and the center would soon be driven back. Among the Jade Falcon forces, only the right flank, apparently inspired by Charlie Assault Nova, was making any headway. Some Clan Wolf 'Mechs were being edged backward toward the slope leading to Blood Swamp. But Kael Pershaw's forces were being separated too widely, divided too much. Only disaster could come of that.

When Pershaw gave the order for strategic retreat, Lanja came quickly on the commline: "It is too soon. You will look cowardly."

"Only for the moment. We need to regroup. We discussed this in our prebattle briefing. You and I agreed that the second phase of the assault was more

than likely to occur. Order your Points back, leaving the packs behind.''

Pershaw knew that his next tactic might be considered questionable in some circles, but as the saying went, nothing was truly unfair in a war.

"They have their tails between their legs, Craig Ward,'' Dwillt Radick shouted excitedly.

"Do not be too sure of that, Star Captain.''

"No. They are weak now. Pursue!''

"Perhaps we should just allow them their dignity and—''

"Dignity! What a foul word! Pursue!''

Craig Ward wondered why Dwillt Radick would place such high priority on courtesy but have no regard for dignity. Now, however, in the midst of combat was not the time to challenge his superior officer. ''Yes, sir,'' was all he said.

As the charging Clan Wolf BattleMechs passed over the packs dropped by the Jade Falcon Elementals, the vibrations of their heavy tread set off the vibrabomb charges in the packs. The force of the explosions and the subsequent shrapnel sent armor flying through the smoke, smashed operating machinery beneath the armor, cut wires and, in one case, sent a *Gargoyle* crashing to the ground. The impact not only killed its pilot but crushed more than a Point of Clan Wolf Elementals that had been pursuing their Clan Jade Falcon counterparts.

In his aptly named *Hellbringer*, Kael Pershaw permitted himself a satisfied smile. The odds were a bit reduced now. They were still in Clan Wolf favor, but for the moment, the retreat was covered.

The next phase of the battle would be near Glory Station itself, where he could run supplies, especially ammunition, out on a shorter line while forcing the Wolves to stretch out their supply lines. He wondered if he should have set up barricades. They would have to be enormous to conceal 'Mechs, and besides, there was something distasteful about entire units firing from cover. Had there been time to construct them, he might have been tempted anyway.

Looking back as the smoke cleared, Pershaw saw the field littered not only with the ruined *Gargoyle* and the fallen Elementals from both sides, but also with hundreds of shards of ceramic and metal, the detritus of the battle. The Clan Wolf forces had apparently ceased their pursuit. Behind them Blood Swamp was catching the light oddly, lending a reddish glow to the entire scene.

He thought of the possible reinforcements somewhere beyond the rim of the swamp and anticipated the difference they could make to this battle. But he had heard nothing from any of them since the departure of Star Commander Jorge and the rescue Star. That meant nothing, for everyone knew how easily the swamp and the jungle beyond it distorted even those communications that did get through. Crash survivors and rescue party could both still be out there.

Kael Pershaw could never have dreamed that he would one day be so devoutly wishing to see Star Commander Jorge and his stinking freebirth miscreants taking their places in a noble Clan battle.

13

"Aid—ah, Jorge, there is something on my shoulder."

"Star Captain Joanna, in this clime some insects find their way into the cockpits, but you need not—"

"No, fool! I do not mean my own shoulder. I mean Ter's."

"Ter's?"

"I forgot, you would not know. I have named my 'Mech Ter. And make no remarks. It is not a mark of admiration, but of hate."

"I thought the two of you were close."

"I served under Ter Roshak. I did not like him."

"You went after me and brought me back to Ironhold for Ter Roshak."

"That is true. But I did not want to do it. And I did not want you to return. That whole second-chance idea of his was madness."

"You think Ter Roshak mad?"

"Jorge, this is useless chatter. What do I do about the thing on my 'Mech's shoulder?"

"What does it look like?"

"I cannot tell. It is a large shape. I can feel the 'Mech tilt to the right because of its weight. It appears to be a catlike animal."

"Oh. That is probably a tree puma. Several of them prowl this jungle. They are black, sometimes even blacker than the jungle itself. We detect them, as you just did, and sometimes there is enough light to reflect off their eyes. It is quite eerie. No one has ever captured one. No one has ever wanted to. It will ride along for a while, then jump off onto a tree branch. They have never been detected on the ground.''

Aidan noted the clamor of sounds all around them. On top of the many wildlife noises and the rustling of leaves was the almost continual crunch of the Point 'Mechs carving a path out of the jungle. Aidan had ordered the most direct route possible to the battle site, figured as accurately as distorted sensor readings could make it. Mixing with these sounds, usually preceded by light flashes, came the sounds of the battle going on in the distance. Aidan was navigating by these as much as from his own calculations.

"It is gone," Joanna said suddenly. "The tree puma. I never even felt it spring. It was there one moment, then gone the next.''

Behind her, Nomad had fallen asleep, a look of pain on his face. He had said that a throbbing in his shoulder worried him, and that he hoped Joanna would rush in and save the Jade Falcons instantly so he could get some medical treatment.

Her primary screen recorded scene after scene of what looked like the same area of jungle. She wondered how anyone could find the way through this wild place. She was about to ask Aidan more questions about the swamp, when Horse's raspy, unpleasant voice cut into the open channel. "Star Commander!"

Anger rose in her at the audacity of the miserable freebirth. She, after all, was the ranking officer, and he should report to her. The naming of Aidan as guide out of the swamp was a delegation, not a substitution. Only the urgency in Horse's voice kept her from some sharp reprimand.

"Report, Horse," Aidan said.

"I have a pair of magnetic anomalies moving toward us right at the edge of sensor range. They could be ours, but I doubt it. One of the signatures is definitely that of a *Stormcrow*. The last *Stormcrow* we had in the Garrison Cluster was the one that malfunctioned and was shipped out.''

"They are Clan Wolf then?''

"I believe so.''

"If we can see them, there is a good chance they have detected us. We will have to take them out, *quiaff?*"

"Aff."

"Commander, let me remind you," came Joanna's cool voice over the commlink, "that I am the ranking officer here. I am the one to decide who is to fight these intruders."

The phrase *with all due respect* was becoming heavy on his tongue, but Aidan used it anyway: "With all due respect, Captain, Horse and I have experience in this locale, on this planet, in fact. We are able to compensate for its difficulties. It would be better for us to face this pair while the rest of you remain back as—"

"May I remind you, Commander, that not only are you the subordinate here, but you also wear the dark band. I have to treat any protest as a violation of the law of the band. You will come with me to face the intruders. Everyone else, remain behind."

As they moved away, heading toward the Clan Wolf 'Mechs, Horse spoke to Aidan over the private commline: "I'll cover you, Jorge. She won't even know I'm in the vicinity."

"Thank you, Horse. If Joanna's folly sends me into the quicksand, be sure and set a memorial stone into the nearest tree."

A quick glance at the configurations of the terrain map now on his secondary screen showed Aidan that they would undoubtedly encounter the interlopers a short distance into Blood Swamp itself. Joanna's inexperience with the jungle and the swamp was slowing them down. Aidan had to act as point and clear the way for her. The positioning might have satisfied her need for tribute, but it did not make for an efficient mission.

As they crossed into the swamp, the passage actually became somewhat easier, but no faster. Aidan was cautious, not wanting to take his *Summoner* into any suddenly deep waters. On the screen he saw that the Clan Wolf 'Mechs had definitely spotted them and were heading their way.

"Jorge."

"Yes?"

"I may be having a neurohelmet malfunction. It feels as if I am walking in a dream."

"It is no malfunction. It is the sensation of the 'Mech's movement through the swamp. Basically, it is no different from a person going on foot through a swampy area. The normal stride changes, which gives a feeling of uncertainty as each foot comes down. The adjustments that a 'Mech must make are quite similar, and we feel it in our neurohelmets. Once you have been in Blood Swamp a few times, you will get used to it."

"I doubt that."

Joanna was wondering if duty at Glory Station was going to be all swamp and disorientation. A warrior was supposed to adjust to whatever conditions he or she found, but all she could see was absurdity in the prospect of battle in this godforsaken region.

As the two pairs of 'Mechs closed in on one another, the TBS began to crinkle with static. Their enemies were apparently trying to contact them, Aidan realized. Working with the controls, he tried to divert the static to another channel and keep the voices on their intended frequency. He could not completely eliminate the static, but he did manage to hear the voice of the *Stormcrow*'s pilot.

"Identify yourself and your unit strength," he was saying. It was the tail end of a ritual of challenge.

"I am not required to—"

"Jorge, it is my right to respond."

"Suit yourself."

"We are Clan Jade Falcon," she said. "I am Star Captain Joanna, of the Falcon Guards. Our numbers do not concern you if you are Clan Wolf."

"We are proud to identify ourselves as Clan Wolf. We are scouts, searching this area. Are you bid into the battle?"

"Of course we are."

"You speak with a freebirth accent."

The insult was deep, a deliberate provocation. Even someone from Clan Wolf would know that there were no freeborns in the Falcon Guards.

Instead of responding with words, Joanna shot off several bursts from her autocannon. Aidan noted that she had obviously powered her weaponry back up. The shots went nowhere. Rustled a few leaves, maybe, woke up a tree puma, perhaps, but they were otherwise no more than the shot across the bow from ancient naval history. Horse, apparently near enough for his voice to travel over the private channel, laughed softly.

Aidan recognized that the other scout 'Mech was an *Adder*. Like the *Stormcrow*, it was lighter than either of the 'Mechs he and Joanna piloted. The swamp tended to nullify any differences in weight or weaponry, however. Of the four warriors, Aidan realized that he was the only one with experience in Blood Swamp. He was elated, thinking that he could not lose. He could, in fact, dispose of both enemies at once.

Without awaiting instructions from Joanna, Aidan literally waded into battle. When Joanna realized what he was up to, she yelled through the commlink: "Stop! I will not have this insubordination. Commander, respond."

Aidan remained silent and moved on.

"For this, Star Commander Jorge, we will meet in the Circle of Equals."

"Kael Pershaw has abolished the Circle on Glory," Aidan said, not stopping.

She watched him through the viewport as he and his *Summoner* disappeared into a heavy mist. Continuing to track him, she saw that he was only thirty or so meters from the Clan Wolf 'Mechs. Following him, she next saw that he had opened fire. His first shots appeared to hit the enemy *Adder* dead-center.

"This is grandstanding, you freebirth filth," she muttered, knowing that Aidan would not be listening even if there had been communications between them. But someone else was, and his voice startled her. She had forgotten that Nomad was even in the 'Mech, secure in a pull-out passenger seat.

"What did you say?" he asked.

She jumped, startled.

"It does not matter what I said, Nomad. I did not say it to you. Hold on tight. We are going into combat."

She headed her *Hellbringer* toward the fray, annoyed

to see that Aidan had already succeeded with one of the Clan Wolf 'Mechs. The *Adder* had fallen backward. Only the trunk of the tree kept it from lying flat in murky water. There seemed to be no movement from the 'Mech or its pilot. Aidan was exchanging laser fire with the *Stormcrow*, and damage reports showed, as accurately as her sensors could, that Aidan was definitely holding the advantage. The *Stormcrow* was rocked by one hit after another.

Suddenly Joanna's *Hellbringer* slipped sideways, as its foot slid into deep muck. Then the 'Mech's other foot also slid forward and seemed about to tip backward on its heel. Using all her best concentration, melding with the pulses from the neurohelmet, Joanna steadied the machine, keeping it from landing unceremoniously on its hind end or back. However, once she was in a vertical position again, she realized that the 'Mech's foot was stuck. Nothing she did seemed to affect the suctionlike grip of the mysterious muck on her 'Mech's leg.

As she cursed her fate roundly, she saw that the battle between Aidan's 'Mech and the *Stormcrow* was moving away from her, the Clan Wolf machine moving backward, either from Aidan's marksmanship or as a retreat. She slapped her throttle forward in a desperate attempt to wrench her 'Mech free. Suddenly the jury-rigged navigation and communications console exploded in a cascade of sparks and the 'Mech shut itself down. She was now on her own in a place she had never been, her 'Mech at least temporarily disabled, separated from the rest of the unit, and with no idea of how to get out of bloody Blood Swamp.

In the pale glow of the darkened screens that turned their faces an eerie gray, Nomad watched Joanna's shoulders slump heavily.

"We seem to be in a bit of trouble?" he said, barely able to keep from showing his own amusement by laughing.

Only the darkness and the restraining straps of Joanna's seat kept her from murdering Nomad on the spot.

14

The hiatus in the battle gave both sides a chance to perform field repairs and recharge weapons. The normal Clan tactic would have been for the Wolves to charge forward and take advantage of the disarray of the Clan Jade Falcon retreat. Kael Pershaw was surprised when Radick and Clan Wolf seemed to hold back. The damage done by the Elementals' subterfuge had apparently made Radick cautious, at least temporarily.

Though the lack of pursuit allowed the Glory Station Garrison Cluster a chance to regroup, it nevertheless disappointed Pershaw. He had planned to send Charlie Assault Nova around to the left flank, where the unit would have attempted to target one or two 'Mechs at the edge, unload their weaponry on them, and take them out of action. The maneuver would have been unClanlike, because it did not pit single 'Mechs against one another, but Pershaw decided that his best chance was to attempt to reduce Clan Wolf numbers through what had once been known as hit-and-run tactics. The fight could resume more ritualistically when the odds were more even. He knew that Dwillt Radick would also improvise if he were the underdog. Situations often demanded compromise, and so he would have to save this particular tactic for another time, perhaps another war.

Pershaw strode on foot around the open area outside Glory Station, taking the time to inspire his warriors. He climbed up to several 'Mech cockpits, disdaining the use of a field howdah. Opening hatchways and shouting through them, he told the pilots that when the battle resumed, they should fire steadily and await their chance to pounce on a weakness. Walking among the Elementals, conscious of how much each one towered over him, he congratulated them on the success of their hastily laid minefield, and urged them to fight on with their accustomed bravery.

Lanja meanwhile left her Command Point and walked over to him. In combat, they were as formal as was appropriate for commander and aide.

"Some news, Star Colonel," Lanja said.

"What is it?"

"We have two more BattleMechs to add to the Cluster. MechWarrior Nis, one of Star Commander Jorge's warriors, has led the 'Mech of a survivor from the DropShip crash into the south gateway to the station. They—"

The information immediately caught Pershaw's interest. "Just two? Just two survivors of the *entire* operation?" In his mind he was already considering alternate plans for the battle.

"We do not know that for certain," Lanja replied. "Jorge's Star encountered MechWarrior Enrique, the crash survivor, wandering alone in the swamp. Apparently he had traveled a great distance under terrible conditions. His 'Mech's leg was disabled in the crash, but we can repair it. Star Commander Jorge directed Nis to return here with Enrique. It was a slow trip, she says, because Enrique's 'Mech could not walk more than a few kilometers per hour. The new 'Mech is being repaired right now, and Nis will join Alpha Star of Trinary First Garrison after her 'Mech also gets some minor repairs. You scowl. Why?"

"Nis. A freebirth. My confidence is not exactly inspired. Order her to await the repair of the damaged 'Mech. Have this trueborn, Enrique, take the place of Nis in her 'Mech."

"Nis has shown herself to be quite brave. At any rate, Enrique is being treated at the med station."

"All right, all right. Allow Nis to join Alpha Star. They have a 'Mech and a pilot out of action right now.

Except for filling the slot, she will probably not make much of a difference.'' He could see that Lanja, whose views on the efficiency of *all* Clan warriors were already known to him, felt that his hatred of freeborns was interfering with his judgment. But loyal as she was, she would never question Pershaw's statements during a combat situation. He was often amazed at how deep her loyalty went.

"Lanja, I need your help."

"What can I do?"

"I have an idea, but it will require one of your Elementals risking his or her life."

"That is the easiest of tasks. Tell me."

"Soon it will be night. I believe Clan Wolf will attack then. We will have to engage them. As long as Radick keeps some units in reserve, the odds are only slightly in their favor. I believe we can hold them, at least for a time. But we need to put more 'Mechs into the field. We need to find out what happened to the Trinary from the DropShip."

"Do you believe, then, that Jorge's Star has failed?"

"I am not sure, but I need to know. If there are any surviving warriors and 'Mechs, I want them here. I would accept even the freebirth Star right now. Lanja, select one of your warriors and order him or her to find a way through the battlefield and into the swamp. We must locate any survivors from the crash or the rescue team, brief them on the situation, and urge them to travel here at their highest speed."

"In the swamp—"

"I know, I know. An Elemental would have to go without his suit of battle armor to avoid detection when crossing Clan Wolf lines. Fate has placed many demands on me and one Elemental is all I can spare. If I truly control my fate, the Elemental will find the Star. If he finds that the search for survivors still continues, he will pass on my order to abandon the search and join us here. So, detach a warrior from one of your Points."

"Unnecessary. I will go."

"But that would not be—"

"Proper? Perhaps not. But I am the fastest runner and the highest scorer in survival techniques, *quiaff?*"

"Well, aff, but—"

"No need to discuss this further. Your order was to detach a warrior for this mission. I have done so."

Pershaw recognized the determination in Lanja's eyes. He respected her, as he respected all his good officers. It had always been his policy not to countermand the orders of one of his trusted subordinates, and he trusted none more than Lanja. If she chose to go, she must.

"If you cannot home in on any of the 'Mechs or even their remnants, do not waste time in a long search. Return at once, *quiaff?*"

"Aff. I will depart as soon as night falls."

"Good. Dismissed."

As always, she wheeled about immediately and strode away. Pershaw felt a rare moment of apprehension. Lanja was the most efficient aide he had ever had. He did not want anything to happen to her. But, of course, they were both Clan, able to easily accept death. There were stories of Clan warriors who had known each other for years, served together, saved each other's lives countless times. Yet, when one died, the other walked away without so much as a backward glance. Would he look back at Lanja if she became a corpse? Once, perhaps, as a tribute to her loyalty, but no more than that.

"I cannot contact Joanna on any channel," Horse reported. Aidan had returned to the remaining seven warriors and their 'Mechs.

"Neither can I. And there is no indication of her on anybody's radar, *quineg?*"

"Neg. Wherever she is, the swamp is hiding her even from electronic detection. You know how it is, Jorge. Out here you cannot trust your equipment. If it says you are under attack, it may be only a tree puma nibbling on your neck. If it shows that a BattleMech is flying, then—"

"Horse, spare me the fanciful lecture. The fundamental point is that we cannot locate our commanding officer, *quiaff?''*

"Aff. Which places you in command. *Back* in command, Star Commander Jorge."

"Agreed."

"I cannot say I regret the change. And I must observe that nothing would be gained in a fruitless search for Star Captain Joanna."

"If she is still the same warrior, she will find her own way out. We have a more urgent mission. We must rejoin the garrison."

"It has been a long time since there has been any sign of the battle in the skies above. Could it be over?"

"I hope not. Let us find out, *quiaff?''*

Except for one Clan Wolf Elemental sentry, whom Lanja quickly disarmed and smothered, the trip across the battlefield was simple. She sensed that the Wolves were now intent on new battle plans, for the Command Star headquarters was obviously busy. A continual stream of warriors went in and out of the geodesic dome set up just behind the wreckage and carnage that warriors from both sides were now cleaning up as part of the one-hour truce Pershaw had negotiated with Radick.

At Blood Swamp she slipped down the slope and into the murky blackness. Once there, she fitted a pair of MAD goggles over her head and looked around. The magnetic anomaly detector was short-range, but in Blood Swamp tended to be more accurate than any installed in a BattleMech. The device also made it easier to travel on foot through the swamp.

Moving quickly and adeptly, Lanja went about a kilometer before discovering the two downed Clan 'Mechs. Their pilots had abandoned the machines, which lay now in swamp water, a pair of drowned giants. Beyond them, however, were faint but clear heat tracings left behind by another BattleMech. The heat signature led in a clear line deeper into the swamp.

For the next half-hour Lanja followed the signature,

which got stronger as she swiftly proceeded. Suddenly Lanja was in a small clearing that her scanner showed crisscrossed with a complicated network of heat lines. As she passed through the clearing, she spotted the clear lines of a unit of 'Mechs—seven or eight, it appeared—heading out of the clearing, in the general direction of Glory Plain. If they continued on their current path, they would emerge right into the claws of Clan Wolf. She had to head them off.

Running, she kept her attention on the heat signatures, which got stronger as they became more recent. Her height allowed her to grab fairly high branches, using them to propel herself forward. She made a few magnificent leaps across deep-water areas.

Suddenly she heard the unmistakable sounds of 'Mechs using their hands to clear a path through trees up ahead. She knew she would be seeing the unit soon. Taking off the scanner, Lanja slipped it into its belt holder without breaking stride.

Passing under a high tree, she heard a rustle in the branches overhead. Before she could even look up, she felt the air change as something descended swiftly toward her. She reached for her laser pistol, the only weapon she had, but not fast enough. In that instant, the tree puma landed heavily on her, forcing Lanja down into stagnant, murky water.

15

It was a pity that the pilots in their 'Mechs and the Elemental with her MAD goggles depended so much on external devices. More reliance on their own eyes, on what the real world offered to their view, and they might have found Joanna easily. The warm red glow of emergency lighting from her cockpit was visible for nearly a hundred meters in the dark swamp. An unwavering illumination ten meters above ground level. If any of the searchers had been able to get close enough, they would have seen the Star Captain staring out the viewport, trying to discern something in a place as black as the heart of a Periphery bandit.

"We could try to get out on foot," Nomad said.

"Are you joking? In your condition, you can barely make headway on flat ground."

"Leave me behind."

"I would do that gladly. However, I have no means of navigating, I do not know what the dangers and pitfalls are, and I would prefer not to abandon a valuable BattleMech because its foot is stuck in something, especially when all available equipment is needed for the current combat."

"Then why aren't you trying to pull the foot out?"

"What do you think I was doing? I think it got stuck when it sank into the muck or whatever is down there. It seems to be tangled in something."

"What?"

"If I knew that, I would have said so."

The light inside the cockpit flickered, but did not go

out. Joanna balled her hand into a fist and punched the inside of the viewport.

"It is that filthy freebirth, Aidan, who is responsible for our being stranded here. He deliberately left us here so that he could reassume command. I will kill him, first chance I get."

"How? There is no Circle of Equals here. I heard him tell you that. And you, Star Captain Joanna, for all your difficult traits, are not a murderer."

"Do not be so sure. I may practice on you."

Recognizing the threat in her voice, Nomad lapsed into silence. She might not kill him, but he knew from experience that she could do significant damage. With his arms already throbbing, he needed no new pain.

After a long period of quiet, interrupted only by odd whoops and other raucous sounds rising like spectral invasions from the swamp, Joanna finally said, "We must get this 'Mech moving."

"Are you going to try to pull the foot out again?"

"No, I am going down there and disentangle it."

"Out there? In the dark?"

"I have a lantern."

Nomad did not know what to say. On the one hand, he admired Joanna's courage in trying; on the other, if she failed and something happened to her, he would be left stranded in this cockpit, his arms injured, plus legs that did not feel so good, either.

It was not worth wasting his breath. Joanna was obviously not waiting for advice as she hastily grabbed some rope and a lantern from her storage compartment. Then, without so much as a fare-thee-well to her chief tech, she forced open the cockpit hatch and slipped from sight. Nomad strained to listen, to distinguish the sounds of feet bumping against the side of the 'Mech from the many other noises around him. He heard little, only a couple of definite clanks and then Joanna uttering one of the more shocking Clan oaths in a voice that could compete with the swamp cacophony. Using his right arm, which still pulsed with pain, he managed to get himself up off his seat. He worked himself over to the viewport and looked down.

All he could see was the wavering and flickering light from Joanna's lantern.

At one point Joanna nearly lost her balance and fell. She was at that moment hanging onto the rope, which she had wrapped around the field mounting unit of her 'Mech's left arm. With one hand still clutching the swinging rope, she reached out with the other to touch the tree next to the 'Mech. What she got was the soft, slimy, spongy matter that clung to the tree, perhaps some kind of moss or lichen. It was colored a sickly gray. The lantern did not pick up much color on anything, perhaps a result of so little light penetrating the swamp canopy.

Touching the side of the tree made her shout out an oath she had not spoken since her days as a training officer at Crash Camp on Ironhold. Composing herself and trying to get a new grip on the rope, she recalled the last time she had cursed so thoroughly, disgusted to recall that this bunghole Aidan was connected with the occurrence. It had been on the day she learned what Ter Roshak had done, that he had killed the free-birth unit merely to give Aidan his unlawful second chance at becoming a warrior. She had raged for nearly an hour, smashing several items in her ill-kept quarters, cursing not merely the actions of Roshak and the boon granted Aidan, but the fact that she had been implicated as Roshak's agent. It was Roshak who had ordered her to find and capture Aidan, then return him to Ironhold.

Steadying herself and the rope as well as she could, Joanna continued downward, gagging and coughing at the repellent odors that rose up to meet her.

Reaching bottom, Joanna saw that the 'Mech's foot was buried in the muck up to about ankle level, the heat sink ballistic cover nearly half-submerged. Clutching the rope with one hand, she tilted her body sideways and reached downward into the muck. The viscous substance seemed so eager to draw her hand in that she pulled it out instantly. Shining her light around, she noted a clutch of dark gray vines hanging down from the tree, but each vine seemed pulled taut. At their bottom ends, the vines were also buried in the muck. Kicking away from the side of the 'Mech's leg, Joanna swung over to the vines and held onto one of them. She could feel its tension. When she tugged at it, it barely moved. Whatever was holding the 'Mech's foot down was connected to these vines. Perhaps some of them had become tangled with the foot. For that matter, the muck itself might be enough to exert significant pressure to hold it down.

She was considering blasting the vines with her laser pistol when an odd vibration of the vine made her look up. She expected to see Nomad pulling at her rope, but what she saw was much worse. Not far above her head, a reptile that looked like some blend of razorback hog and alligator, as dark and gray as the swamp itself, was clinging to the side of the 'Mech. For a reason known only to it and whatever deity watched over reptiles, the creature was happily chewing on the rope, apparently making great headway.

Drawing her pistol, Joanna fired it upward at the reptile. Her shot was right on target and some of the reptile's razorback went flying. It slipped off the 'Mech, but its mouth continued to cling to the rope. Aiming carefully, so as to miss the rope, she fired again. As the creature fell away, she felt a tug on the rope. The beast was falling directly down at her. Kicking at the 'Mech leg, she swung out. The reptile fell right past her, making a small splash as it hit the muck and then disappeared. She was ready to breathe a sigh of relief as the rope finished its outward arc and came back toward the 'Mech, but the relief turned to fear as she felt the rope separate. Beginning to fall, she grabbed at a vine but missed, then she too went, feet first, into the muck.

Oddly, the muck seemed to break her fall. After she had gone down only a few centimeters, her movement slowed. Yet, at her feet, she felt a definite sensation of suction. She was being pulled in, but whatever the muck was, it was patient in claiming its victims. She wondered what had happened to her laser pistol. She did not remember dropping it. Shining the lantern around her, she spotted it just beyond the rim of the pool of muck, just beyond her reach.

She had been pulled in up to her knees. Looking down, Joanna watched as the line of detestable sediment slowly rose higher.

Nomad had located a small pair of binoculars in Joanna's storage bin. Ignoring the pulsations in his wrist as he tried to hold onto them, he focused the view on her and saw how she was being sucked downward. His sense of her position suggested that the 'Mech's foot must be just slightly to her right.

He could not use her neurohelmet to work the controls, but if only he could use his hands, he could bypass the helmet to work the foot. Well, one hand, at least. Its damaged wrist would give him ferocious pain, but it would function.

Pulling away a panel beneath the joystick, he wrenched out the wires to the neurohelmet. Joanna would scream when she saw what he had done. But the very fact she saw it would mean he had rescued her and returned her to the cockpit to resume her continuous harangues.

Taking the joystick, lightning flashes of pain erupting from his wrist, he worked with the 'Mech's foot. He could tell it was prevented from rising, but he felt a slight give left and right. Checking the viewport, he saw that Joanna had now sunk to her waist in the muck. His quick calculations told him that her feet would contact the upper surface of the 'Mech foot either just before her head sank below the surface level of the muck, or just after.

With severe effort, his eyes filling with tears from the furious pain, Nomad worked with the joystick. At first, the foot seemed unwilling to move. He pressed harder, and the pain got worse. Then, with a sudden jerk sideways, the foot moved just enough to place it under the sinking warrior. The muck was up to her shoulders now.

His arm throbbing with pain beyond any he might have dreamed he could endure, Nomad staggered to the viewport and looked down. Joanna had dropped the lantern. It bobbed on the surface of the muck, casting a thin, wobbly light over her. She held her arms high. The level of the muck was just below her neck.

Joanna had calmly accepted her imminent death, especially after being forced to fling away the lantern. Looking up, she saw Nomad staring down at her from within the light of the cockpit. This must be stimulating for him, she thought. Watching her die was probably something he had dreamed of for years.

They said that people often reevaluated their lives when they knew they were about to die, that sometimes their lives flashed before their eyes. There were many instances of conversion to ancient religious beliefs on the part of dying individuals. Many people regretted the actions of their lives. They made their peace with the human race, it was said.

Not Joanna. She would make peace with nobody, she thought. She had spent most of her life hating everyone. Why regret that now? She had found little reason to change her mind about the hatefulness of others. She would die contented that she had viewed life correctly. But that was about all she would be contented about. Mostly, she was angry. What an absurd way to die! She was a warrior, and a warrior was not supposed to die in a pool of filth, not unless he or she had been put there by an act of combat. What she regretted more than anything was that she would die without having earned a Bloodname, without contributing her genetic legacy to a gene pool.

She felt the disgusting sludge against the skin of her neck. Soon she would slide under. With her upraised hands, she worked off the gloves that were the symbol of her achievements with the Jade Falcon Clan. Studded with metal stars, they represented to Joanna her success in several combats. She did not want them to slide into the muck with her. Throwing them as well as she could, she watched them disappear into the darkness. But she heard them land. No splash accompanied their coming to rest, and so she knew that they would be retrieved by another warrior, perhaps used again by their new owner.

Resigned, she waited for her death. Which made the moment her feet landed on the upper surface of the 'Mech foot all the more startling. She felt the impact all through her body, even to the top of her head.

Suddenly she was not dead yet. But she was still neck-deep in muck, her arms flailing upward, rotten, odorous air seeming thicker just above the swamp surface, the suggestion of dangerous animals in every dark patch, her 'Mech disabled, a malfunctioning chief tech up in the cockpit, all communications gone. Death, she thought, might just have been better.

══ 16 ══

In a bizarre concatenation of circumstances, Kael Pershaw, Lanja, and Joanna were all in life-threatening danger simultaneously. Were an attentive god watching over his human minions, he or she might have been busy coordinating the fortunes of all three at once. Fortunately, Clan warriors did not have much use for gods and were, in fact, aware of only a few of those that were a part of human mythology. Those who speculated about gods generally concluded that a Clan warrior must rely on him or herself and not bother any god about anything.

Kael Pershaw's 'Mech was being rocked by a series of direct missile hits, most of them centered on the torso. With his thumb, he frantically pressed the enabling switch for the anti-missile system, but it was not working. The Wolf warrior on the other side apparently realized that and was shooting off a whole rack of SRMs at him.

With enemy Elementals swarming about his limbs as they tried to disable the 'Mech, and the awesome firepower being directed against him, only one response was possible. He must wade forward, all his weapons blasting away at once, hoping for a lucky series of hits.

What made matters worse was that the battle was being lost all around him. Every single Jade Falcon 'Mech was in serious jeopardy. The Jade Falcon Elementals had been pushed backward, behind the line of their 'Mechs.

Pershaw could not help wondering if the Elementals would have been pushed back so easily if Lanja were here.

Lanja was in the battle of her life. Had she been a normally constructed human being, she would be dead by now. Holding her head just barely above the stagnant water, she had managed to toss the tree puma off her body once, then turned around onto her back so that she faced it. It attacked again, its face coming so close that its foul breath seemed like some more pronounced extension of the swamp's putrescent odors.

The animal was small, which gave her some advantage because of her own great height. Somehow gaining leverage with her feet, she managed to hold the puma away from her. But she could not stop it from struggling and swiping at her with its paw, sometimes tearing skin. The strength she felt surging through the beast told her that it could wear her down. She had her own advantage, of course, for the beast had not been trained in battle skills. If she could just get to her laser pistol, she would let technology decide the issue. The only problem was that if she gave up her hold on the animal to reach for the weapon, it would get to her throat first.

Tension caused a new aching in Joanna's arms as she continued to hold them high. She did not know how long she could keep them there, but she emphatically did not want to let them fall into the muck.

She did not really know that she was now standing on her 'Mech's buried foot. For all she could tell, she was standing on a hidden rock or perhaps a muck animal. When whatever it was moved, she felt an irrational urge to draw up her legs. The muck would not allow any of her lower body to budge.

The thing jerked again, the movement pushing her forward. Her left arm dropped inadvertently, and before she could pull it out, sank into the muck. Another sudden move and the right arm nearly dropped. She felt herself slipping sideways, and might have slipped beneath the surface if the foot had not moved again and propelled her upward.

Now, her main problem, as the foot cleared the top of the scummy mud and the vines broke free, was to maintain her balance and keep from falling off. Especially when several of the vines came swinging past her, some of them hitting and stinging her face on their way.

The gods who might have been neglecting Kael Pershaw, Lanja, and Joanna might have been directing their attention at others. Not everyone was in jeopardy, after all. But no Clan warrior wanted to hear that some god was meddling in his life, in his achievements. Let the gods stay where they belonged, and if they would not, Clan warriors would bid against them in a battle to claim spiritual rights.

Most times, Dwillt Radick would have thrown out of his cockpit any god who had the bad judgment to appear there. At this moment, however, he might have been genial instead because of the chance it would give him to boast of his impending and impressive conquest of Kael Pershaw's Jade Falcons.

"Do not let up!" he shouted to his warriors.

Listening to this and Radick's other urgings, Craig Ward began to worry. If Radick had asked him, he would have admitted that Clan Wolf had the edge in this battle, but he was amazed at the tenacity of the Jade Falcons. His analysis showed that casualties were about the same on both sides. There was no superior strategy, tactics, or even firepower from Clan Wolf. Only attrition would give Radick the victory. And that, to Craig Ward, who was among the most fierce of warriors, would be a tainted triumph.

Aidan had turned his 'Mech to check on the status of the other warriors and their machines. If not for that he would never have seen the activity behind them.

"Horse, something is going on back there. It looks like a fight."

"Probably just two swamp animals having fun," Horse replied.

"No, it does not look like that. I would swear that one of the fighters is human. I have to go back there, check it out. It could be Joanna, separated from her 'Mech and coming after us."

"If it is her, there is no need to go back."

"Horse, we are Clan. We cannot let one of us die."

"I hear the words, Commander. I'm just not sure about them."

Aidan ordered the others to stay where they were. He descended from his *Summoner* and came down onto relatively firm soil. It squished a bit with moisture when he walked on it, but he *could* walk on it. There was a clear path of firm ground, nearly up to where the fight was taking place.

As he neared, he saw that the battle involved a tree puma. Knowing that, he took his laser pistol out and made sure it was on full charge.

Whatever the god's participation, often things just worked out. Lovers came together, families were reunited, good governments ousted bad governments. People in jeopardy found themselves, astonishingly, rescued. And occasionally one or two of them were grateful.

Kael Pershaw was only half-lucky. His automatic ejection mechanism got him out of his BattleMech before it fell. It did not explode, nor did it go down in pieces, but it was now clearly inoperative. As his ejection seat reached ground, five of his Elementals immediately surrounded him, fending off personal attacks from Clan Wolf Elementals. In a battle for a bloodline, capturing or killing the holder of the gene heritage would end the conflict, and so it was essential that Pershaw be kept alive and out of enemy hands.

When he walked back through his lines, he saw fallen BattleMechs all around him. His had not been the only one. Stepping over the dead warriors, he recognized among them the freebirth MechWarrior named Nis.

Joanna did slide off the foot, but only after Nomad had laboriously succeeded in making it take a step onto normal terrain, or at least what passed for normal terrain in this repulsive swamp. She fell to the ground. As she got up and brushed herself off, she looked up at Nomad, who was rather frantically gesturing for her to climb back up to the cockpit.

He could wait. She had to retrieve the gloves. When she found them, after skirting the pool of muck, she also found another of the reptilian creatures inspecting them, its mouth tentatively nibbling at a finger. Cursing silently, she picked up the laster pistol, which was still lying nearby, and blew the reptile's head off.

Aidan's well-aimed shot could have gone awry as Lanja managed to push the animal sideways, but it did not. The fire from his laser pistol entered the tree puma's brain, first going through its ear, transforming it into tiny fur and hide missiles. The animal went slack, its weight falling on Lanja, pushing her back into the water. Her head vanished beneath the water's surface, then her body, then the puma on top of it.

Aidan rushed to her. Reaching into the water, he found the puma's neck and yanked hard. The animal was heavy, damn heavy. But the water gave Aidan enough leverage to lift the animal off Lanja. It was too heavy to lift out of the water, but with a gigantic heave, he managed to fling it aside. Lanja did not reappear above the surface of the water. Wading in further, he reached down and paddled his hand around for her. At first he thought he had lost her. In the darkness he could not go underwater to look for her. He would not see anything.

Suddenly something bobbed up a few meters away. It was Lanja, on her stomach, her head still in the water. He swam to her, brought her head up, then dragged her back to the water's edge. He lay her down on the firm soil and started breathing into her mouth.

With a violent thrust upward, she started breathing again. Mustering all of his strength, Aidan grasped the massive woman's shoulder and then pulled and pushed and shoved until he had Lanja on her belly. Then he pounded on her muscular back to get the water out of her lungs. With 2.3 meters of her to handle, none of this was an easy task.

Nor was it easy to carry her back to the 'Mech. She had tried to walk on her own, but collapsed after a single step, passing out for a moment. By the time they reached the 'Mech, however, she was fully conscious again, insisting that Aidan put her down. Horse stood by Aidan's 'Mech, waiting for them. Aidan started to explain what had happened, but Lanja interrupted.

"The battle is not going well," she said. "Your units are badly needed, which is the message Kael Pershaw ordered me to relay to you."

Then she explained in precise detail what had occurred before she had started on her mission. Horse noted that the battle must still be raging, judging by the distant sounds of warfare and the way the night sky seemed light gray instead of deep blue.

Turning back to Lanja, he gestured to several cuts on her face and neck. "Those cuts are bad," he said.

"That does not matter," Lanja told him. Nevertheless, Horse quickly got out the medkit and started working on her.

"I am using bloodpetals," Horse said. "They will suck out any infections, then accelerate the healing of the cuts."

Lanja did not seem to be listening to Horse's comments. She turned to speak to Aidan, urgency in her voice: "If you continue on your present course, you are likely to come out just behind the Clan Wolf forces. That is, if my calculations are correct. We know how easily data can become distorted by the conditions of this place."

"Knowing we will emerge behind Clan Wolf could

be a strategic advantage," Aidan commented. "But we are only eight. That would not be enough for an ambush, *quineg?*"

"Neg," Lanja replied.

"Then we need a diversion."

"A diversion?"

"Yes. Can you get us close enough to Glory Station to establish a commlink?"

"Of course. There is a rise in a clearing about ten kilometers from here. From there, I should be able to establish both voice and digital secure link with Cluster headquarters."

She waved Horse away, even though he was still working on her wounds. Her gesture indicated that was all the medication she would accept right now.

"All right, then," Aidan said. "We will go on foot. Horse, bring the Star as close to the Wolf lines as you can without leaving the swamp. Have one of the extra pilots from Joanna's Trinary pilot my 'Mech there. I will join you there."

He turned to Lanja. "Let us go. And, Lanja, you will have to intervene for me. Because of this"—he pointed to his dark band—"Kael Pershaw does not have to talk to me. Even without this, he might not want to take advice from a freeborn."

Lanja thought that was true enough, but chose not to say it. She had a sense that Jorge might be the solution to what might otherwise be certain defeat.

17

Joanna wondered if Nomad's meddling with the neu-rohelmet had severely damaged it. Even though he had reconnected it, the helmet now felt exactly as when she had first been fitted for one so many years ago. There was a kind of throbbing dizziness in her head, a sense that, even though the 'Mech was apparently functioning normally, it was actually walking around in a daze.

She wondered if he had sabotaged the device. It would not be beyond his capabilities.

She took a deep breath. The air scrubbers were not working, and the smell of vomit hung in the air. No-mad's pain had become so intense that he had thrown up after completing the great effort of operating the 'Mech's foot. He had managed to clean up most of it, but the smell was taking its time. He had seen no point in trying to air out the cockpit. Not only were the air scrubbers down, but the air outside was even worse than this smell.

After sulking for a while, Nomad had fallen asleep again on the passenger seat. The sulking was because Joanna did not thank him properly for saving her life.

"It is your duty to rescue your commanding offi-cer," she told him. "It is not some act of generosity that endows you with special qualities. You are still the same worthless sub-caster you always were. I will commend you properly in my report. That is all the gratitude that a Clansman deserves."

"Have it your way, Captain," he muttered.

"Look, Nomad, if it satisfies you to know, I am content that I will have more opportunity to serve the Clan. For that, I realize you are responsible. I respect those who perform their duty, so I respect you for doing it. Does that make you happier?"

"I'm not even sure I understood it."

She was glad that he slept now. His incessant footnoting of her every word was getting on her nerves. She had no idea where they were, could not use a single instrument of her control panel to find out, and had to—as the saying went—walk blind. They could use nothing in the swamp for a guiding mark. Every part of the place seemed to look almost exactly like every other part.

Something in the neurohelmet was giving her a headache. She shut her eyes and for a moment seemed to see a fully operational cockpit. She was knocked back to reality when the 'Mech stepped into a small pond, and she had to switch her concentration to navigating through water. The pain in her head grew even stronger when the 'Mech tripped over something and careened against a thick tree. She thought she sensed something rattling around in the compartment beneath the cockpit, but then decided it must be just her imagination or the malfunction in the neurohelmet.

Joanna was sure they were traveling in a circle, as so often happened to 'Mechs without sensors in unknown areas. There was no sense of what was behind or in front of her, to the right or the left. She might as well stand still as continue this blundering search.

She stopped the 'Mech and ate some rations she had stored away. She could not get much down, the cockpit odors not being conducive to a heavy appetite. Looking out the viewport, she saw she was facing a clump of tall trees, trees that seemed to stretch above the canopy. Their branches and leaves were in sporadic motion, as if animals were jumping from branch to branch, perhaps excited by the intruder in their midst. She had heard that some animals lived their entire lives in the upper areas of swamps, jungles, forests, never coming down to ground level. The ground must be a wondrous land, something few of their kind ever saw. For Clan warriors the Inner Sphere was such a wondrous place of mythology. Generations ago, the ancestors of the Clan had left there to seek a new home among the distant stars. They were not even Clans then. Since that time, warriors of every generation hoped to be part of the invasion of the Inner Sphere when the Khans decided that the Clans possessed sufficient military strength to accomplish their goals.

She stopped thinking of Clan things when a head suddenly appeared, peering through leaves in one of the trees. Though she realized it was some kind of animal, it was like nothing she had seen before. The thing was monstrous, horny-headed, with a thick snout and sharp teeth that overhung its lower lips.

She hated looking at it so much that she aimed her left-arm PPC and shot it out of the tree. Watching it fall, Joanna felt a sense of satisfaction. It had been like defeating a monster in a nightmare.

She traveled on.

As she walked over a particularly malevolent-looking bunch of shrubs and creepers, her commlink suddenly, with a warning crackle, came back on. Though she immediately began to send out a vocal signal, she was surprised when a response came back within a minute. "I hear you, Star Captain Joanna," the voice said. She recognized it as belonging to one of the freebirth filth in Aidan's unit.

"Where is Star Commander Jorge?" she demanded.

"He is . . . he is not with his BattleMech and has left me in charge."

"You in charge!"

"Yes. Do you object?"

"You know I do. Four of your . . . your warriors are from my Trinary. You cannot command them. One of them must be chosen to lead. They cannot be led by freebirth scum!"

The commlink was silent.

"Star Captain Joanna, I thought you would have joined us earlier."

"My inertial guidance and scanner units are out of

commission. So was this commlink until a moment ago. I have been guiding my BattleMech through this infernal place. Why did your unit not search for me?"

"It was deemed of lower priority than to rejoin the Glory Station forces."

The words irritated her, especially when spit out from the mouth of a freebirth, but she refused to engage such a lowlife in rational argument. He would not understand reason.

"And why have you not rejoined the garrison forces?"

"Our commander ordered us to go to the rim of the swamp, then await his orders."

"I am your commander again. You will do what I order."

"You are not here."

"When I am there then."

"How will you get here? You said yourself that your guidance system is inoperable."

"You will send one of the warriors to guide me to you. And one from *my* Trinary, none of your filthy freebirths whom I cannot trust to lead me to a drinking trough of swamp water."

A strange sound came over the commlink, but Joanna could not interpret it.

"Begging your pardon, Captain, but I recommend that you allow one of us . . . us freeborns to come for you, filthy though we might be. We know the terrain and can get there faster."

For once Joanna found a freeborn's argument compelling. She told Horse to dispatch a warrior in a 'Mech immediately. He said he would do it before then.

Horse wished Aidan would return. MechWarrior Prent, whom he had sent out for Joanna, would follow Horse's orders to move slowly, then pretend to have encountered obstacles along the way. It was a stalling maneuver, but he had not known what else to do. Because of the communication difficulties, he could not contact Aidan for orders, so he had to stall Joanna until the real officer came back to give real orders. He did not mind giving her a wild goose chase until then.

Lanja was as good as her word. After ten grueling kilometers through the muck and mire of Blood Swamp, half-carrying, half-dragging Aidan all the way, she set up her communications gear and carefully aimed the parabolic antenna toward Glory Station. Within minutes, Kael Pershaw's face appeared on the diminutive screen.

"You said you got your idea for the diversion from some book," Kael Pershaw said to Aidan. "A *book?* Where does the likes of you find a book?"

Aidan almost said that he had found it during his days in the sibko, but then he remembered that, as far as Kael Pershaw knew, he was freeborn and never was anywhere near a sibko. Not wanting to confess his secret cache of books in the freeborn barracks, he tried a lie: "I think, when I was a child, a woman used to come to my house and care for me when I was sick. I believe she brought the book with her. Took it away again later, for that matter."

"And this was what kind of book?"

"A great book, written in poetry and full of battle."

"So you are asking me to perform a diversion based on, as it were, battle intelligence from centuries ago. And written in poetry, at that."

"That about sums it up. We need the diversion so that the other part of the plan will work."

"What has made you think I would even consider a plan that comes from a stinking freebirth?"

"Because, Star Colonel Kael Pershaw, I know that you are a master strategist who can see the merit in anyone's plan, even a freebirth's."

"Even a freebirth wearing the dark band, whom I am encouraging to talk much beyond the small liberties permitted by the band."

"With all due respect, sir, I do believe the rites of the dark band should be suspended during a battle. They interfere with—"

"Yes, yes, Jorge. But, when I do allow you to talk, it is difficult to shut you up. How do you expect me to do what you want? It is quite a logistical monstrosity, your plan."

"But it can work."

"It worked in a story. Anyway, I will do as you say. Short of retreating all the way to Glory Station and allowing Clan Wolf to overrun us, I am out of schemes to use in this battle. Lanja!"

"Sir?"

"I think this plan will work better if we use your Elementals. Can they squeeze into such a small area?"

"It is large enough for two or three of them."

"Two will be sufficient. And can they find their way across the field without being detected?"

"I cannot guarantee it. But we will try."

"That is sufficient. Jorge, you are dismissed. Return to your unit and await my signal. If we cannot reach you on any communications line, we will send up a flare. When you see it, start your attack."

Aidan nodded and left Lanja alone on top of the knoll. Pershaw, disgusted at having to deal with a freebirth, rubbed sweat off his forehead.

"That cost you a lot, did it not, Colonel?" she said.

"You know that any contact with freebirth warriors irritates me. I suppose, though, that it is better to get help from freeborns than to let my gene legacy wind up as Clan Wolf property."

"You are not accepting something from just any freeborn. This one has distinguished himself."

"How can you say that? He has killed one of my officers and been insubordinate on many occasions."

"And he has rescued the survivors of the crash, enlarging your complement of warriors. For what it is worth, he also saved me from being mauled by a tree puma. Then he saved my life again when I almost drowned. Jorge has shown bravery and resourcefulness in spite of the accident of his birth."

Pershaw understood what Lanja said, but in his heart he deeply resented Jorge and all his deeds, however useful and miraculous.

"Rest," Lanja said. "I must meet my team on the battlefield. There will be another battle soon enough, and we will see how well Jorge's plan works."

"Your cuts are almost healed."

"I hate to tell you this, but the medicine was originally discovered by a freeborn warrior and administered to me by another freeborn warrior."

Pershaw shuddered. Thoughts of coupling with Lanja turned sour. He was afraid he would sense the freeborn touch on her skin.

18

Lanja had been in a 'Mech cockpit before, but those machines had been upright for inspection tours, not twisted and lying on their sides on a ravaged battlefield. To squeeze into this *Fire Moth,* her fellow Elemental had ripped out the command couch and half the control panels so the two of them could fit in their full battle armor. Others had found clever concealment beneath the detritus of battle.

They were operating under radio silence, Kael Pershaw having decided that the risk of Clan Wolf picking up some stray transmission was too great. In the dark confusion of her battlesuit, Lanja waited in isolation for the flare Pershaw would send up when he decided the time was right.

"Clan Wolf must attack," he had said. "The plan will only work if they are on the move."

Lanja had noted that whenever Kael Pershaw mentioned the plan, he never attached Jorge's name to it. It was as though he wanted to prevent anyone from knowing that the plan had originated with a freeborn. Though Lanja had always assumed that she despised freeborns as much as anyone of her caste, next to Kael Pershaw's hatred, hers seemed like the whim of a child.

In the dome housing the command center, Star Captain Dwillt Radick was planning one final thrust. Repairs had brought the two Supernovas almost up to full strength again, though his Elemental force had fallen to twelve, little more than two Points. By his rights under bidding protocols, he called upon the Battle-Mechs of the Cluster's Supernova Third to reinforce his command, bringing his total 'Mech force up to twenty-three. He dismissed the aerospace fighters, however, for rank did not come to those who used more than enough strength to achieve objectives.

With all his forces already at their start points, Dwillt Radick reviewed his operations order for the next attack. He would launch a massive assault directly against Glory Station. He would then pursue the remnants of Persaw's forces all over the wretched terrain of Glory until the sweet moment of their inevitable surrender.

Radick was awaiting the final reports of his officers when Kael Pershaw's surprisingly placid voice came over the commlink. "Are you sleeping, Dwillt Radick? If you wish to give up your foolish quest and become my bondsman, I am ready to go through the rituals now. You cannot win, *quiaff?*"

"Kael Pershaw, I will not even bother to waste feeding you as our bondsman. You should surrender now so your gene heritage can find a dwelling place more suitable than a stinking Jade Falcon home." "Home" was the common term for the scientifically supervised caches where genetic materials were stored. If Clan Wolf won this challenge, the Pershaw line would be ceremoniously transferred from the Jade Falcon vaults in the cache to those of the Wolf Clan.

"We are bored with your idle boasts, Dwillt Radick. If you wish to fight, fight. Combat instead of bombast, *quiaff?*"

"You had better be ready to count your casualties, Kael Pershaw."

Dwillt Radick slammed his chair backward and shouted at the command center personnel to activate all warriors. "This will be the final battle before we claim victory," he said, then watched as the communications personnel swung into action. They were the heart, the center of the battle, coordinating information among Supernovas, keeping the flanks steady as the center moved ahead in the wedge formation that Radick favored. He urged them on one more time before racing to his own *Mad Dog*. He hoped to meet Kael Pershaw in a one-on-one engagement. It would be the greatest of pleasures to slice Pershaw's 'Mech in two from the head downward, halving Pershaw along with his machine.

In his own command dome, Kael Pershaw nodded at his subordinates, a signal that he had prodded Dwillt Radick into action. He then went directly to his new 'Mech, a shiny *Warhawk* whose regular pilot was injured. Looking up at the 'Mech, with its flat head and double extended-range PPCs in each arm, he wondered, as always, if this would be the 'Mech in which he would die. If so, he would not mind. It would be the death he had always craved. Sometimes Pershaw believed he must have come out of the canister wishing for an honorable death.

Joanna scoffed at Aidan's strategy.

"Attack from behind? That is absurd. As soon as we emerge from the swamp, their sensors will pick us up, and they will turn around and massacre us."

"Clan Wolf will be advancing with all their forces," Aidan said. "Their rear will be vulnerable. Only think of how hard it is to change a 'Mech's direction once an assault has begun. No, I suspect that we will meet no more than some guards left behind, perhaps just Elementals."

"I do not approve suicide missions."

"Fortunately you need not. Kael Pershaw already has."

"He does not know conditions here, nor the damage to some of our 'Mechs."

"I am sure he would not care. His back is against the wall. He cannot win without us."

"I do not see that to be so."

"Then stay back and watch from behind some tree while we fight."

Aidan enjoyed the wrath in Joanna's eyes. She was the type of warrior for whom even a hint of cowardice was the deepest of insults.

"If Kael Pershaw has approved the plan, then we must implement it. I am willing to lead us into the battle, no matter what my opinion of the plan. That is the way of the Clan."

If Aidan had permitted himself a gleam in his eyes, even a twinkle, it would have showed at that moment. From the side pocket of his jumpsuit, he drew out a facsimile of the orders, which he had demanded from Kael Pershaw before rejoining his unit. Silently he handed it to Joanna.

"What is this?"

"The authorization for me to take command of this operation."

If Joanna had been an LRM, she would have shot right off the rack at that moment. "You! He assigned you the mission! I am the ranking officer."

"I told him that. However, he accepted my argument that I would be more qualified in the terrain and in Glory Station tactics because you are new to Glory. He has given me a temporary field promotion to Star Captain so that you will not be dishonored in any way."

Joanna fumed. What did he know of dishonor? Pershaw would never have done this to her if she were Bloodnamed. And what did terrain and tactics have to do with a piddling operation like this? It was a hit-and-run action. Nothing was ever accomplished with hit and run. Toe to toe, that was Joanna's way.

But she saw that she could not argue. The careful wording of Kael Pershaw's order took away her command without making her subordinate to Aidan by assigning her a role as a kind of free-lance combatant. Without saying another word, she wheeled around and strode away, her heels coming down with such force that her steps sent missiles of water droplets out of the wet, swampy ground.

"I would watch your back with that one," Horse commented. He had observed the whole exchange with evident pleasure.

"No. Joanna's as mean as a rogue surat, but she would not attack dishonorably. She is Clan through and through."

"All right then, don't watch your back. Watch your throat, especially when there is a knife anywhere within a kilometer of her."

"That I will do, Horse. That I will do."

The Clan Wolf forces came thundering across the plain like a giant city on the move. Keeping his 'Mech still, Kael Pershaw watched them with the detached admiration he always felt when viewing a line of advancing 'Mechs. Although of different designs and sizes, although configured differently, although each had its own style of movement, each was a beautiful and graceful symbol of unity and strength. To Pershaw the 'Mechs represented the Clans themselves. Each Clan had its own unique configurations, its own rites and customs, but all followed the basic Clan rituals. Each Clan took pride in its own achievements and was willing to fight others to assert them, while all would unite for a grand battle, then return to the Inner Sphere. Each Clan had its own ways, but over all was the way of the Clans.

Pershaw had a direct sensor link from Bravo Striker Nova, which was tracking the advance of the Wolf Clan forces. Right now he saw the Wolves nearing the line where the Elementals had hidden themselves during the night. Only a moment more and the battle would begin. Pershaw readied his 'Mech to lead his Cluster, or the remnants of it. He was as apprehensive as any commander in an odds-against status, yet also thrilled that the challenge had been reduced to one grand do-or-die gesture. It would either turn the tide of battle or send the Jade Falcons to a humiliating defeat. A military leader could hope for no more exciting moment.

Pershaw kept his concentration on Radick's *Mad Dog,* in the lead as was only proper. The moment Radick was two steps past the hidden Elementals, Pershaw would give the signal to attack.

An instant later, Radick's 'Mech was crossing the fallen 'Mech in which Lanja and another Elemental were hiding. For a moment he feared the foot would come down on her, but it narrowly missed the 'Mech. Then it took another step. And another.

"Now," he said into the commline, his voice quiet but steady.

The flare went up.

To Dwillt Radick the flash looked like distant lightning through his viewport, but his secondary screen identified the illumination as a flare. It was early morning, still dusky but with clear visibility. Why in the name of Nicholas Kerensky would Pershaw send up a flare?

For Lanja, the light of the flare came through all the open cracks in the wrecked cockpit. Her huge muscles straining from being packed into the tight cockpit, she did not think the signal came a moment too soon.

Weapons activated, she and her fellow Elemental rose from the fallen 'Mech like specters from the mist. Unlike such a phantasmal creature, however, she was already firing at the BattleMech that rose above her but that had yet to see her. Indeed, none of the enemy 'Mechs were prepared for the concentrated attack from below, giving the ambushers a chance to inflict heavy damage in those first few seconds alone.

To Joanna, the flare was the kind of flamboyant tactic she would have expected in any plan originated by Aidan. The grand gesture, the overreaching move, the plunging forward against all logic—Aidan had been that way even as a cadet. Now that he was a warrior, those characteristics would continue to be his downfall. She despised his individualistic bent. It was some kind of odd blessing, she thought, that circumstances had forced him into the false identity of a freebirth

MIKE·N 91

filth. That meant he could never earn a Bloodname. Perhaps it was only bitterness at having failed thus far in her own Bloodname trials, but Joanna genuinely believed that a Bloodnamed Aidan would be a disgrace to all that the Clans represented.

At Aidan's signal, she began to move her 'Mech forward, the resentment only increasing at the idea of having to follow even a single one of his commands.

Aidan welcomed the light of the flare. He yearned for nothing more in the universe than to distinguish himself as a warrior. It did not matter whether others believed him freeborn or trueborn. The battle was all, the battle and the honor to be earned in it.

Giving the signal to advance, he led the way out of Blood Swamp, the 'Mechs looking monstrous in the quickly fading light of the flare. Moisture from the swamp dripped from their limbs. Stray leaves and patches of moss had rubbed off on their surfaces. Mud and muck smeared their feet. They looked like antediluvian creatures just aroused from beneath the deep waters of the swamp.

The last flicker of the flare was a momentary brightness and then the battlefield was bathed only in the half-light of dawn. In the distance, the Clan Wolf battle line, now a bit uneven, looked gray in the dim morning light. Beneath it, lines of fire from both the weapons and the jump packs of the attacking Elementals rose up around them like a fiery net.

19

Once out of the swamp, the tread of Aidan's *Summoner* seemed to lighten, climbing the slope with sure, almost carefree steps. Though Aidan felt a touch of disorientation from being so long in the swamp and jungle, his 'Mech easily topped the slope, where the fire of the rear-guard Wolf Elementals was disorganized and ineffective. As Aidan had suspected, Radick had underbid his Elementals, which left too few in the rear. A burst of rapid pulses from his medium laser and a whole line of them lay either still or squirming on the ground. The *Summoner* stepped over them as Aidan guided it forward. His primary screen showed an LRM coming toward him, but he blasted it out of the air with his anti-missile system before it could do any harm to the Jade Falcon warriors. Instead, much of the shrapnel dropped onto Wolf warriors and support personnel, setting small fires and ripping sections off some of the domes housing supplies.

Some of the pleasure Pershaw felt at the entrance of his gallant swamp warriors into battle derived from seeing the battle turn, some of it from imagining the confusion and irritation on Dwillt Radick's face. Even now, the man's 'Mech seemed to waver, as though not sure whether to shoot at the Jade Falcon 'Mechs in front of him or turn back to demolish the small enemy contingent at his rear.

The confusion gave the Jade Falcon warriors just enough time to execute the next phase of Aidan's plan.

The *Mad Dog* that Lanja had so severely damaged when bursting from her hiding place looked ready to topple. Knowing it would be easy prey to a blast from the Jade Falcon 'Mech now closing in on it, she opened the commlink to order her armored soldiers to move toward the Wolf Clan command dome.

Screaming high on their jump jets, the Jade Falcon Elementals were a fearsome sight against the lightening sky. The Wolf Elementals, already decimated by the Jade Falcon attack from the rear, turned toward the new attack with the same confusion being shown by the Clan Wolf 'Mechs in the middle of the field.

In the Wolf Clan command dome, tacticians fired off messages to both 'Mechs and Elementals, trying to coordinate the triad of Supernovas in the field into a unit, assigning each element to specific parts of the widely spaced battle around them. Messages flew back and forth across the commlinks.

On the other side of the field, Kael Pershaw saw that the Clan Wolf 'Mechs were closing their lines to fend off the attack coming from the three advancing Jade Falcon forces.

If Jorge did not perform his mission soon, the tide of battle could turn in favor of the Wolves. Could? It definitely would. Kael Pershaw did not have the personnel for a long stand-up fight. Attrition alone would win Clan Wolf the day.

Joanna saw that Aidan was in deep trouble. An enemy *Dire Wolf* had just gone striding through the line of Jade Falcon Elementals, injuring a couple with glancing blows from its footfalls. When its left-arm SRM got off a cluster, Aidan did not see it in time. The missiles exploded against the chest of his *Summoner,* gouging out a large chunk just above the fusion engine casing. Another successful hit and the 'Mech would be disabled, unable to finish its mission and perhaps cause a Jade Falcon defeat. Knowing she was too far from the command dome to successfully take over Aidan's mission, Joanna saw her best bet was to plunge forward, coming at the attacking 'Mech from the outside angle, firing everything she had. She was definitely closest to it, while the other swamp 'Mechs were under fire in their own difficult circumstances. One of her Trinary 'Mechs was tottering from a concentrated Elemental attack.

Zeroing in on the imposing and well-armed Clan 'Mech, Joanna pressed her own machine forward with the determination that had won her as many curses as praise in all her warrior assignments. Once within range, she launched a cluster of short-range missiles. Her hope was that the *Dire Wolf* pilot, intent on destroying Aidan, would not notice her entrance as a tiny symbol on any of his cockpit battlescreens. The high-velocity missiles sailed toward the *Dire Wolf*, but Joanna did not wait for them to hit before launching a backup set from both her hip-mounted launchers. If the first cluster did no damage, the sudden appearance of the second probably would. But she was not content to await the flight of the second missiles. Bringing her *Hellbringer* to a full run, she started firing the PPCs in both her 'Mech's arms.

Rivers of sweat poured from her as the cockpit's temperature soared. She fired off the trio of medium lasers in the *Hellbringer*'s chest, then slapped the override on the fusion plant's automatic shutdown sequence. It did not matter how much firepower she used. It did not matter if her ammo cooked off from the searing heat of the stressed fusion plant. It did not matter if she were broiled alive in her cockpit. This was the only battle she had to win, the only enemy 'Mech she *had* to vanquish.

And all, she thought, bitterly, to save Aidan, that sanctimonious imposter who had become more freebirth than any freebirth.

Aidan, rocking from the *Dire Wolf*'s hits, did not at first detect Joanna's entrance into the fray. For a moment, he thought his own weak ripostes were causing the awesome damage to the *Dire Wolf*. After the explosions from the first missile clusters ripped a long scar across the enemy 'Mech's chest, the second group appeared to pierce the wounds created by the first. Then he saw her *Hellbringer* coming down into a landing, firing off PPC beams at such a high rate that she was obviously risking heat buildup just to go for the kill.

It was a moment before he realized that she was in the act of saving him. The bitch Joanna was rescuing him! Stealing the kill. The *Dire Wolf* pilot ejected high out of his 'Mech just as the entire machine seemed to dissolve in a series of small explosions. Aidan raged with anger and frustration, but he fought to regain control. By her action, Joanna was making it possible for him to continue with his mission and to come out of it with even greater glory.

Quickly checking his damage on his secondary screen, he saw that one of the *Dire Wolf* blasts had disabled his right arm with its PPC. That weapon had been a major part of his plan because of its accuracy, so now he would have to rely on missiles, plus whatever damage his left-arm autocannon could do.

No matter. If his plan was good, he would win even with all his weapons disabled. If it was not, he deserved to become ashes that would scatter over the battlefield or be lifted by the breeze into the murky atmosphere of Blood Swamp.

Lanja took note of the trio of BattleMechs that had broken from the Clan Wolf line to take care of the intruders from the swamp. Taking advantage of the confusion, she timed her jump-jet leap with the kind of precision for which Elementals were so famous. She rose swiftly to the back of a passing Wolf *Executioner,* and sank the claw of her battle suit's left arm into a joint between the armor plates. Jamming her laser into the crack, she pumped megajoules of energy into the interior of her victim. Then some sixth sense inborn to Elementals made her suddenly whirl and jet off the 'Mech, jumping as far away as possible. Hitting the ground, she went into a long roll that took her behind a knoll.

From there she watched the *Executioner*'s back explode outward in a gout of flame as its ammunition erupted. For a moment, the 'Mech continued forward, then its left leg shuddered and collapsed, throwing the 'Mech sideways. She had expected it to fall immediately, but the expert pilot inside stubbornly refused to eject and kept his machine going in a stumbling, sideways stagger. It was moving in Lanja's general direction.

Lanja realized immediately that she had miscalculated. As the 'Mech teetered and began to fall, it was coming right down at her. She tried to leap again, but her jump jets had lost too much charge.

As the huge machine bore down to crush her, she stared up at it in horror, but made no sound. Elementals did not scream.

Pershaw, knowing Lanja's plan, kept track of her on one screen while watching Jorge on another. At the same time, he was able to fire off a cluster round at an advancing *Ice Ferret*. The Clan Wolf 'Mech had stopped firing, however, its PPC hanging uselessly from its left arm and its right-arm missile box open and empty. It was a child's target. Pershaw would gain no honor from finishing it off, but neither did he want to lose his blood heritage.

The *Ice Ferret* retreated, but not fast enough to evade Pershaw's incessant autocannon assault. He also saw Jorge, who had nearly been knocked out of the action, now advancing toward the command dome while another warrior finished off the 'Mech that had nearly taken Jorge. At the same time, two more BattleMechs from the opposite flank were closing in on him.

He saw which of these 'Mechs Lanja had targeted. Pleased, he watched her ascend the 'Mech's leg, while he simultaneously fired the shots that sent the *Ice Ferret* crashing to the ground. He watched the explosions form a garter of smoke around the 'Mech leg, then saw the machine begin to descend to the ground. Before it crashed, Pershaw realized that the Elemental beneath it was Lanja. It looked as though she was trying to get out of its way, but some debris falling from the 'Mech obscured his view just before it hit the ground.

Pershaw's mouth felt dry as he realized that Lanja, his aide and lover, was most likely dead. Then he focused his attention back on the battle, watching Jorge's advance with single-minded concentration.

Aidan's concentration was just as fierce. He was aware of other things happening on the field, but he chose not to interpret them. He fired a stream of missiles at the command dome. Apparently someone there was tracking them and had engaged a static anti-missile system located just on the other side of the dome. It took care of the missiles easily, but a few pieces of shrapnel did some damage falling on the dome. He had not figured on the ground anti-missile setup, but neither could he have foreseen the damage the falling shrapnel would do. He fired off another cluster, which the anti-missile system countered a bit more quickly, so that less shrapnel fell on the dome. But enough did hit the dome, making the cracks wider. Through his viewport, Aidan glimpsed movement in the dome, cool technicians busy getting control of their side of the battle. There was no time to lose.

"Aidan!" It was Joanna, and the damned woman had used the wrong name. Had anyone heard her? When she used the name a second time, he had to answer. All he needed was for the shrewd Kael Pershaw to overhear and start asking questions.

"What is it, Joanna?" He deliberately did not use her rank in retaliation for her lapse of judgment. If she noticed the insult, her voice gave no indication.

"You are under attack. To your right, an *Ice Ferret!*"

She was right. And it was close.

He estimated that he had just enough time to get to the command dome before the Clan Wolf 'Mech could do any real damage. Simultaneously with the thought, he engaged his own anti-missile system to destroy a rather weakly launched cluster of missiles.

There was no time to counterattack the *Ice Ferret*. He had to complete his mission. The Clan Wolf pilot could do what he wanted. Aidan must take the chance that it would not be enough damage to block him from his objective.

Piloting the *Ice Ferret*, Craig Ward was both angry and puzzled. The guerrilla-like tactics of the Jade Falcon Clan seemed unfair, though he knew that Clan warfare did not acknowledge any tactic as unfair.

He was beginning to think that these Jade Falcons were lucky, damned lucky. But buzzards might have been a better name, for falcons had too much nobility. The enemy should never have been able to survive the Wolf Clan onslaught for this long, yet they had. They should not have had enough firepower left to destroy the other two members from his Star who had been detached to handle this attack, but they had. Now this damned pilot in his damned *Summoner* was firing off rounds at the communications dome. So far he had not made a major hit, but with luck going the way it was for the buzzards, Craig Ward began to fear that this enemy 'Mech, this monster that had risen from the murk of the swamp, was about to get even luckier.

Furiously, and without the tactical wisdom that he usually displayed, Craig Ward raised his *Ice Ferret*'s right arm and launched a pair of missiles at the *Summoner*.

Aidan, his attention too divided, did not activate his anti-missile system in time. Both missiles struck the side of his 'Mech, with some severe damage to its already gouged torso. Another strike might explode the whole 'Mech with a direct hit on the fusion engine. He had to get the dome now.

Advancing, he managed to shoot down another flight of missiles from the *Ice Ferret*. The next one, he realized suddenly, he could use to his own advantage.

Ripping at the dome with his autocannon, he visited

more wreckage to its roof. From the other side, some Wolf Elementals desperately fired off their arm-mounted lasers. Short-range missiles leaped from their backs toward the *Summoner*. Their shots were low, he noticed, but they were chipping pieces off his leg armor.

The *Summoner* could not last much longer, but that was all right. One more step and his 'Mech would be in position, nearly towering over the dome. He tried more shots with the autocannon, but one of the Elemental's return fire hit the *Summoner*'s arm, sending it shooting upward.

Well, no matter. He was close enough now.

Aidan turned the 'Mech slightly toward the Clan Wolf *Ice Ferret,* which was now only a few meters away, firing desperately with its PPC, each hit rocking the *Summoner.* Calculating the arc of the fire emanating from the *Ice Ferret,* Aidan leaned his 'Mech just slightly toward the dome like some giant bestowing a blessing.

The *Summoner* had been a good 'Mech, Aidan thought. It had served him well at Glory Station, but its time had come to die. He was neither more nor less sad over that prospect than he would have been over the death of any valiant warrior.

Then came the impact he was waiting for, blasting against the 'Mech's right shoulder just below the cockpit. It was his signal to press his ejection button. He had not ejected from a 'Mech since his first Trial of Position, and the fierce rush of Glory Plain air nearly knocked him out when it hit.

As Aidan had calculated, his ejection seat sailed over the Clan Wolf command communications center. Because he was facing away, he did not see his *Summoner* slowly fall onto the command dome, did not see its impact send pieces of dome erupting skyward like shrapnel, did not see the 'Mech crumple onto the building itself, did not see the Clan Wolf techs frantically scrambling from their consoles and monitors to find a way out of the dome before being crushed, did not see the sparks, smoke, and fires that consumed the dome and its destroyer.

Aidan was happy as he guided the para-wing-equipped ejection seat to the ground. He did not even mind nearly falling into the arms of a pistol-waving Wolf Clan MechWarrior, who, in spite of his weapons and evident physical advantage, proved to be a rather easy victim to Aidan's best weapons, his bare hands. He crushed the other man's throat between them. The sensation of this victory reminded him of that other satisfactory killing, the death of the vicious Star Commander Bast. Blood was splashed all over his ripped and shredded dark band, but Aidan did not mind.

20

Trudging on foot across the battlefield, Aidan had to dodge Clan Wolf warriors, 'Mech pilots who had ejected from their machines and now staggered about clumsily, looks of disbelief on their faces. He would not have minded a few skirmishes with these warriors, just for the exercise, but the battle was over and the Jade Falcons had won. Aidan saw no point in dying *after* a battle, when some other time a warrior could die *in* one. Still, the frustrated Clan Wolf warriors were angry enough to engage in useless combat, and so Aidan stayed out of their way.

One of his boots had split open during the battle with the Elemental, and he had cast it away. The ground beneath his bare foot was hot, making him step gingerly. The burning hot steps, alternating with the booted ones, were clumsy, so he cast off the good boot in order to walk more rapidly. The ground heat urged him forward and definitely helped him to pick up his pace.

He found Lanja trapped beneath a large piece of armor that must have fallen with the 'Mech beside which she lay. He would not even have noticed her except that his burning feet had forced him to stop and sit on a jutting sliver of the fallen 'Mech. The place where he sat was quite warm, but at least it was a new area of his body that was getting singed.

He did not notice Lanja until she groaned. It was an abrupt sound, more an expression of frustration than pain. At first all he saw was the twisted armor of her battle suit sticking out from under the metal fragment. Walking around it, he saw Lanja lying in the shattered hallmark of her trade.

"Are you all right, Star Commander Lanja?"

"No. You can tell that easily, *quiaff?*"

"Well, aff. But I thought it was polite to ask."

"A freebirth who is polite. What a novelty. What has happened in the battle?"

"It is over." Aidan told her what he knew about it, including his own crushing of the command dome.

"So your plan was a success," she said. "And your dark band. It is ripped."

He looked down. "So it is. I had a bit of a skirmish back there. Happened then."

"You are a good warrior, Jorge."

"It must cost you a great deal to say that. I have always known you despise us, *quiaff?*"

"Freebirths? I have always hated freebirths. I hate you now. But you are a brave warrior."

"I am about to complicate your hatred even more."

"Oh? How?"

"I am going to carry you to the med dome, Star Commander Lanja." Ignoring her look of disgust, he summoned up nearly all his remaining strength, lifted the metal piece, and then pushed it off Lanja. When it was safely aside, he looked down at her. Seeing her body, twisted as it was, crushed in the upper legs, even his emotionless Clan demeanor gave way. Lanja undoubtedly saw the slight flinch in his eyes.

"Can you move?"

"I feel very little sensation, but I will try."

Her arms responded naturally and she was able to lift her neck.

"Your back seems to be all right, and your upper body. We will have to get you out of here."

"We?"

"Figure of speech. We freeborns do n—don't speak just right, you know that?"

Working quickly, Aidan fashioned some pieces of shrapnel and wire from various exposed places in the fallen 'Mech into a kind of metal cot, a device called a traverse that he must have read about. Ripping out some electrical cable, he made a usable handle with which to pull the flat metal construction.

The hardest part was extracting Lanja from the remnants of her battle suit and onto the makeshift traverse. She was covered with the black goo that the suit's medical system expelled to stabilize injured Elementals. The goo, combined with Lanja's massive frame, made it difficult to maneuver her onto the traverse. Using more electrical cord, he fastened her body firmly onto the construction. When he was sure that she would not slide around unnecessarily and harmfully, he grabbed the cord handle and began to pull.

Almost immediately he realized that he could not progress quickly. The weight of the traverse, so much greater than any real medical conveyance, plus the care needed to keep the ride smooth over some fairly rocky ground, forced him to move slowly. Each step he took seemed to burn his feet even more.

It was not long, however, before the ground cooled as he drew away from the battle site. Then he was spotted by some Jade Falcon Elementals, who rushed up to take over transport of the traverse. Weary and exhausted, Aidan was grateful for the strength of these towering, sinewy warriors.

Aidan barely felt his last steps into the Jade Falcon encampment. He stumbled into the center of camp, then fell unconscious at the entrance to the command center. Kael Pershaw was there. He had watched Aidan's progress the whole way, ordering his subordinates not to give the exhausted warrior any help.

Pershaw was feeling extraordinarily good at that moment. He had just signed off from Dwillt Radick's surrender acknowledgment.

"I am to be your bondsman then," Radick said.

Pershaw chuckled to himself before responding, "There will be no need for that. Your defeat came at the hands of a freebirth. I cannot have such a humiliated warrior as my bondsman. You may return with your Cluster to your home world.''

"Kael Pershaw, you *must* take me as bondsman. It is Clan law.''

"No, not law. Only custom. I reject the custom. If you were my bondsman, I would remember your shameful history every time I saw your face. To lose a battle because of the actions of freebirths. I could not bear that. If you must have the custom, I take you as bondsman and immediately free you. May you come to understand Kerensky's blessing, Star Captain Dwillt Radick.''

He could sense Radick fuming at the other end, but the Wolf Clansman could do nothing. It was not mere custom, but Clan law, that gave Pershaw the right to dictate all terms. Pershaw thought the defeat, against odds and with so much freebirth help, was humiliating enough. Why subject Dwillt Radick to any more? He would carry this shame with him long enough, perhaps for the rest of his life.

Then a messenger came to him with the news. Lanja was alive but injured, and the hero of the battle had returned, having dragged Lanja across nearly a third of the battlefield.

As Jorge staggered toward him, Pershaw could not repress the disgust he felt for this man's freebirth origins.

When Aidan woke up later, lying on a cot in Pershaw's office back inside Glory Station, Pershaw was sitting beside him, idly fingering the severely ripped dark band.

"Bast's picture is gone," Pershaw said laconically.

"Must have dropped off. I am sorry. I am not supposed to speak without permission.''

"Under the circumstances, we can ignore that rule. We can, in fact, ignore the dark band.''

With a pull that sent pain down Aidan's back, Kael Pershaw ripped the dark band off.

"Now you can speak as you always have, disrespectfully and rudely. Consider it your reward for winning the battle. Quite the opposite of the dark band. For now, do not even discuss this with me. I despise the fact that you must be honored now, and I will hate every moment of my participation in honoring you. But your act, especially for its capable improvisation, is deserving of the medal we are forced to award you.''

"Do not award me anything. I am Clan. What we must do, we do.''

Pershaw laughed abruptly. It was a chilling sound. Aidan wondered if anyone on Glory Station had ever heard Pershaw laugh. It was not real laughter, of course, but more the delighted growl of a creature about to pounce, the happy scream of the jade falcon before it seized its prey on the mountainside. It was the laugh of nightmare monsters.

"You are such a fraud, Jorge. I could almost like you. 'What we must do, we do.' Spoken like a true-born, Jorge, but filth in the mouth of a freebirth.''

Pershaw stood up and walked to the window behind his desk. Aidan tried to sit up, but the immediate dizziness forced him to lie back.

Standing with his back to Aidan, Pershaw spoke without turning around. "I have just delivered the vilest humiliation to the leader of the Clan Wolf warriors. I could hear his hatred in his voice. And despite my satisfaction at winning, I suffered my own humiliation. I am grateful that my gene heritage did not go to the Clan Wolf vaults, and I have you to thank for that, Jorge. It was your plan and your subsequent deeds that protected my Bloodright. But this victory will, in all our codexes, always be tainted. We trueborns should not have to thank a freebirth for our victories, and I will forever be conscious of the shame.''

Aidan could find nothing to say. He had no wish to be arrogant, no need to exacerbate the shame.

"How is Lanja?'' Aidan asked.

"She died,'' Kael Pershaw said quietly.

"I am sorry.''

"Yes. Your courage in dragging her to camp has proven to be fruitless.''

"That is not what I am sorry about.''

"I do not know what you mean, but I order you not to tell me. When you are well enough to go, you are dismissed."

Pershaw walked out of the room. His strides were long, longer than usual, as if he needed to hurry away.

Aidan closed his eyes. In his mind's eye, he saw his *Summoner* fall onto the command dome, this time with him in it. That might have given him some feeling of victory. Nothing Kael Pershaw had said could provide it.

As his eyes came open suddenly, he wondered how much longer he could bear the trueborn's continual scorn.

Dwillt Radick raged at his subordinate, Craig Ward.

"If you had seen his objective, perhaps you would have taken care to shoot better, hit the freebirth's 'Mech at an angle to force its fall in another direction."

"It was not possible. I was attempting to protect the dome. He unexpectedly bent his 'Mech over the dome before I had a chance to divert fire. He was deliberately drawing the fire in. He—"

"I know all that! I have studied the tapes. You failed, Craig Ward!"

The accusation was too much, the charge that set off the explosion.

"Perhaps I did misjudge! We all do in the heat of battle. Even you."

"Not to that degree, Star Commander."

"Then let me ask you this, Dwillt Radick. What misconception of strategy led you to establish a permanent command center instead of accepting the responsibility of directing the battle from your cockpit in—"

"I could charge you for that."

"Take it to a Circle of Equals."

"Perhaps I will. When we return." Radick took a deep breath. This Craig Ward, he felt, would plague him for years to come. "Establishing a permanent communications center is more efficient than directing from a command 'Mech. The techs can follow every phase of the battle as the leader directs while fighting off the enemy.''

''And leaders have done so for centuries. You cannot give over the battle to techs. You must—''

''I set up the battle like a soldier, like the great military experts of former times, using all the facets of strategy, tactics, and logistics.''

For a moment Craig Ward remembered his place. ''With all due respect, sir, perhaps thinking like a soldier is inferior to thinking like a commander.''

''As you did? Blundering into an engagement where you had the clear advantage, but then losing it? Was that action from the mind of a commander?''

Craig Ward saw, from the way Dwillt Radick shook with fury, that he had overstepped his bounds. Quickly he invoked all the cautious subordinate rituals that slowly defused Radick and brought the two of them back to their normal, uneasy peace.

21

Kael Pershaw's glare was more piercing than a xenon searchlight. Any other recipient of that gaze would have reconsidered the action that drew it. But Aidan was not just any other. He thrived on glares. Especially from Kael Pershaw.

"I knew you were freebirth, Jorge, and I knew you were arrogant and stupid, but I did not think you would interrupt a sacred ritual with a foolish and insulting gesture. If not for the valor of your recent performance, I would consider shooting you on the spot."

"If you do not accept my case, then I promise to meet you in the Circle of Equals to prove it."

Resplendent in their ceremonial dress, the gathered Jade Falcon warriors muttered among themselves, an ominous sound. Some of them would gladly join with Kael Pershaw to kill this upstart freebirth who had so airily insulted one of their most cherished rites.

"What manner of case could you have, freebirth?" Kael Pershaw shouted, his voice still in the timbre of the ceremony Aidan had interrupted. "Freebirths may not compete for a Bloodname!"

"That is true. As a freeborn warrior, I would have no right to make the claim, and you would be justified in shooting me immediately."

"It seems you have just called for your own death, *quiaff*?"

"On the contrary. I said *if* I were a freeborn. You see, Star Colonel Pershaw, I am not freeborn. My birth is just as true as yours, and that of every trueborn here.''

The murmur of the assembled warriors grew louder, as did its angry tone. Never in memory had a single warrior crammed so many insults into so few words. How dare this freebirth claim to be trueborn?

Kael Pershaw raised his hand to silence the warriors. He was certain now that something had affected Jorge's brain. Perhaps the battle had jarred some synapse, or perhaps the man's own inferior genetic strain had stirred up some chemical imbalance that had finally pushed him over the edge. Pershaw nodded toward his Personal Guard to come nearer so that they would be ready to pounce on Jorge if he started to run amok.

''I will disallow what you have said thus far if you will sit down and be silent, Star Commander Jorge. Your recent valor may have earned you a fraction of leeway, but it is now used up. Understand this: You may not compete for a Bloodname and may not put forth a claim.''

''You have not been listening. I may make a claim. I am canister-born and sibko-bred, from the Mattlov-Pryde genetic line. My name is not Jorge; it is Aidan. Clan law permits me to compete for the Bloodname of Pryde, which was that of my genemother Tanya Pryde. She is a former Galaxy Commander whose exploits are well-documented in Jade Falcon annals.''

Aidan's neck tingled, and he wondered if it was a reaction to the combined rage of the warriors gathered around him, most of whom looked as though they could kill him immediately.

That was not going to stop him, though. Without a pause Aidan began the story of his life on Ironhold, as cadet, as failed Trial participant, as successful freeborn qualifier.

Joanna was beside herself. The fool! Ter Roshak had warned him never to reveal his trueborn origins. Roshak had promised to kill Aidan if he ever confessed that Roshak had manipulated events to give Aidan a second chance at becoming a warrior. What stupidity could have made him claim the right to a Trial of Bloodright now?

Even as the thought crossed her mind, Joanna knew the answer to the question. How often did a warrior get a chance to earn a Bloodname? She knew from her own experience how few and far between were the opportunities. Aidan had probably been planning to make this claim for some time. Overall, the Bloodname of Pryde was a mixed one, with some good lines and some mediocre. This particular line, however, one of the twenty-five that had come down through the generations from its original holder, Aeneas Pryde, had been claimed two generations ago by a Jade Falcon hero named Teukros Pryde, and until recently by Ileana Pryde. It was a particularly noble and intrepid line, one for which only the best warriors could compete. In his announcement of the new Trial of Bloodright, Kael Pershaw had cited Ileana Pryde for her courage in backing her BattleMech against a high cliff wall and fighting off a succession of Snow Raven Clan 'Mechs in a fierce battle for territory on the planet York. Ileana had met her own death in that battle, he said, and thus did the Bloodname become available.

Her predecessor as nameholder, Teukros Pryde, had accomplished a list of achievements that was the envy of any warrior. Teukros Pryde had, in fact, killed many times to earn that reputation. And this Aidan, a true-born who had failed his Trial of Position because of an arrogant attempt to attack his three opponents simultaneously, who had to pose as a freebirth in order to become a warrior at all—what right had he to take his own tainted name into a struggle for such a proud Bloodname? Even in the unlikely event he won the name, his previous history would tarnish it even before he could ever serve it as warrior.

Listening to Aidan recite his history amid the incredulous expressions of his listeners, Joanna contained a rage that might have wiped out half the Jade Falcons assembled if she were to loose it. She knew she was far from the ideal of a Clan warrior. Though she had striven to be one all her life, her fierce animosities had too often consumed her when she should have been honing her skills instead. It was not just a matter of distaste for everyone she met. Had it been only that, her career as a warrior might have gone forward with more certainty. But, no, she hated everyone. Oh, she had experienced a few temporary alliances back in sibko days, but when those companions had flushed out of training, she had despised them for their inferiority. It was true that she had felt some respect for perhaps three commanding officers, but each had inevitably fallen in her esteem, whether because he did not fight hard enough, complain loud enough, or kill skillfully enough. She hated Nomad, too, but that at least was a cheerful hatred, one she rather enjoyed. Indeed, they would be back to exchange barbs as soon as he was well again.

There was probably no one in Clan Jade Falcon who hated as fiercely as Joanna did, nor any who hated as well.

Yet she knew that with a more balanced view of life, she might have won a Bloodname. She vividly remembered a recent attempt, when she had been one of the final contenders. In previous attempts, she had failed the Trial of Bloodright earlier, That was either her shame or an indication she was being saved for some later Bloodname prize. She could always hope for the latter. But at twenty-eight her time was running out. In the Clans, old warriors did not win Bloodnames, but usually ended up as volunteer cannon fodder in some battle diversion.

As she studied Aidan's calm in claiming the Pryde bloodline, she hated him more than ever. During the training years on Ironhold, she had sometimes believed that, of all that sibko, Aidan was her personal curse. Subsequent events had done little to change her thinking. If it were not contrary to the way of the Clans, she would have run up to him this very moment, her knife drawn to slit his worthless throat.

Kael Pershaw was rarely, if ever, at a loss for words, but right now he had not a clue what might come out of his mouth when, according to ritual, this Jorge/Aidan reached the end of his claim. He regretted not having Lanja near to send him the kind of signs and signals that had so often helped him render judgment. It was the first time Pershaw had thought of her since announcing her death to this piece of decaying matter speaking before him. He would not recall her again for some time.

Finally Aidan's speech came to an end.

"And that is the word of a trueborn warrior of the Jade Falcon Clan, direct, blunt, and true in every detail. My case is just. I would leave this duty to compete for the Aeneas Pryde Bloodname."

Aidan looked around at the others, as though they might suddenly affirm his claim by solemnly uttering, "Seyla," the ritual response of affirmation. No one spoke.

"What is your judgment, Star Colonel Kael Pershaw?" asked Star Captain Shan Zeke, who was performing the role of Loremaster. He looked as astonished as every other person in the gathering, except for Aidan and Joanna.

Kael Pershaw scrutinized the assembly, then shouted: "I cannot make a proper judgment unless someone steps forward to endorse the claim of this . . . of this warrior."

When Horse immediately came forward, he looked every centimeter the freeborn he was. At least with him the warriors gathered here knew there would be no controversy about birth origin.

"I know this to be true, Star Colonel," Horse said. "I trained with Star Commander Aidan after he was transferred to my unit. I recognized him as a trueborn because I'd faced him in an earlier training exercise."

Horse went on to tell the story in detail. Certain warriors flinched when Horse mentioned how he, a mere freeborn, had nearly beaten Cadet Aidan by planting a satchel charge on the back of a 'Mech shell the other was using in the exercise.

"MechWarrior Horse, is your memory so sharp that you could be sure this Jorge was the cadet you fought in that training exercise?"

"Yes. And when I confronted him, he admitted his identity to me."

Kael Pershaw slowly shook his head. "No, MechWarrior Horse, that is not enough. It verifies only that one apparent freebirth by name of Jorge transferred into your unit after an unfortunate accident on a training field. That he was the Cadet Aidan you battled earlier is not proven. Further, your evidence does not verify any other points of Star Commander Jorge's story. Step back, MechWarrior Horse."

Horse looked as though he wished to say more, but then he shrugged, performed a ritual salute to Pershaw, and walked away. Many of the warriors growled and sneered as he passed, making no secret of their disapproval that he had come forward at all. In response, Horse twisted his mouth into an obvious expression of defiance.

"Does any other member of this assembly verify the rightful claim of this warrior?" Kael Pershaw asked.

The silence hung heavy, as though not a single warrior moved or breathed. When Pershaw let his gaze sweep the throng, the rustle of his cape, the clank of his adornments echoed all the way to the rear of the crowd.

The next sound was the shuffle of feet as Aidan turned to face the Glorry Stateion warriors.

"Yes," a voice said finally, "I can verify this man's true identity." Roughly pushing several subordinate warriors aside, Joanna reluctantly made her way forward.

22

Joanna had weighed her responsibility against her shrewdness, and responsibility had come heavier on the scale of her judgment. Or perhaps she was merely out of her mind. She had no special desire to verify Aidan's claim, but it *was* the truth. Worse, she was one of the few people in the universe who knew it, and unfortunately for her, she happened to be at Glory Station exactly at the moment when she *could* verify it. If it were only up to her, she could happily have remained quiet and watched the despicable pseudo-freebirth gag on his own words. Oh, she knew that eventually he could have proved his identity through genetic tests, but it would have taken so long that the Bloodname battles for the Aeneas Pryde name would long have been over. Then would have come a period of shame. No matter what proof existed of his lineage, Aidan's freeborn years would mark him as an inferior warrior, despite his birth. She would have enjoyed witnessing even a fraction of that. But it was not fair to remain quiet at the moment of his claim or to ignore whatever fate had brought her to Glory Station, where she now forced her feet to take her ever nearer the platform where Kael Pershaw stood waiting.

"*You* have evidence, Star Captain Joanna?"

"Yes. I was this warrior's training officer on Ironhold."

A murmur passed through the crowd. Aidan had omitted all names from his tale, concealing Joanna's participation in it.

"Then he speaks the truth, *quiaff?*"

"Aff."

"And you have knowledge of the deception he describes, the masking of his identity to participate in the second Trial?"

From the moment Aidan had begun his claim, this was the moment, the question she had been dreading.

"I not only know about it, Star Colonel Kael Pershaw," Joanna said, "I participated in it."

That revelation produced a shock as great as any of Aidan's. Few of the warriors present knew Joanna, who had arrived on Glory only in time for the battle, but they respected her for downing the BattleMech that might have defeated Aidan, crashed the mission, and ended the conflict over the Pershaw gene legacy.

At Pershaw's behest, Joanna told tersely and with some bitterness about how a superior officer had sent her to pursue Aidan after he had been relegated to the tech caste and escaped Ironhold. She had found him, brought him back, and drilled him to enter the freeborn training unit. She explained her assumption that he was merely replacing a freeborn who had died accidentally. Only later did she learn that the cadet's death and the deaths of the entire freeborn training unit had been arranged. In the meantime, events transpired to force her to take command of the freeborn unit containing Jorge. (Joanna carefully neglected to mention the mysterious death of one of the freeborn unit's previous training officers, about which she was quite suspicious.)

She concluded by saying, "After Cadet Aidan qualified as a warrior through unorthodox strategy and teamwork with the freebirth who has just given witness, he was assigned elsewhere. I did not see him again until I came here, nor have I heard anything of his exploits as a warrior. As a loyal Clan warrior, I am forced to observe that his actions in the recent battle were distinguished enough to merit mention. That is all. These are the direct, blunt, and true words of a trueborn Clan warrior."

Kael Pershaw stared at Joanna for a long while before he began to speak in the quietest of tones. "You have both related a strange story of defiance and deceit," he said finally, "yet you both neglect to mention the name of the officer responsible for the wretched deeds you describe. What is his name, Star Captain Joanna?"

This moment, too, Joanna had been dreading.

"Falconer Commander Ter Roshak," she said, making each word precise and crisp. "He was commander of the Bravo Division of Cadet Training Ironhold."

"Does he still hold that post?"

"I believe so, Star Colonel. The last I heard he had won a citation for turning out more successful warriors than any other training commander."

"The last detail is unnecessary, Star Captain. All this individual's achievements, all the high points of his codex, are rendered meaningless by the evidence you and Star Commander Jor—Aidan have given. Ter Roshak has injured us all. He has insulted the Clans and perverted our ways. I have no choice but to put Star Commander Jorge, Star Captain Joanna, and MechWarrior Horse into custody for transport back to Ironhold, where I am sure a Grand Council of the Jade Falcons will convene to examine and render judgment on the case."

At a snap from Pershaw's fingers, two Elementals immediately took hold of Joanna on either side. Two others had taken Aidan into custody. Far in the back of the crowd, ripples from a struggle showed that apprehending MechWarrior Horse was not going so smoothly.

"Further," Kael Pershaw announced, "as commander of the base where this treason has been exposed, I will travel to Ironhold to give evidence. And your conviction, Star Commander Aidan, will give me the greatest joy."

"Permission to speak, sir," Aidan shouted.

"Granted."

"I accept your judgment and transport back to Ironhold, but I request again that you render judgment on my claim.''

For once Kael Pershaw appeared rattled, but he recovered quickly. "I have no choice in the matter, Star Commander," he said. "If what you say is true, and your matrilineal line is Pryde, then of course you may compete in the Trial of Bloodright. I doubt that any current Bloodnamed warrior will sponsor you, though.''

"I will present myself at the Grand Melee."

"Oh? That is your choice, of course, but do not make your plans too soon, Star Commander. You must first go before the Grand Council, which will determine the disposition of your case. In all likelihood, you will not have to worry about the melee. Executed warriors do not usually compete in any phase of the Trial of Bloodright.''

Aidan was enraged by Pershaw's sarcasm, but he forced his face to remain expressionless. "I accept your judgment and any other judgment to come," he said steadily, "as well as the Clan rituals that support them.''

"Take these people away," Pershaw ordered. "A JumpShip will be charged and ready within a week. All those involved with the Aidan claim will travel from Glory to Ironhold on that ship.''

Though Joanna protested mightily, the Elemental guards placed her and Aidan in the same jail cell. Because so few violations were deemed worthy of incarceration, Glory Station's prison was small and only two cells were currently available. Custom dictated that trueborns and freeborns be separated during imprisonment, which put Horse alone in the other cell.

"You are a fool, Aidan," Joanna muttered under her breath, "but you have gall, going for a Bloodname, with your history. How egotistical of you to even think it possible. And do you not see any violation of the code?''

"Code? What code?''

"If you do not feel it, then of course you do not

mind violating it. The code I speak of is among warriors. We depend on one another and we support one another, in battle and in all other action.''

''Strange words coming from you, Joanna. You have no comrades.''

''That is true, but it does not mean I will not close ranks with fellow warriors under attack or in a crisis. The code states that you should protect Ter Roshak, not reveal his treachery to the universe.''

''Treachery such as Ter Roshak's should not be permitted. To do so would make us as decadent and weak as the people of the Inner Sphere.''

Joanna was taken aback. ''What do you know of Inner Sphere history?''

''I have made a study of it, from some . . . some sources I have discovered.''

''I do not know about such decadence, but I do know we must maintain the code of loyalty.''

''Why?''

''I do not understand you, Aidan.''

''I am asking why loyalty is preeminent. What loyalty did Ter Roshak show by involving us in his schemes?''

''He gave you a second chance.''

''Which I was not supposed to receive.''

''But you got it, and you should have been satisfied.''

''As a freeborn?''

''You are a warrior, are you not?''

''That is true, and living as a freeborn, I respect them and—''

''*Respect?* You can respect a freebirth?''

''Freeborn, you must say freeborn. And, yes, I can. I have served with nothing but freeborns these last few years. Their inferiority is only in the minds of others. Given a chance, they perform as well as any other.''

''I cannot believe you would utter such filth, Aidan. Stop now. A freebirth is a freebirth, and that is that. Whatever else you have come to believe, you are a trueborn. You will always be that. You can assume an identity with the ease of a tribesman disguising himself in an animal skin, but your real identity comes from your birth. However you may have adjusted to being a freebirth, do not try to convert me to your ideas about freeborns.''

''All right.''

''So, I ask you again why you have decided to ruin Ter Roshak's career—and your own?''

''Anything is worth the risk if the ultimate prize is a Bloodname.''

''Whatever happens on Ironhold, you will not earn a Bloodname. You will never get that far.''

''There is always a poss—''

''There is no possibility! You and Ter Roshak have broken Clan law, violated Clan custom. And I, by being a cog in Ter Roshak's plot, will be dragged through the muck along with you. And I have been dragged through enough muck lately, thank you.''

Aidan smiled, a rare event for a Clansman. ''Yes, I heard you nearly drowned in the swamp. Joanna, I truly regret what is happening now. If I had thought that you would be—''

''*If* you had thought. That is your problem. You do not think, you act. Back in your first trial, you went for too much, and in your second, you were lucky with some improvised tactics. So this time, you over-reached in another way. First, you announced your candidacy at the wrong time. You should first have determined whether you could legitimately compete for the Bloodname.''

''I did not, as you say, overreach. Every move I made today, everything I said, was planned. Calculated. I have every right to compete for the Bloodname. And I will.''

They fell silent. Aidan turned away from Joanna to gaze out the small window of the cell at the compound. Nothing was moving out there. Pershaw's council must still be in session.

''At any rate,'' Joanna said, ''now Ter Roshak must answer for his deeds. I wonder if he will reveal his motives. There is much I would like to know. Although I could pass on learning the information if it meant I would not be executed.''

"You will not be executed. You were merely an accessory."

"Practicing the words to be used before the council, are you?"

Again the two fell silent for a while, then Joanna said, "You have not learned, Aidan, that deceit is the real sin among the Clans. Your second chance, your life as a freebirth, your assumption of someone else's identity—it is all deceit. They have a good case against you."

She laughed harshly, a true sign of her mirth. "Perhaps the name *should* be yours," Joanna said. "Who else would find the name Pryde so eminently suitable?"

Horse and Aidan sat together while they and Joanna were being transported to the shuttle area. "I wish you victory in all things, Aidan," Horse whispered.

"Your support means much, Horse."

"Support? Please do not call it that. I do not support you. I am ashamed of you."

"Ashamed?"

"You renounced your freeborn identity for the sake of competing for a Bloodname. Deep down you were trueborn after all. Deep down you hold us in contempt just as the others do."

"That is not true, Horse. It is—"

"No. If you really respected us, as you claimed, you would not have renounced your freeborn identity. You are like the real jade falcon, which flies everywhere but always comes back to the mountainside where it was born. You may have flown as a freeborn, but now you return to your trueborn nest."

"Horse—"

"Or should I say trashborn?"

"Do you not wish me to win a Bloodname, to contribute to the gene pool?"

"Truthfully, I do not. I do not care what happens to you now. I will be your comrade in all things, but

I do not care what happens. Freeborns do not demean themselves for Bloodnames, nor would they wish to contribute to the gene pool. You may win this contest, or you may die. Whichever, I will be by your side if you wish it. But I *am* ashamed.''

"It is the Bloodname, Horse."

"I know that. And it is no excuse. You have more respect from me as Jorge than you will have as Aidan Pryde.''

The conversation ended there, but for the rest of the trip, Aidan savored the sound of the name: Aidan Pryde. An almost lustful surge of will went through his body. The name had such a natural ring to it. How could he not succeed in winning it? In spite of the turmoil he had stirred up with his desire for it. In spite of the agony he would have to endure to fulfill the desire. In spite of the dangers on the long road to the Bloodname.

Joanna decided the game was up as soon as the Jade Falcon council members filed in. BattleMechs charging and firing in the midst of combat looked friendlier than these Bloodnamed warriors. There were so many of them, most arriving on Ironhold from far-off outposts, answering the call to council. Some Clansmen, as was their right, claimed duty prevented their attendance at the trial. Many more, however, chose to come and sit in judgment on this unusual case. Joanna had heard that nearly 475 of the 960 qualified warriors (well, two less, with Ileana Pryde's demise and Ter Roshak on trial) were on Ironhold now, and more might arrive during the course of the trial. Video cameras would record every bit of testimony for examination across all the Jade Falcon worlds. The crime involved was so unusual, so grotesque that council members were flocking to Ironhold to be, perhaps, a part of Clan history.

She had also heard that one major reason for the ardent interest in this trial was the stature of the Bloodname in question. Its original holder, Aeneas Pryde, had been a member of Aleksandr Kerensky's command staff even before the Exodus. As a Star League officer, he had distinguished himself in battle as a member of the 131st Battle Division, the so-called "Hercules Division." So daring were the celebrated exploits of the 131st that they had been compared to the arduous tasks of a mythical hero named Hercules.

Joanna did not know of this Hercules, but on the

trip to Ironhold Aidan had explained that he was a fabled hero whose feats of prodigious strength went beyond normal human prowess. Though she scoffed at Aidan for accumulating such useless knowledge, she was secretly impressed. Something had undoubtedly happened to him during his years pretending to be a freebirth, for intelligence had not been an outstanding trait of the Aidan she had once known. What might have changed him she could not guess, nor did she care. One trait, however, had not changed a bit. The fact that he planned to compete for a Bloodname without anyone's approval showed him to be as determinedly stubborn as a warrior as he had been as a cadet. However, even Aeneas Pryde would probably have felt revulsion to see Aidan presuming to win his name.

Ileana Pryde, the previous holder of this version of the Bloodname, might have been more sympathetic to Aidan's cause, for she was known for a similar stubborn persistence and fortitude.

Joanna had known her, a warrior no better or worse than many others. Tall and beautiful, with a regal manner, Ileana was already famous as a warrior when her path crossed Joanna's. She had tried to engage Joanna in a discussion about specific strategies that led to a wasteful, bloody skirmish between the Ice Hellion and Mongoose Clans. Ileana's ideas were precise and insightful, but Joanna would not give her the satisfaction of agreeing. Soon the two were arguing in a way just as wasteful as the strategy in question. When they reached an impasse and agreed to abandon the argument, Joanna noticed that Ileana glowed from the intensity of their talk. Guessing that Ileana might be just as mean as she was, her respect for the noted warrior increased.

Joanna and Aidan sat together at a table near the center of the massive Council Hall. From her vantage point, the tiers occupied by Bloodnamed warriors seemed endless. Dressed in their ceremonial masks and garb, each with its particular resplendent flourishes, the effect was of an enormous patchwork quilt spread unevenly across one side of the room. At the main table sat the

Loremaster, the Advocate, the Inquisitor, and the current Khan of the Jade Falcon Clan, Elias Crichell. Elias Crichell had earned fame as a great warrior and shrewd politician. He was also said to be a harsh judge, who believed in severe punishment for even the smallest offense. Many credited him with the Jade Falcons' success among the seventeen clans.

Joanna ceased scanning the council, suddenly aware of a strong gaze upon her. She knew whose it was even before turning to look, for she had learned that Ter Roshak, primary offender in this case and the highest-ranking officer, would be seated alone at the center table. Looking back in his direction, she was astonished at the change. Once bulky and impressive, Roshak seemed to have shrunk. His face, once so sculptured in its hardness, looked softer, as if formed of lumps and bulges instead of cliffs and crevasses. But his eyes had not changed. They glared like beacons, penetrating as a beam from a pulse laser. With a start she realized that Ter Roshak was not looking at her. His hatred was directed purely at Aidan.

Aidan had watched Ter Roshak come in. The two had not met since Aidan left Ironhold several years before. Roshak had vowed to kill Aidan if he revealed any part of his deception. Though the threat had not frightened Aidan, he had remembered it often enough.

He wondered briefly if he should regret his action, which would surely ruin Roshak's career. But what good was such a career if the man violated Clan law? Of the three under various accusations here in Clan council, Roshak was the only one who deserved to be on trial. Neither Aidan nor Joanna had ordered murder. Of course, murder was not the issue. Few of the Clansmen sitting in judgment would think twice about the elimination of a sibko of freeborns. No, it was Roshak's manipulation of events in defiance of Clan law that was the terrible deed.

Aidan, however, was appalled by the murder that Roshak had planned with such calculation. Perhaps the Terran books in Aidan's secret library had corrupted his mind.

Clan culture did not hold life so dear as did Terran, he knew, but the killing of cadets with warrior potential merely to create an identity for him was not moral. Yet sometimes he even scoffed at himself. What did he care about morality? Murder like the one Roshak had committed might have been a mistake, an error of command judgment, but morality was not a factor in Clan actions.

Warriors were still filing into the chamber. It would be some time before the trial would begin, and Aidan was restless. He wanted to speak with Joanna, but they could drag him out of the room for so much as nodding to her. Silence was the order of the day, not only for the defendants and the witnesses, but for the warriors sitting in judgment. In council and in warfare, it was the Jade Falcon way to focus all attention on the matter at hand. During the actual session, a warrior could speak if he or she stood and was acknowledged by the Loremaster, who acted as director of the proceedings.

The only speech allowed at present was between the officers of the court, who were sitting at the long table across from Roshak. They maintained an incessant if undecipherable murmur. In the whole time since Roshak had entered the room, he had not looked at any of the officers of the court.

The Advocate for all three defendants finished off his conversation with the Inquisitor and with Khan Elias Crichell, who sat aloof and, truth to tell, apparently oblivious to events. The Advocate stood up and walked toward the table where Aidan and Joanna sat. His name was Beck Qwabe, which was about all Aidan knew about him. Almost Aidan's height, he was as tall as the Inquisitor was short, and had unusually gentle eyes for a Jade Falcon Clansman. Aidan had seen falcons with such eyes, and they generally proved to be poor hunters. He hoped that the comparison would not carry over to Beck Qwabe.

"The proceedings will begin soon," Qwabe said. "I am instructed to tell you that you may reduce participation in the trial by admitting guilt, invoking the rite of forgiveness, and taking your chance on whatever punishment the Khan chooses for you. Based on what I know about the two of you, I believe that you would reject such an offer, *quineg?''*

Both Aidan and Joanna ritually responded, "Neg."

Beck Qwabe gave them their last instructions on trial procedures. Aidan had received this same briefing so often since arriving on Ironhold that his mind wandered. As had Joanna's, his gaze traveled out toward the warriors looking down at the defendants. If the cruelty in many of those eyes was any indication, he and the others did not stand a chance.

Suddenly one pair of eyes caught his attention, not because of their malice or even their coldness, but because of their familiarity. They belonged to someone sitting far up in the tiers, so far away that the eyes were little more than dots. Yet Aidan knew from the eyes and the erectness of her posture that it was Marthe staring down at him. It could be no other.

And it was logical. With two victories in her Trial, one of them over Aidan, Marthe had entered the warrior ranks at the level of Star Commander. Enough time had passed for her to rise further and to have fought for a Bloodname, for another of the Pryde Bloodnames. Though this was the first time Aidan had chosen to compete for a Bloodname, he had known of two other times that a Pryde Bloodname had become available during his years as a warrior. Marthe must have fought for one of them and won it.

He did not know why, but he felt some satisfaction that Marthe had preceded him to Bloodname status. Because they had been so close in the sibko, he had always expected them to succeed together in all Clan enterprises. When she had surged ahead of him in cadet training and subsequently cooled toward him, Aidan had been unhappy for a long while. Perhaps a very long while. Perhaps until now.

Beck Qwabe was summoned back to the Judgment Table, and at a nod from Khan Elias Crichell, the trial began.

24

"MechWarrior Horse," said Lenore Shi-Lu, the Inquisitor, her voice oratorical in its resonance. Aidan found it much more impressive than Beck Qwabe's rather thin tenor, especially considering the difference in height between the two court officers. Lenore Shi-Lu was as delicate and pretty as Beck Qwabe was lumbering and homely. Just as with Beck Qwabe, Aidan noticed the hint of falcon in her eyes. Again the difference was pronounced. Shi-Lu's eyes were not gentle like Qwabe's. Hers were the eyes of a hunting falcon, like the one named Warhawk Aidan had known in his own youth.

"MechWarrior Horse," she said, "that could not be your real name."

"It's not," Horse replied. "I don't give out my real name." The words, though spoken softly, echoed through the enormous room.

A shudder went through the observers at the coarse sound of Horse's reply, not only for the contractions, but for the suggestion of defiance. Defiance from a freeborn was not to be tolerated in official ceremonies. Most of the warriors in the chamber had had little contact with freeborn warriors.

"However that may be," said Lenore Shi-Lu, with some contempt for the freeborn in her stentorian voice, "This is an official proceeding, and for official proceedings we must have official records. You must tell us the name you were born with. Come, Mech-

Warrior, no hesitation. We can derive it from your codex anyway.''

Horse nodded, knowing that the Inquisitor already knew the name and merely wanted him to speak it. ''It's Tyle. My real name is Tyle. I am named after my father.''

The word *father* also created a stir among the observers, for it was a reminder of the foul origins of a freeborn. Genefather or genemother was a term of honor. But the naked words *father* and *mother* were so obscene that they were not uttered even as curses.

''Thank you,'' the Inquisitor said smugly, then led Horse through a series of questions that revealed Aidan's participation in the freeborn training unit. She allowed him to describe the Trial during which he and Aidan had cooperated to defeat two opposing BattleMechs and earn their warrior status.

''And you were aware at the time that this Aidan— Jorge, as you knew him—had already failed in an earlier Trial?''

''He told me, yes.''

''Then you also must realize that your own qualifying as a warrior was the result of fraud.''

''No, I don't *realize* that at all. I would've qualified, with or without help. I'm as good as any trueborn warrior any day.''

Had weapons been allowed into the chamber, Horse would have been the victim of multiple shots fired from the council seats.

''It seems,'' said Lenore Shi-Lu, with an eye toward the angry crowd, ''that Star Commander Aidan's arrogance and defiance have influenced your own, MechWarrior. Let me remind you that this is an official proceeding, and any violation of Clan custom will be recorded on your codex.''

''I know that.''

''And you do not care?''

''No, I don't.''

Lenore Shi-Lu nodded and glanced toward the Loremaster, whose gesture indicated that she be done with this witness.

"One last question, MechWarrior Tyle."

"Horse. I don't know how to answer to the name Tyle."

"You will answer to whatever name with which I and the council choose to address you, freeborn. My question, MechWarrior Tyle, is this: Should a warrior whose status came as the result of fraud be allowed to compete for an honorable Bloodname?"

"It don't matter none to me." Horse's use of improper grammar in conjunction with the contraction caused some nearly violent reactions among the Clansmen. "Aidan fought better and was a fairer officer than all the trueborns I have ever encountered."

The Loremaster made a gesture toward Lenore Shi-Lu to end her interrogation of the witness. She seemed pleased to tell him that she had no further questions.

Beck Qwabe then conducted a brief interrogation of Horse intended to establish that Aidan had the respect of his warriors and had fought courageously, especially in the battle over the Pershaw gene heritage. In his mind, Aidan decided that Horse's positive testimony would have no effect on the judgment of the Council. Indeed, to the ears of these Bloodnamed warriors, Horse's words were no more than the unnecessarily provocative utterances of a freebirth.

"Star Colonel Kael Pershaw, you have described well the valor of Star Commander Aidan during the engagement with Clan Wolf," said Lenore Shi-Lu. She had drawn from Pershaw vivid details of the battle. "You have credited him not only with the act that finally won it, but with the strategy that eventually achieved victory."

"That is correct."

"But only days before you had placed the emblem of deep shame, the dark band, on this same man after, as you testified, he had refused to invoke *surkai*. Did you not feel shame at giving this recalcitrant warrior such prominence in the combat?"

Kael Pershaw had not expected to have his own name tainted with the brush of Aidan's crimes. A loyal

Clansman, he had come here to give evidence *against* the man. Ordinarily he did not take advantage of his right as a Bloodnamed warrior to sit in council.

"Circumstances dictate improvisation. Any commander in the field knows that." He stared at Lenore Shi-Lu, as if to infer that her experience did not provide her with a true comprehension of the actions of warriors on active duty. She had come out of cadet training as a warrior with an extraordinary cadet record, but Khan Elias Crichell had ordered her immediately to his command staff, where she was one of his top advisers. She had seen very little battle.

"Star Commander Aidan's plan had merit," he said, invoking his command voice. "There were the unknown combatants obscured from normal detection in the swamp, and Clan Wolf's forces were stretched out across the battlefield. Clan Wolf was thus attacked from front and rear—and, for that matter, from underneath, by an Elemental assault. Where the plan of battle originates is of less importance than the judgment of the commander. I, as commander, approved the plan. It could not have gone forward without me. That is the kind of improvisation under battle stress of which I speak, Inquisitor."

Lenore Shi-Lu had performed enough council interrogations to know when she had been successfully countered, and she bowed her head slightly in acknowledgment of his skill.

During his question period, Beck Qwabe returned to the matter of the conflict with Clan Wolf. "Then do you say that Star Commander Aidan's battle prowess and his strategy do not necessarily qualify him to compete for a Bloodname?"

"No, they do not. They are no more, and no less, than I would expect from any warrior under my command."

"Yet you have verified his claim to compete for the Bloodname."

"He is allowed, by virtue of the matrilineal name. The deplorable facts of his life have no effect on that. I was forced to approve the claim."

The Loremaster interrupted. "Beck Qwabe, we do not need any further verification of the warrior's claim to the Bloodname. It is not his achievements as a warrior or the matrilineal genetic ancestry that are at issue in this council. We are concerned with the circumstances by which Star Commander Aidan earned the privilege of warrior status. The council must judge his right to that status before he can be allowed to battle for a Bloodname."

"I stand properly corrected, Loremaster," Beck Qwabe demurred. "I merely wish to establish that Star Commander Aidan's codex is untainted, even if his character may be."

"A worthy purpose, Beck Qwabe. Please go on."

In his final statements, Kael Pershaw indicated that Star Commander Aidan, in spite of his achievements, was difficult to control and discipline.

"Kael Pershaw," Lenore Shi-Lu said, in her second round of interrogation, "do you believe that Star Commander Aidan's first failed Trial is the one that should apply, that the second Trial should be canceled out and he reassume his caste role as tech? You hesitate. Why?"

"With all due respect, Lenore Shi-Lu, I must say that I roundly despise Star Commander Aidan. However, your questions trouble me. If he has effectively carried out his duties as a warrior, which I believe he has, then should his codex be summarily erased?"

"I believe it is my role to ask the questions here, Star Colonel."

"And my role is to be honest, *quiaff*? And, in all honesty, I believe that Star Commander Aidan performed his duties with ability and, as noted, valor. He has been a warrior. Fraudulently earned or not, his status may indeed be verified by his actions. I came here to condemn him, yet I must say that the only blemishes to his record under my command are related to personality traits and not actions. I begin to wonder if perhaps his second Trial was, after all, the correct one."

Again sensing her disadvantage, Lenore Shi-Lu

quickly dismissed Kael Pershaw, who resumed his seat on the council. Aidan studied the man, at least as well as he could from a distance. He found no clue in the officer's expression as to why he had actually given Aidan's cause some support. There never would be, Aidan suspected.

A few character witnesses came forward to verify Ter Roshak's military records, then the trial went into the next phase: the interrogation of the accused parties. Joanna took a deep breath as she heard her name being called.

25

Lenore Shi-Lu led Joanna through her questions meticulously. Almost all her questions, and those of the Advocate, came from the council members, via computer monitors. The questions reflected the warriors' concerns in this very delicate matter, while it was the Inquisitor's task to frame the questions in the way that would have the most impact. Lenore Shi-Lu rose brilliantly to the occasion. It was only minutes before the woman's politely phrased queries began to exasperate Joanna, but she realized that anyone's questions, conducted over a long period of time, would probably do so. Her testimony was rendered even more difficult because she could sense, even without looking, the intense gazes of both Aidan and Ter Roshak upon her.

Ter Roshak had spent the last evening writing in a journal he had kept since his cadet days. In it he poured out his thoughts.

He wrote that, whatever happened, his career as a Clan warrior was now finished. Even in the unlikely event that the council cleared him of all charges, he could never return to his position as Falconer Commander of training. His authority would be undermined by the cloud of doubt and suspicion that would follow him everywhere. He could not have that.

And he was now too old to return to active duty as a warrior. Age was the one unpardonable sin among the Clans, and few had been able to surmount it.

He could have requested demotion to a lower caste,

to live out his life performing some useful service, becoming proficient at some craft. But what real warrior could accept that? What glory could he find in adjusting a calibration or shaping clay into pots?

No, only death awaited him now. And he aimed to face it with the will and ferocity of a proper Clan warrior. This trial was merely a tedium he had to endure. He knew the outcome, almost to the exact numbers. Oh, it was possible that some council members might switch their vote at the last moment, but it was not likely to change things.

In the days before the trial, Roshak had spoken with all the Bloodnamed warriors he knew, especially those who owed him favors. Persuading several of them of the inevitability of the verdict, he told them he wished to reduce the level of dishonor so that he could take proper measures. If he could get the verdict down to three-to-one, or at least four-to-one, he could enact his plan, the one recourse that would allow him to finish off his life with some sense of honor, but the one secret he could not commit to his journal.

Whatever happened in the council, he wrote, the life of Ter Roshak is over. There is no more need for this journal.

When he had closed the covers of the last volume of his journal, he took the many he had filled over the years and fed them to a fire he built outside his quarters. Watching the flames consume the pages was like watching the destruction of his life. Each page was a period of time. As it went up in flames, that period disappeared, as if eliminated by the hand of an unseen god. There was no god, seen or unseen, Roshak thought. Or perhaps he, Ter Roshak, was the god. He took some satisfaction in enacting his supreme judgment on the life of one of his imperfect minions. The pages, as they gave themselves to the fire, did not curl submissively. Rather, like the man who had written them, they danced among the flames as if defying them.

Ter Roshak had not expected that Star Captain Joanna would be one of the witnesses. Her role in his deception had been so small, at the level of a functionary running errands for him, that he lamented her becoming one of the defendants. But, with all her

cleverness and wary suspicion, she had uncovered just
enough of his deception to make the accusation justified. She should have turned him in back then, but she
had not, and so her career would be dragged down
along with his and Aidan's.

Unless, of course, his new plan worked. There *was*
an outside chance of that happening, but victory was
not his goal. He merely wanted to die, and to die in
the same manner he had lived. As a warrior. Dying as
a warrior meant more to him than any achievement in
his past, and certainly more than any fraud.

"Star Captain Joanna, you knew Star Commander
Aidan was being given a second chance, *quiaff?*"

"As well you know."

The Loremaster interrupted. "There is to be no sarcasm,
insult, or anger in your responses, Star Captain Joanna."

She glanced at the Loremaster. She did not know
his name. He was a bit old for a warrior, with many
touches of gray in his hair and weariness in his eyes.

"I am sorry, Loremaster. I intended no disrespect,
but I will be more careful in my words."

"Thank you, Star Captain Joanna."

"What did you know at that time?" Lenore Shi-Lu asked.

"I knew that he was being given a second chance.
I trained him in how to act his role of freebir—of freeborn. In the last days of training, I was the training
officer for his unit. I was also in the BattleMech that
ended his Trial after he had made the required kill."

"Then it is safe to say that you were implicated in
the fraud, *quiaff?*"

"Aff. Quite safe to say, Inquisitor."

"How do you justify your concealment of the
facts?"

"Orders. I was following the orders of Falconer
Commander Ter Roshak. Furthermore, he had solicited my vow of secrecy before I knew about what he
had planned."

"Once you discovered that Ter Roshak's orders were
based on fraud, did it not occur to you that this released you from vows of obedience and secrecy?"

"No, it did not. Vows must be kept."

"There is not a higher vow, that owed to your Clan?"

Joanna felt trapped by Lenore Shi-Lu's grim words. "Inquisitor," she replied, "I am aware of the theories of the higher vow, and I have considered them often. But I did not want to see a capable officer destroyed, one whose record as a training officer has been, I believe, unsurpassed. I believed that Ter Roshak's abilities surpassed the higher vow, and I still do."

Ter Roshak's eyebrows shot up at Joanna's remark. He knew that she had many good warrior qualities, but had not suspected loyalty to be one of them.

"You have a unique sense of Clan philosophy, Star Commander Joanna."

"Perhaps it is because on the field a warrior must go up against scum—"

"Star Captain Joanna!" the Loremaster shouted, and she quickly apologized.

"I believed I did right," she said quietly.

"Purely out of loyalty."

"No, not just loyalty. I realized that Star Commander Aidan would not have a real warrior's life by posing as a freebirth. Even if his qualifying broke the rules, he would get no real reward for it, considering the kind of workhorse backwater assignments that would be, and have been, his destiny. I did not see any harm as long as he could not do any harm. I had not anticipated the harm he has done."

"Well-spoken, Star Captain. However, as your forced presence here shows, your action was, at the very least, questionable, *quiaff?*"

"Aff."

"Do you believe that Star Commander Aidan is worthy of the Bloodname he seeks?"

"With all due respect, Inquisitor, I thought that his Bloodname worthiness was not an issue in these proceedings."

Lenore Shi-Lu smiled. "You are correct, Star Captain. But most members of the council wish to know. I nevertheless withdraw the question. Let me substitute another that is also on the mind of many council members. Do you believe that Ter Roshak's actions were in any way justified?''

"No!"

"You have no sympathy with his backing of a warrior candidate whom he apparently believed to have suffered an unfortunate defeat in his Trial?''

"No! Star Commander Aidan, regardless of his considerable abilities, had failed. If a cadet fails, he gets no second chance. That is the way of the Clan.''

"But he has received a second chance and done well, *quiaff*? Why do you remain silent? Would not the defenders of Glory Station have gone down to defeat if not for the valor of Star Commander Aidan?''

"They would. But perhaps that might have been for the best.''

"Oh? Explain.''

"The shame that he has brought down on the rest of the warriors of Glory Station may not be worth the victory.''

"You consider defeat better than victory for reasons of, well, ethics? An intriguing view, Star Captain.''

"I know nothing about ethics. I only know the shame.''

"You have explained yourself honestly, Star Captain Joanna. I have no more questions.''

Beck Qwabe's interrogation was brief and perfunctory. He obviously did not want to confuse the council members with any more of Joanna's strange responses, most of which were dangerous to his case. And at the moment, it looked as though any case he might conceivably make was rapidly fading from view.

As Joanna went back to her seat at the table, the Loremaster called on Aidan to bring forth his testimony. When Aidan stood up, his face was remarkably calm.

26

Aidan did not know what the outcome of this trial would be, but believed the justness of his own cause would prevail. There was a poem in one of the books of his secret library. It dealt with some old, now-forgotten hero whose strength was that of ten men because his heart was pure. Aidan could not be sure of the purity of his heart, but he did feel inordinately strong.

As Lenore Shi-Lu approached, he thought idly of what an odd pair they made—he so tall, she so small. Looking down at her, he experienced a strange attraction. It was not the first time he was attracted to a woman, of course, for there had been Marthe, Peri, and a few others he had known only briefly. This time seemed peculiar, however. This woman held his fate in her hands. He should neither respect her nor find her intriguing sexually, yet he felt both.

As Lenore Shi-Lu scanned the computer screen, Aidan took the opportunity to cast his eyes about the audience looking for Marthe. She was still there, watching impassively. And she did not look away. He wished he could talk to her.

"Star Commander Aidan," Lenore Shi-Lu said abruptly, startling him out of his reverie. The loudness and authority in her voice made his awareness of her sexuality drift away with her words. "Are you well?"

"I am fine."

"I thought we had lost you there for a moment. Before I begin my interrogation, the Loremaster informs me that he must speak to you first. Loremaster?''

The Loremaster glanced at Khan Elias Crichell, who signaled his assent with a nod. ''Under the authorization of the Khan, I have made a formal poll of the members of the council,'' the Loremaster announced. ''The outcome of the poll is that the council will agree to reduce all charges against you, including the charge of treason, in exchange for one thing.''

The Loremaster paused for a moment, letting his words sink in. ''If you will give up your claim to eligibility to compete for a Bloodname, we are prepared to excuse most of the other infractions. Before you respond, I must explain the reason for this unprecedented offer. Khan Elias Crichell is willing to verify your warrior status as long as you are not Bloodnamed. It is, he believes, a worthy compromise that endorses your performance of duty as a warrior while taking into account the fraudulent means by which you earned the status. Further, it is his judgment that, regardless of your origins, you have lost the right to compete for a Bloodname because you failed in your first and only official trial. He believes you are an estimable warrior who might ascend to the highest ranks of command. However, should you win a Bloodname, you would burden it with a serious taint. More than two-thirds of the Bloodnamed warriors present agree. What say you, Star Commander Aidan?''

Aidan's calm left him in a rush, and he wanted to let out a scream of rage. The next moment, he reminded himself of his vow to conduct himself with dignity. He did not want to give these warriors any satisfaction, any endorsement of their view that he was tainted, or a fraud, or such a coward that he would accept this insulting offer.

''With all due respect, Loremaster, to you, to all warriors present, and to the honored Khan Elias Crichell, I cannot accept.''

The rest of his speech was drowned out by the commotion that immediately erupted. Some warriors stood up, shaking their fists. A few tried to climb over their tables to rush down at him. Others merely roared their disapproval. He heard their cries as a long, scrambled message, one voice weaving in and out of another. "Freebirth! You are a disgrace to . . . right have you to dishonor the . . . to be strangled until your face turns . . . guts ripped out and eaten by . . . dare you refuse the Khan's generous and . . . will kill you! I will . . . cut them into a thousand pieces and—"

It was all the Loremaster could do to bring the uproar to a semblance of order. It took a long time, during which Aidan stood impassively, not looking at anyone, but not looking down either.

Joanna was impressed. Aidan kept surprising her, and this was one of the best shocks yet. She almost admired him for it. She knew that the offer, though presented in generous terms, was absurd, offensive. How could any trueborn warrior accept it? From the moment a trueborn dropped from the canister, he or she was geared to fulfill his or her destiny, especially through prowess in warfare, with the single goal of earning a Bloodname and contributing to the sacred gene pool.

The council's gesture was political, an attempt to extricate the Clan leadership from a serious dilemma. But Aidan had probably doomed himself with his refusal. Sentiment would go even stronger against him now. The Khan had backed him into a corner and directed the vote. This council session would, in effect, block Aidan from going after the Bloodname. Khan Elias Crichell was known for crafty political strategies. Well, Joanna thought, he had just brought off another coup.

Though some warriors continued to squirm in agitation, all the while speaking to one another in angry whispers, the room returned to relative quiet. Lenore Shi-Lu began her interrogation. Her first questions concerned autobiographical details, which Aidan provided succinctly and without emotion.

"Star Commander Aidan," she said suddenly and with no preparatory questions, "when you were posing as a freeborn here on Ironhold, were you aware Ter Roshak had violated Clan law?''

''I knew that I was not supposed to receive a second chance.''

''Yet you took it when offered, *quiaff?*''

''Aff. I only wanted to be a warrior. I had failed the first time because I was too bold. If not for that, I would have succeeded in my Trial.''

''You would have won, you say, if you had modified your strategy. Yet, how can a Clan warrior be *too* bold? Can you answer that?''

''No. I cannot. I believe I misstated. I lost, as cadets do, because I deserved to lose. I accept that.''

''As you so easily accepted the second Trial.''

''Yes, I suppose you could put it that way. Inquisitor, I have been a warrior for a while now. As a warrior, I can look back on that time and say, in all honesty, that I should have not been granted a second chance. But I also believe it is too late for the Clan to renege. I have served the Jade Falcons well, and as a warrior.''

''Then in your estimation, pragmatism replaces proper procedure, *quiaff?*''

''Aff. Whatever happens here, I am a warrior.''

Though spoken softly, Aidan's words reverberated through the chamber, which immediately erupted into a new babble of protests.

Aidan stood, alone and calm, at the center of a whirlwind. Joanna, in spite of herself, admired him.

He was right in a way, she thought. His brand of defiance, of standing up to others, of speaking his mind at all costs—that too was part of the Clan. The refusal to step back, that was the way of the Clan as much as any other rite or custom. Aidan never stepped back. Who could expect him to do so now, renouncing the means by which he had earned his warrior status? Though such speculation might upset some of the assembled warriors, it made perfect sense to Joanna.

In a strange way, Aidan is my ally, she thought. The two of us are much alike. Perhaps that is why I hate him more than any other. And perhaps that is why my destiny seems so entwined with his.

Aidan's responses to Lenore Shi-Lu's subsequent questions were desultory. No, he had not known how Ter Roshak had manipulated the events leading to his second chance. Yes, he had suspected chicanery and confronted Ter Roshak with his suspicions. No, Ter Roshak had admitted nothing of substance to Aidan. (Ter Roshak, almost everyone knew, would have been too shrewd to make that error.) Yes, the Trial of Position had been run fairly, and he had earned his warrior status through superior strategy.

Beck Qwabe's few questions added little to Aidan's testimony. When Aidan returned to his place at the table, he did not quaver before the rumble of sustained hatred against him; his calm remained. During his interrogation, he had not become ruffled, an achievement that—for Aidan—approached the superhuman. He knew what he would do, and as he heard the Loremaster calling Roshak's name, he already suspected what Ter Roshak would do.

The man stood up. His spine erect and his shoulders militarily straight, for the first time he looked like the Roshak of old.

27

"Ter Roshak? Did I hear you right? Do you mean to tell us that your motives for the crime of which you are accused were both honorable and benevolent?"

The usually detached Loremaster could not keep the disbelief from his voice. He had interrupted Lenore Shi-Lu's current line of questioning with more abruptness and less politeness than was his usual wont.

"That is correct, Loremaster."

"Ter Roshak, as a Bloodnamed warrior with a fine combat record, we must listen to your defense, but I must say that I fail to see how the terms you propose offer any justification of your acts."

"If you will hear me out, Loremaster."

"By all means. Go on."

Roshak glanced at the tiers of Jade Falcon warriors, most of whom were leaning forward with expressions of doubt on their faces.

"It has been said repeatedly during these proceedings that I arranged for Cadet Aidan's second trial because of some special potential I saw in him. Though I did recognize such potential, it was not sufficient to merit a violation of Clan law to award him a second chance. I have seen too many cadets with just as much potential end up in lower castes or dead on a scarred battlefield. If anything, Cadet Aidan's potential was almost negated by his cocksure, rash, often arrogant tactics. Daring too much may sometimes result in impressive individual heroism, but it is more likely to lead to overbidding, then humiliation in battle.

"In his official trial he came close to qualifying, but fate took his chance away. I have often believed the Clans should provide a second Trial for certain cadets, but I would not have gone against Clan law and custom for any but the most extraordinary reasons."

"It is to learn those, as you say, extraordinary reasons that we wait with bated breath," Lenore Shi-Lu commented drily. "Please abridge your prologue to the main points and provide us the evidence we require."

"I am sorry. I had wished to be as meticulous in my testimony as the Inquisitor is meticulous in her questioning."

"Flattery is an Inner Sphere weakness, Ter Roshak. Please continue without it."

"Yes. Just a bit more prologue, if you please. It is significant to this case that I previously served with Ramon Mattlov, one of the greatest Galaxy Commanders in Jade Falcon history."

Lenore Shi-Lu tapped something onto the keyboard of the computer console set into the main table, then scanned the monitor. "Mattlov is the male progenitor of Star Commander Aidan's sibko, *quiaff?*"

"Aff. He was a great hero in his life, Ramon Mattlov, and I watched him die as one. When I left warrior duty and took command of the Ironhold training center, I dedicated my service to him. Indeed, Ramon Mattlov was often in my thoughts as I went about my duties. I considered his views whenever I made my own decisions, and in my briefings and meetings with my training officers, I often repeated Ramon Mattlov's views and beliefs verbatim. There were times—and I must ask the council's indulgence for uttering such unClanlike sentiments in this official session—when I almost believed I *was* Ramon Mattlov. I would dress down a cadet just as he would have, I would demonstrate a fighting technique exactly as he had demonstrated it to me, I would conduct surprise inspections just as brutally as he did."

Perhaps, Joanna thought, you also got falling-down-drunk just like Ramon Mattlov, mistreated your subordinates just like Ramon Mattlov, foolishly defied fate just like Ramon Mattlov.

For once Lenore Shi-Lu seemed ill-at-ease. She glanced toward the Loremaster for guidance, but his attention was so focused on Roshak that he did not notice her silent plea. Finally, she turned back to Roshak: "I am sorry for being obtuse, Falconer Commander, but perhaps you can explain how this—may I call it obsession?—with Ramon Mattlov relates to the accusations and concerns of this assembly?"

"It will become clear."

"I am relieved. Go on, sir."

Roshak paused for a moment, seeming lost in his thoughts. Actually, he was marshalling them into ranks so that he could march them past the council members with military precision.

"On the day Cadet Aidan's sibko arrived on Ironhold, I thought I was seeing a ghost when I looked at the young man. It was as though Ramon Mattlov, a bit younger than when I had first known him, were back in the flesh before me. Oh, others in the sibko also resembled my former comrade. That was only natural in a group with the same genetic background. Another one of them, a young woman, also strikingly resembled Ramon Mattlov. She is among us now, an honorable warrior who has won the right to the Pryde Bloodname."

A few in the audience glanced at Marthe, who showed no expression.

"But I saw something more in Cadet Aidan than a mere resemblance. At first sight I almost believed he was the reincarnation of Ramon Mattlov."

The gathered Clan warriors muttered at this last statement, which seemed a clear indication that Ter Roshak was mad. Insanity among Clan warriors was rare, but not unknown.

"Cadet Aidan not only looked like my former commander, he stood like him, with a defiant tilt to his shoulders, with his feet placed on the ground as though ready to spring. None of the other sibkin displayed that posture. When I noticed him speak to Cadet Marthe, he had a way of leaning his head toward her that was a duplicate of the way Ramon Mattlov instructed another officer.''

"That is all quite remarkable, Falconer Commander,'' said Lenore Shi-Lu, ''but how does it justify your subsequent acts?''

"Bear with me, Inquisitor. That day I studied Cadet Aidan secretly. When, as his commanding officer, I got close to him, I stared into his eyes. Cool, confident, they were the eyes of Ramon Mattlov. Not only that, I saw in them the same hint of danger.

"At that first encounter, the training officer gave the cadets the usual beating every newly arrived sibko deserves. When Falconer Joanna picked out Cadet Aidan for the most ferocious punishment, he gave back more fight than any cadet I have ever seen. And that, too, made him like Ramon Mattlov. Knocked down once, he got up again. Severely beaten, he continued to fight. He would not admit defeat. Again, all traits of Ramon Mattlov. I had seen all those qualities over the course of various battles. I fought alongside Ramon Mattlov, and now I was seeing his ferocious tenacity all over again.

"As training continued, the resemblance became even more pronounced. And the major likeness was to Ramon Mattlov's tendency to go for the big strike and his unwillingness to accept defeat under any condition. Ramon Mattlov turned the tide of battle several times at a moment when most warriors would have been submitting terms of surrender. So extreme were his tactics that he often risked losing a battle. He would underbid his firepower, for example, or choose tactics so unorthodox that even seasoned combatants tried to change his mind. He was lucky, though, and usually achieved his objective. He had earned his right to contribute his heritage to the sacred gene pool long before his death in combat.''

Roshak glanced around the room, silent now during his eulogy to Ramon Mattlov. Lenore Shi-Lu quietly broke the stillness: ''Go on, Falconer Commander.''

"It was this that fed my desire to see Cadet Aidan

succeed. It was why I prodded him, pushed him, and made sure my officers did the same. His successes in early tests were denigrated instead of praised to spur him to try all the harder. His lapses were magnified so that he would brood on them and seek ways to eliminate them the next time around. During that time I had few actual encounters with him, but I do recall once coming upon him suddenly when he was standing guard. For a moment, I mistook him for Ramon Mattlov. I knew then that if Cadet Aidan did not win his Trial, it would be a dishonor to the memory of Ramon Mattlov.''

''I am not certain I follow your reasoning, Falconer Commander,'' Lenore Shi-Lu interrupted. ''In the Clan, as you know, metaphysics are discouraged. How might the very real achievements of Ramon Mattlov be dishonored by a cadet who had a mere physical resemblance to him?''

For the first time Ter Roshak looked flustered. ''You misunderstand, Inquisitor. His resemblance was not a *mere* physical one. I believed him to be the embodiment of all Ramon Mattlov had been. That meant he must be the best in all Clan combat activities. When the young man failed his Trial of Position, I could not accept it. He should have won. Anyone who examines the records or tapes of that test would agree.

''Even then, I would not have interfered if Cadet Aidan, by now astech Aidan, had not escaped from Ironhold at the first possible opportunity and begun to seek his own fortune. In similar circumstances, Ramon Mattlov would have done the same. That was when I knew what I must do. I had to create the circumstances for another Trial.''

''And to do that,'' Lenore Shi-Lu interrupted again, ''you found it necessary to arrange for the death of a freeborn to give a new identity and another chance at the Trial to this cadet you favored so much?''

''That is essentially correct.''

''Essentially?''

Ter Roshak seemed to hesitate before responding. ''I did not merely *arrange* for the freeborn's death. I personally planted real explosive charges in a training minefield. When the only survivor of the explosions was the freeborn cadet whose place Cadet Aidan was to take, I killed the cadet, too.''

Aidan was surprised. He had not known the extent of Roshak's personal involvement.

''We are grateful for your honesty, Falconer Commander, but in truth, the deaths of a few freeborn cadets have little bearing on this case. The issue is *why* you engaged in deceit, not *how*. Are we to understand, then, that loyalty to Ramon Mattlov underlay all your actions regarding Star Commander Aidan?''

''Expressed so succinctly, your statement diminishes the gravity of my objectives, but what you say is quite true. Loyalty is the way of the Clan, and my loyalty to Ramon Mattlov overrode other considerations.''

''Loyalty to a *dead* commanding officer, I am forced to point out. Loyalty in the extreme. Meritorious on some level, I am sure, but not worth defying Clan law.''

The approving murmurs in the hall seemed to endorse Lenore Shi-Lu's words.

''If you so believe, Inquisitor, I would not attempt to disagree.''

''Why not, Falconer Commander? When you have disobeyed Clan law, why not disagree with one of its loyal minions?''

''With all due respect, Inquisitor, I believe I have established my motives in the actions for which I was called here. Judgment follows. I have no more to say.''

Ter Roshak did, however, speak more, responding tersely to Beck Qwabe's questions, which Roshak's own previous testimony had rendered irrelevant. Foreseeing the outcome of the case, Qwabe was merely going through the motions, presenting the questions submitted by those warriors sympathetic to the Advocate case. He had been surprised at the numbers who seemed to support the defendants until he noted that most of them were of Ter Roshak's generation, aging warriors in their last years of service. Roshak had called in some favors, Qwabe was certain. The vote would be closer than Qwabe had originally expected.

When all the testimony was complete, the Loremaster polled the council members. Of the 493 warriors who voted, 372 voted against Ter Roshak and Aidan. Joanna, whose case was considered separately, received approval from 167 of the warriors, with 326 against.

As soon as the Loremaster announced the vote, both Aidan and Ter Roshak stood up. Roshak, as senior officer, would speak first.

"I do not accept the judgment of this council. I demand a Trial of Refusal."

"I also," Aidan shouted.

The Khan nodded wearily, then signaled to the Loremaster. Most of the warriors in the room recognized that the officers of the court were not surprised by the request. Aidan speculated on the likelihood that Roshak had called in favors from old comrades to influence the proportions of the vote to acceptable levels. He quickly calculated that the odds against them in the Trial of Refusal were three-to-one. They might be formidable odds, but at least, Aidan thought, it gave him a chance. Even before coming here, he had planned to invoke the Trial of Refusal, at that time figuring the odds against him would be much worse.

A Trial of Refusal was the right of any warrior to protest a judgment against him by the council. Conceived in the early days of the Clan, it permitted a warrior to verify his cause or his case by going into combat against some of the best available warriors of the Clan; the number of opponents was based on the odds of the vote. Because the vote against Aidan and Ter Roshak was three-to-one, they would have to face six warriors in their Trial of Refusal. Tough odds, Aidan thought, but with some skill and a well-modified 'Mech, they could be overcome. They were certainly better than the six- or seven-to-one he might have faced if not for Ter Roshak's political acumen.

As the Loremaster announced the terms of the Trial

of Refusal, Joanna astounded everyone by rising to her feet with a request to speak.

"Yes, Star Captain Joanna?" the Loremaster said.

"My name is tainted by the judgment against me. Two-thirds of the warriors present believe I have committed a wrong. I will not have that. I demand to be included in the Trial of Refusal."

"But, Star Captain, your vote was different. With only two out of every three voting against you, you need not fight at three-to-one odds."

"I wish to. I am implicated in their deeds. I will exonerate myself. And the odds mean nothing to me. What is one BattleMech more or less?"

The officers of the court conferred, then the Loremaster announced that the Trial of Refusal would take place in two days, with the three tainted warriors meeting nine of their Jade Falcon judges in a contest of BattleMechs.

As they left the chamber, Aidan caught up with Ter Roshak. "When will we discuss tactics?" he asked.

"You presume too much, as always. We will discuss nothing. I have no intention of cooperating with you. Why did you not hold your tongue, as I instructed you?"

"You should know that better than I. No true warrior can pass up the opportunity to win a Bloodname. I must have mine."

"What a fool! You will not live to compete in the Trial of Bloodright. I will take great pleasure in watching you die on the battlefield. Goodbye, Star Commander Aidan. We will not speak again."

As Aidan watched Ter Roshak walk away, he wondered if the man was mad. At the very least, he seemed disoriented. Finally he decided that Roshak's actions were consistent with his past. The Falconer Commander's actions had always been difficult to read.

"What was that all about?" Joanna asked, coming up to Aidan.

"Ter Roshak refuses to discuss tactics for the Trial of Refusal. I do not think he cares whether or not he succeeds."

"Perhaps he wishes to die in a cockpit, and this is his last chance."

"If that is true, it considerably increases the odds against us."

"Yes, I do not approve of the idea of Ter Roshak acting out his own personal tragedy, all the while taking us down with him. Still, as I said in court, what is one BattleMech more or less? Or two?"

"You should have stayed out of this, Joanna."

"Do not address me familiarly."

"All right, Star Captain Joanna. I will not blame you if you withdraw. You could still initiate your own separate Trial of Refusal."

"No. I stand by my words. Besides, perhaps this will show me if there is any sense in what Ter Roshak said in his testimony. Perhaps the spirit of Ramon Mattlov does live in you."

"He said nothing about spirit."

"You were not listening. It was *exactly* what he said. So, we have two days. Let us discuss what we must do. This Trial will, after all, not be like any to which we are accustomed. All the 'Mechs in the field will go against us simultaneously. There will be none of the single engagements we are used to in Trials. In a Trial of Refusal, the odds against the challenger must be maintained. We must plan on several contingencies. Especially with Ter Roshak now an unpredictable factor."

"I agree. We must—"

Aidan suddenly stopped speaking when he saw Marthe approaching. He stared at her the whole way. She must have been conscious of his gaze. For an instant, her eyes seemed to flick past his, then she walked on without speaking or acknowledging him in any way. At one time, he might have run after her, demanding that she speak. But now, with her a Bloodnamed warrior and wearing the insignia of a Star Captain, he would not give her the satisfaction of snubbing him further.

"Look at her," Joanna said. "I trained her. I instilled in her a respect for the Clan and a desire for a

Bloodname. Now she has the Bloodname and she walks by without speaking. I hope she is in one of the 'Mechs at the Trial so that I can destroy her.''

Aidan's thoughts were less aggressive and his hope was not in any way related to Marthe in a BattleMech. ''If it is all right with you, Star Captain,'' he said, ''I would like to plan to dispose of all our adversaries quickly.''

''Any reason for that?''

''Yes. The Grand Melee for the House Pryde Bloodname commences the next day. Without a warrior to sponsor me, it is my only path to the Bloodname.''

Joanna sighed and gave Aidan a rare smile. ''At this moment, I do not know who is more lunatic, you or Ter Roshak. On second thought, maybe I am the crazy one here.''

28

Nine BattleMechs came over the crest of a wide hill together, rising into the sky like rockets in some kind of slow-motion launch.

"Nine little BattleMechs tempting cruel fate," Aidan whispered to Joanna over the commlink. "One got religion, and then there were eight."

"What in the name of Kerensky are you talking about?"

"Something I picked up somewhere, listening to a child's game, I think. Eight little BattleMechs reaching up to heaven, one fell to hell and then there were seven."

"Doggerel. Do not give me doggerel now, Aidan."

"All right," he said, "let us do it as we planned. Let us move out."

"What about Ter Roshak?"

"Since he has carefully disabled all his communications systems, he will just have to follow us, or not."

Slowly, they began moving toward their nine opponents. "Nine little BattleMechs . . . ," Aidan muttered to himself, softly so that Joanna would not hear.

Although Joanna had been reluctant to break with Clan trial traditions, Aidan had persuaded her that their only chance lay in the unexpected. As they lumbered forward, he in his favorite 'Mech type, a *Summoner*, she in a *Mad Dog*, Aidan was astonished by the array of heavy 'Mechs against them. Ahead he saw a *Dire Wolf*, a pair of *Warhawks*, an *Executioner*, a *Mad Dog*, and a *Gargoyle*. As some of these 'Mech types were not typical of Jade Falcon forces, they must have been shipped in just for this battle or else were part of the Ironhold refresher training courses. The other three BattleMechs were another *Summoner* and two lighter 'Mechs, a *Stormcrow* and an *Ice Ferret*.

Aidan had considered going out in a lighter 'Mech, but he did not want to give up that much firepower. He had changed his *Summoner*'s primary weapons configuration, removing the right-arm PPC in order to increase the size of his shoulder-mounted LRM rack and also mount a Streak class short-range missile-launching system. But this also precluded his mounting an anti-missile system, something he liked to have regardless of his 'Mech's configuration.

"All right, Joanna, remember the drill?"

"Of course. Which one first?"

"The *Stormcrow* seems to be moving out ahead of the pack. All right?"

"I am with you."

Aidan and Joanna had realized that the odds in a Trial of Refusal were formidable in terms of firepower and maneuverability. It was one thing to go up against other 'Mechs one at a time, but when a line of them came at a warrior all firing at once, the target could not know where to direct fire. It was worse, in fact, than a Grand Melee, in which every 'Mech was on the same footing, the opponent of every other 'Mech on the field, all going for the same goal, the odds the same for every combatant. In a Trial of Refusal, the adversaries were all concentrated against the challenger, with not a single one of their shots intended for one another. The odds for the lone warrior were, therefore, actually better in the Grand Melee than in this Trial. Treating each opponent as if he were the only enemy of the moment allowed for less waste and more possibility. No matter how much Aidan ran the numbers through his mind or a computer, however, there seemed no way he and Joanna could win, especially with Ter Roshak out on his own instead of working with them.

He and Joanna had nevertheless agreed to start with

a plan and stick to it, unless unexpected tactics from the other side forced improvisation. Both Aidan and Joanna targeted the *Stormcrow.* Sixty fiery arrows leapt from the shoulders of their 'Mechs and streaked toward the 'Mech. The pilot did not expect such a deluge of missile fire and seemed to have frozen into inaction at the sight. Most of the missiles impacted on the *Stormcrow*'s upper torso, blasting out a great hole. Another quick launch sent the 'Mech reeling backward. It teetered for a moment, then its middle chest exploded and the 'Mech fell. As the *Stormcrow* disintegrated, the thin line rising above it was its pilot ejecting. Surprised by the tactic, the other 'Mechs had barely touched the 'Mechs of Aidan and Joanna.

"Nice work!" Joanna yelled.

". . . and then there were eight," Aidan muttered. "That takes care of the advantage of surprise, Joanna. Now is the time for cowardice. Get moving."

Ter Roshak watched Aidan and Joanna fight with an almost academic interest. He had been responsible for the training of one and had been served by the other. They polished off their first kill quickly, taking little damage.

Then, as their opponents came at them, the two underdogs actually turned and ran! Joanna's 'Mech moved swiftly across the terrain, while Aidan's used a leap to move even further ahead. Back at the enemy line, the *Executioner* detached itself from the others and made its own sudden leap forward. The jump was graceful, especially for a 'Mech of such considerable tonnage. It was not, however, perfectly calculated. The *Executioner* came down just short of Joanna's swift *Mad Dog.* Having tracked it well, she was already countering its fire even before its pilot could orient himself.

Ter Roshak turned his 'Mech, a rare *Nova,* one of two presently on Ironhold, and fired off a cluster of LRMs from the right-arm rack that replaced the 'Mech's usual medium lasers. The long-range missiles would surprise the *Executioner* because a *Nova* was not usually equipped with them. The missiles' flight was true, their arcs high to make up for the relatively short distance, and the missiles coming in at an odd angle that apparently the *Executioner* pilot did not detect in time. The other 'Mech was already reeling from the concentrated attack by Joanna's left-arm laser, whose large pulses were making an asymmetric tattoo on the 'Mech's chest. Two of the LRMs made direct hits against the *Executioner*'s upper torso. The damage would not normally have removed the 'Mech from battle, but the pilot's cockpit was split open and its inhabitant killed instantly, never knowing what hit her. As Joanna's *Mad Dog* sprinted away, the *Executioner* was left standing in the field, a shell whose upper surface was slashed open in many places.

For a moment, Ter Roshak was exhilarated. Killing the 'Mech reminded him of his days fighting side by side with Ramon Mattlov. Now he was focused on his cockpit sensors and the *Mad Dog* that was heading his way, its large lasers already firing and doing glancing damage to Roshak's *Nova*.

"And then there were seven," Aidan said softly as he noted the *Executioner*'s fall. "You did that with just your lasers, Star Captain Joanna?"

"Truth to tell, I had a little help." She explained how Roshak's direct hit to the cockpit had annihilated the *Executioner*.

"The sleeping giant awakes early," Aidan commented. He saw that the *Mad Dog* was closing in on Roshak's *Nova*. The contest was something of a mismatch, with the *Mad Dog* so much heavier than the *Nova*, but Ter Roshak had a couple of advantages over his opponent. First, he was a seasoned pilot, of an age not usually seen piloting a 'Mech. Second, the *Nova* was a relatively unknown quantity on a Jade Falcon planet.

"Should we help him?" Joanna asked, her tone almost analytical rather than sympathetic to Ter Roshak's plight.

"No, we must not waste firepower. He left us to

fight without his help. Let him fight this one out on his own. Have we run far enough?''

''I think so. We seem to have two ranks of pursuit. I think it is time to take care of the front line. In the meantime we need more split in their ranks. You veer off to the right. I will join you in a moment.''

Joanna was surprised to note how quickly she followed Aidan's directions. Perhaps he was a natural warrior, after all.

Aidan's *Summoner* turned and took a short jump toward the leading trackers, one of the *Warhawks* and the *Ice Ferret*. Simultaneously he noticed that two of the other four 'Mechs, the *Dire Wolf* and the *Gargoyle*, had begun to go specifically after Joanna. The gap between the groups of 'Mechs was widening, what with the *Mad Dog* engaged in a rough contest with Ter Roshak's *Nova*.

As Aidan landed his *Summoner*, he glanced toward the two lead 'Mechs and thought of a little variation on that childhood rhyme that kept running through his head: ''Seven little BattleMechs, thinking they were alive. Two tripped on wires, and then there were five.''

Ter Roshak had come into the Trial of Refusal not caring whether he won or lost, lived or died. Dying would not, in fact, be so bad. He would have challenged the council instead of accepting the shame; fought in a final Trial instead of winding up in a useless life; died with honor in the Trial instead of dying as cannon fodder. Battling with the *Mad Dog*, trading it blow for blow, he felt some meaning had returned to his life. And to think he had been so ready to die only a few moments ago.

He had mounted a pulse laser into the left side of the *Nova*'s torso. Right now he was cycling through the lasers on that arm and firing off the pulse laser in the torso in an effort to keep his heat under control.

The *Mad Dog* was under no such constraints. It carried only two weapons, Gauss cannons that would spit out a melon-sized ball of hardened steel at Mach 2 every ten seconds. Twice the melons struck home, shattering most of the armor plate protecting Roshak's right and center torsos. Roshak now had to keep the exposed side away from the *Mad Dog,* which meant that he could not use the missile rack mounted in this 'Mech's left arm. Circling and weaving around his almost stationary opponent, Roshak stayed in almost constant motion, his slow and steady fire gradually chipping away the *Mad Dog's* armor. His opponent had yet to score another hit with his Gauss cannon, but Roshak knew it was only a matter of time.

Suddenly he wondered if he might not turn the *Mad Dog* pilot's immobility into an advantage. He had to do something soon, he thought, as the muzzles of his opponent's weapons sent silver streaks speeding past his cockpit viewport.

Quickly calculating the range, Aidan fired a salvo of the Thunder LRMs at the *Warhawk* and the *Ice Ferret.* He watched as the missiles fell in front of their targets, exploding just before hitting the ground. The two 'Mechs were fooled enough to try to knock them out with their anti-missile systems, whose shots were too short.

If either 'Mech suspected what was coming, neither showed any reaction. They did not diminish their speed, as they might have, although Aidan calculated that even a slowdown would have taken them directly into the minefields that the Thunders had laid down. As his opponents' massive 'Mech feet came down directly on clumps of mines, three of the four legs were instantly blown off below the knee. The *Ice Ferret* crashed to the ground, setting off more mines and undoubtedly killing the pilot, while the *Warhawk* tilted forward on its one leg. With superhuman effort, its pilot managed to force his 'Mech sideways, away from the minefield. Then it, too, fell to the ground. In a moment the *Warhawk* pilot had ejected. Watching him sail upward, Aidan realized immediately that the man's angle was wrong. The arc of his flight was taking him to the outer edge of the minefield. Aidan felt the pilot's death would be useless, but fate was stronger. As the man's ejection seat touched ground, a small tower of explosion enveloped both him and his ejection seat.

"I think the observers must be getting a bit restless," Joanna commented over the commlink. "The odds could be in our favor any minute. Unless these fellows coming at me get lucky. By the way, you did promise to get back to me, did you not?"

Without responding, Aidan set his *Summoner* on a two-jump trip to the point where Joanna was trading fire with the *Gargoyle*. The *Dire Wolf*, a notoriously slower vehicle, was closing in. Aidan calculated that they had approximately twenty seconds before the pilot could bring the 'Mech's massive firepower against them.

"I cannot see why you need me, Joanna."

"Do not make jokes. You know I do not understand humor."

"I was not joking."

"I suggest you occupy the *Dire Wolf*'s attention."

"Gladly, Joanna."

As Aidan moved toward the *Dire Wolf*, he sang, louder this time: "Five little BattleMechs, playing tough at war. One got a stomach cramp, and then there were four."

Just as he was launching a salvo of SRMs at the *Dire Wolf*, he glanced through his viewport and saw that Ter Roshak was definitely in dire trouble with his *Mad Dog*.

Roshak should have seen the move coming. The *Mad Dog* pilot suddenly pointed his Ultra autocannon down and chipped away at the *Nova*'s right-foot armor. Feeling shudders up through the 'Mech's right leg, Roshak knew something important had been hit.

There was no longer any sense in going head to head with this BattleMech, he thought. Engaging his jump jets, he leaped nearly the full capacity of 150 meters, getting closer to where Aidan and Joanna were in the midst of a furious battle. When he landed, however, it was on the damaged foot, and his 'Mech lost its balance. It would have fallen flat on its back had Roshak not manipulated the joystick frenetically to bring the 'Mech down to one knee, with the other leg slightly sprawled out. As it came to rest, the *Nova* was slightly tilted but operable.

It had to be operable, for the *Mad Dog* was lumbering slowly but steadily toward it.

Aidan did not cease his onslaught as he closed with the *Summoner.* He spent his remaining Thunder LRMs, but the *Dire Wolf* pilot merely steered his ponderous machine around the bomblets they dropped. Aidan recognized that the pilot of this 'Mech was a conventional warrior, the kind who plods on and usually wins through sheer endurance and determination. That is, until he or she runs into a particularly daring or foolish opponent. Aidan knew he qualified in one of the latter categories, but was not sure which.

The *Dire Wolf* pilot, to avoid the heat buildup of its massively augmented weaponry, was firing only two of its large lasers at a time as he slowly moved to close the range. As for Aidan, he had no intention of overheating his machine in a long-range duel, and to trade blows at close range was suicidal. It was time to test fate once again.

Turning directly toward the *Dire Wolf,* Aidan brought his machine up to full running speed. As the distance closed, he watched his secondary screen.

600 meters.

400 meters.

Seeing Aidan moving directly toward him, the *Dire Wolf* pilot stopped, heat visibly venting from the 'Mech's legs and back.

350 meters.

200 meters.

The arms of the *Dire Wolf* came up and pointed directly at the charging *Summoner.* As the eight arm-mounted lasers were brought up to full charge, static discharges crackled across their muzzles.

175 meters.

150 meters.

Raw energy leapt from the *Dire Wolf*'s extended

arms as Aidan slapped the jump switch. Up over the deadly fire, Aidan's *Summoner* rose. The arms of the *Dire Wolf* tried to track the airborne target for a second shot, but it was too late. Seventy ugly tons of BattleMech landed feet first onto the cockpit of the *Dire Wolf*.

As Aidan worked his 'Mech free from the wreckage, the rhyme kept running through his head: "Four little BattleMechs, sliding down the scree. One ate a *Summoner*, and then there were three."

Aidan could not, for a moment, decide which way to go. Coming fast toward the fray were the two 'Mechs that had not yet played any significant part in the battle, a *Warhawk* and a *Summoner*. Nearby was Joanna, holding her own against the *Gargoyle*, though she could probably use help by now. And Ter Roshak was half-down, his 'Mech looking almost numb as the *Mad Dog* approached.

What good was life without choices, Aidan wondered.

Ter Roshak was indeed numb. Not only had he reached the end of his rope as an effective warrior, but he had no feeling in his legs. There was no wound there, no way any shot from the *Mad Dog* could have reached his legs. Perhaps the numbness was from sitting too long in his pilot seat, the stiffness just one more sign of age.

The battle had taken too much out of him, so apparently they were right about the uselessness of old warriors. He never wanted to admit his age to himself, but this test had brought out his infirmity only too well. He was old. He deserved to die. Why could not this *Mad Dog* fire the shot that would finish him off once and for all?

He closed his eyes, waiting for the final moment. He would not eject, he knew that. Then his eyes shot open again. That was neither the way of the Clans nor the way of a good warrior. If he was to meet death, it must be with his eyes open.

* * *

Aidan did not know whether it was wise to tackle the *Mad Dog* coming at Ter Roshak. His 'Mech's legs were damaged from the jump onto the *Dire Wolf*. It looked like his engine shielding had taken a hit, too, for he could not move at full speed. Lastly, his long-range ammo was depleted, leaving him only the short-range missiles and autocannon.

Coming at the *Mad Dog* from the side, in a tactic sometimes known as blindsiding, Aidan fired off a cluster round from his LB 10-X, grateful for its greater range as it did considerable destruction to the heavy 'Mech's left side. The autocannon would normally have been no more than the sting of an insect, but Roshak had already created deep lines of damage in the machine of his relentless opponent. A sheet of flame erupted from one of them, shooting out like a flamethrower.

The *Mad Dog* came to an abrupt stop, the pilot apparently dealing with whatever had caused the sudden fire. For a moment, Aidan drew a blank. He did not know what to do. The pilot of this 'Mech would regain control of his machine and return to the battle. The two oncoming 'Mechs would arrive. Joanna's battle would end in victory or defeat. There were too many factors and insufficient solutions.

He wanted to curse, but the only one strong enough among Clan Warriors was "freebirth," and his experience among freeborns had removed that oath from his vocabulary. The way this Trial of Refusal was working out seemed unfair. They had, the three of them, started out against nine. Already they had defeated *five*. Five was an impressive number, but in a Trial of Refusal, the challengers could win only by defeating every one of their opponents. They had come close, but that was not enough.

And his chance to win a Bloodname was riding on this Trial.

Gritting his teeth, he rejected the odds and went after the *Mad Dog*. Firing his LB 10-X rapidly, he was surprised to make another strong hit as the *Mad Dog*'s right arm dropped. Aidan had hit something there, perhaps just the right clump of myomer tendons, that had disabled the arm. The *Mad Dog,* looking as wild as its name, rotated on its torso to face Aidan.

"Be careful, Aidan," came Joanna's voice over the commlink, "this is one time not to give the battle all you have. Your 'Mech looks like the only things holding it together are spit and wishes. Do a feint, something. I am on my way."

"What happened to the *Gargoyle?*"

"What do you think? It is finished. And if you have not noticed yet, the odds are now even, three against three. Of course, two of those are just entering the battle without having used up much firepower or energy."

Aidan had forgotten the childhood rhyme again until now. He had been making it up for the last couple of verses, anyway. "Three little BattleMechs, none of them new. One lost its nuts and bolts, and then there were two." If only he could concoct weapons instead of verses. One might be able to slay dragons with metaphors, but a BattleMech was another matter entirely.

Ter Roshak wished now he had not disabled his communications systems. He wanted desperately to coordinate the rest of the battle, but could not. Perhaps this was another sign of advancing age.

Ever since his 'Mech had dropped to its knees, he had been looking at things from a skewered viewpoint. Everything outside the 'Mech seemed at an angle. Although he knew that the two BattleMechs he could see were upright, they appeared to lean to their right on a sloping landscape.

The *Mad Dog* was about to finish off the *Summoner,* Roshak could see that. Had the *Summoner* been fresh, it would have been another matter. The *Mad Dog* was severely damaged, both from its battle with Ter Roshak and from its present conflict with Aidan. No matter what type of 'Mech it was, it could be beaten.

On his secondary screen, now being used to get an overhead view of the 'Mechs left in the field, Roshak saw the advancing opponents as well as Joanna's 'Mech reentering the fray, although a distance away.

Having rotated toward the *Summoner,* the *Mad Dog* rocked it with a hit from its remaining Gauss cannon. A glow from inside the cockpit of the *Summoner* indicated to the experienced Ter Roshak that the engine shielding had been breached and waste heat from the fusion fires powering the 'Mech was being dumped into its interior. Perhaps that was why Aidan seemed to be moving back from the fight. Too much damage, combined with too much heat to risk an ammo explosion.

Well, at least the *Mad Dog* had given up on Roshak and his *Nova.* He wondered if he would ever pilot a *Nova* again. It had been the wrong choice. He had desired its maneuverability, but had ended up needing more power. Of course at that time he had not cared whether he won. Still, in a battle of three-to-one odds, the *Nova* was a nearly suicidal choice. Its maneuverability had only prolonged his meaningless survival. When the *Mad Dog* returned its attention to him, it would take only one solid hit to topple him.

Then, he realized suddenly, there was no reason for him to make a final stand. What did he have left? He had spent all his missiles. The left-torso laser was destroyed. Only the left-arm medium lasers remained. They could erode some of the other 'Mech's open gashes, but that was about all. It was what he had, though, and a good warrior always fought with what was at hand. He activated all six medium lasers, directing four of them toward various slashes and gouges in the *Mad Dog*'s armor, the other two toward the Gauss cannon that was the 'Mech's left arm. Because the *Summoner* had disabled the 'Mech's right arm, the hope of ruining the other one was too tempting to resist.

Suddenly the *Mad Dog* was taking fire from two directions. When it swung its arm toward the *Nova,* blasting it with its autocannon, Ter Roshak felt his 'Mech sway and threaten to fall. The *Mad Dog* might have fired again and put the *Nova* out of its misery, but Aidan ripped off a large chunk of armor with a fusillade from his LB 10-X, diverting the pilot's attention back to his *Summoner*.

On his primary screen, enlarged for a closer view, Roshak saw the two untouched BattleMechs within range. The *Warhawk* sent Aidan's *Summoner* into a half-spin with pulses from its extended-range PPC, but Roshak kept the *Mad Dog* from going in for the kill with his fusillade. The heavy 'Mech had to turn its attention back to Roshak.

As Roshak steadied himself for the final shot, he lightly touched the lever of the ejection seat that he had vowed not to use even if it meant being charred to a crisp in the cockpit.

But suddenly the *Mad Dog* exploded. A flight of missiles glided in to demolish it with a direct hit. They had come from behind Roshak and could only have been launched from Joanna's 'Mech. If the *Mad Dog* pilot survived, which was unlikely, he or she would undoubtedly complain about being caught in a roughly triangular attack by the three defendants.

Then Roshak's 'Mech shifted abruptly, and he felt it drop further. Something, perhaps an unnoticed hit, had made the other leg go down. Now, he realized angrily, there was little more he could do in this Trial of Refusal that he had demanded for his own honor. Worse, not only was the battle up to Aidan and Joanna, but he was in a 'Mech that was kneeling in the center of a battlefield as if in prayer. What an absurd sight we must be, Roshak thought, my 'Mech and I!

"Two little BattleMechs, coming at a run. One chewed the grass, and then there was one." Joanna's grunt of disgust told Aidan that he had inadvertently communicated his verse over the commlink.

"Consider," Joanna said. "The odds are now in our favor. Three to two."

"Joanna, Ter Roshak's BattleMech is not moving, nor can it stand. You are stretching a point with your three-to-two odds."

"Perhaps. But technically Ter Roshak is not yet defeated. I agree it will only take a push from a baby's finger to send him flat, but he is still upright, and upright counts. But at least we have evened up on the odds."

Another hit from the *Warhawk*'s ER-PPC sent tremors through Aidan's cockpit. The truth was dawning on even his stubborn brain that he could not defeat this massive and efficient machine.

He might do better to surrender. The council had not formally invoked the death penalty when announcing their decision. Perhaps they might simply send him to a lower caste. No, damn it, that would not be better. It would be the worst thing imaginable. He had to go on. Better to die than to capitulate, especially at this point.

Joanna was suddenly hit by missiles from the enemy *Summoner*. Five explosions flashed on her 'Mech.

"I have not got much left, Aidan."

"I know. Do not even bother with more than a desultory response to the *Summoner*. I will take care of that one at the right time. The *Warhawk* is our concern now, and we will take it together."

"I do not see how."

"But I think I do, and there is no time to explain it. Star Captain Joanna, rush the *Warhawk*. Use the rest of your ammo, missiles, whatever you have, as you go. Take its attention away from me."

"I do not have the firepower to win against a *Warhawk*, particularly one that has barely been in the battle and is fully charged, ammoed, and racked."

"Do not argue logic with me, Joanna. Just do it."

"I will be wiped out."

"Exactly. Keep your hand on your ejection lever, and when I tell you to eject, eject. Go."

"Aidan, if this—"

"GO!"

Joanna, mumbling to herself, started her *Mad Dog* toward the formidable *Warhawk*. As ordered, she was firing everything. Her hands manipulated her joysticks madly. Only a few of her shots hit the mark, and then causing only minimal damage. The *Warhawk* pilot must have thought he was being attacked by a warrior gone berserk.

Getting closer, she took hit after hit to her torso, her limbs. But she came on. Her 'Mech's left knee was nearly shattered, but Joanna managed to keep the *Mad Dog* upright, and she came on. Armor fell off her 'Mech's chest like feathers off a molting bird. Her heat buildup was reaching the dangerous levels. And she came on.

"Aidan, I am close now. I am almost out of—"

"Closer."

She pushed her 'Mech on, feeling it limp and stagger beneath her. More armor flew off.

"Aidan, there is no more I can do. My weapons—"

"Keep on going. Get closer."

"Damn it, I am practically on top of him now."

"Just a few meters now. A few more. Almost there."

The pilot of the *Warhawk* was just toying with her now. He knew the win was a sure thing. That was the way a warrior always felt when an opponent was no longer offering a response and becoming a closer target by the second.

"Aidan, the heat buildup is too much. I am getting dizzy. I have to—"

"Two more seconds. Keep going. Going. Good. Now, Joanna, now. Eject!"

She did not have to be told twice. She was in the ejection seat and flying over the head of the *Warhawk* pilot almost immediately.

At the same time, Aidan launched his six short-range missiles. The *Mad Dog* was beginning to fall slowly forward now. It was between Aidan's *Summoner* and the *Warhawk*. Just where he wanted it to be. If the *Warhawk* had an anti-missile system, the *Mad Dog* would be in the way. That did not matter, really. The missiles were not targeted for the *Warhawk*. They were aimed directly at the middle of the *Mad Dog*'s back. The overheated, coolant-churning, tottering *Mad Dog*.

Joanna's BattleMech exploded in a fine mushroom-like blast, for a moment obscuring the *Warhawk*.

The blast, with its fierce explosion, massive shrapnel, and forward-falling 'Mech, knocked the *Warhawk* off its feet, incidentally destroying its cockpit and piercing the neck and head of the pilot.

The *Warhawk* and the *Mad Dog* became an instant tangled, smoking mess. The techs would be weeks sorting out which part belonged to which 'Mech.

In the distance, Aidan saw Joanna's ejection seat settle almost gently onto the ground. She undid its straps and got out of it violently. It was obvious she was all right. He could turn his attention to the remaining BattleMech, the *Summoner*.

It stood, quiescent, a few hundred meters away, most of its weapons still fully loaded and charged. Its pilot had not yet engaged in much fighting, and the 'Mech had almost no surface damage. The odds were definitely against Aidan.

But what were odds? he thought. They had started as three BattleMechs against nine. Now there was just a one-against-one contest to settle.

Aidan had no worries now. He had piloted *Summoners* during most of his career as a warrior. In his trial he had qualified in a *Summoner*. He knew every move that was possible with this type of 'Mech. No pilot on this planet, or even in the entire globular cluster of Clan worlds, could out-fight him in a *Summoner*.

Ready to engage in battle, he started toward the opposing BattleMech. If he had been the type of warrior who permitted himself a laugh just before victory, Aidan would have been laughing hard right now.

Heading toward victory, he sang softly to himself, "One little BattleMech, with nowhere else to run . . ."

29

As the three victors joined one another next to Aidan's 'Mech at the center of the field, dumbfounded Jade Falcon warriors walked around the scene, surveying the damage. They had been judges and observers during the Trial. By the looks on their faces, they did not comprehend that a trio of discredited warriors could do so much havoc. BattleMechs and pieces of them lay all over the field, smoke rising from scarred chunks, little fires still going here and there, mixed odors of burning liquids and charred metal drifting on the air. Survivors of the contest sat by their 'Mechs and stared ahead, trying to analyze what they had done wrong. Those who had not survived were being carried off the field by medical techs.

Roshak was the last one to join the trio. He climbed laboriously out of his ruined *Nova*.

Aidan stared silently at Ter Roshak. The man looked weary and seemed to have aged another year or two since two days before in the council.

Returning Aidan's stare, the other man said, "If you do not wish to talk to me, Star Commander Aidan, I can understand why."

Aidan continued his scrutiny a moment longer, then said, "No, I do not mind talking with you, Ter Roshak. I would hope, though, that it will not happen too often."

"You wanted to be a warrior. I provided you that."

"That is true, but it does not require that I become your emotional bondsman for giving me the chance. We had it all out once before, and our testimonies only made me more aware of the price I have paid to be a warrior.''

''Take it back then. Certain Jade Falcon warriors would be delighted to see you gone from their ranks.''

''No, I have earned my status and my rank. Let us not continue this conversation. I wish to thank you for your actions in effecting our victory today.''

''I should be thanking you. You have both reversed a harmful judgment against me.''

''And ourselves,'' Joanna interjected.

''Nevertheless, my life would have been over, ended in a dishonorable manner. I may not be able to restore my honor even now, but winning this Trial of Refusal goes a long way toward validating my actions.''

As the three of them fell silent, Aidan saw several warriors who had been inspecting the battlefield send hateful glances his way.

''Well, Star Commander Aidan,'' Joanna said, returning to Clan warrior formality of address, ''what now?''

''Tomorrow is the Grand Melee for the thirty-second slot in the Bloodname competition. I will compete.''

Joanna nodded. ''I admire your willingness to enter the melee, but I must say that, no matter what your abilities, the Grand Melee champion is not necessarily the best warrior of those who go into the field. Winning the melee is more a matter of survival than skill.''

''I seem to have some abilities along those lines.''

Joanna's eyebrows raised. ''Granted. Just remember, you can be demolishing an opponent with all the best moves you have and some other idiot with no skills can sneak up behind and lay the both of you out with a single salvo. There is no military or even common-sense logic to it. Anything can happen in a melee.''

''Which makes it something like today,'' Aidan responded, pointing to the debris on the battlefield. ''This may have been a good practice run for me.''

''After today's fight, you will be exhausted.''

''I have no choice. They are not going to postpone the Grand Melee so I can get proper rest. In fact, I do not intend to sleep. They will not let me have a tech to help get this 'Mech back in shape, and it is going to need everything—repairs, reload, the works.''

"Nomad is here on Ironhold. His arm is better, if a bit stiff. He will help."

Aidan was astonished at Joanna's offer.

"Do not interpret the act as friendship," she said quickly. "I despise you and what has brought you to this point as much as ever. Perhaps even more because you were willing to pose as a filthy freebirth. But you fought well today, and I probably owe my life to you. It is a debt I would like to settle quickly. I will send Nomad here as soon as I can locate him."

Aidan refrained from thanking her, knowing that gratitude would irritate and insult her.

"You will need people to help you in other ways, an entourage. We will work out strategies. Perhaps you can persuade one or two others to join us."

"Horse. I would like Horse."

"That freebirth filth!"

"Yes. Does that bother you?"

Joanna seemed about to say yes, but then thought better of it. "If it is Horse you want, then Horse it shall be. My name is already dishonored. Serving on a Bloodname entourage with a freebirth cannot soil it much more. Somehow it even seems appropriate."

"But from now on, you must not call him a freebirth until I either succeed or am eliminated."

Joanna scowled. "You are a strange person, Star Commander Aidan. A trueborn warrior who is an advocate of freeborns. That combination should be enough to hold you back for the rest of your career, no matter what happens during the Trial of Bloodright. But I accede. I will not call MechWarrior Horse a freebirth to his or your face. How I speak elsewhere is another matter."

"Well bargained and done."

"I did not realize we were bidding, but, yes, I see what you mean. So, how do we complete your entourage? I cannot think of anyone else who can help."

They both glanced down at Ter Roshak, who immediately began to shake his head. "You do not want me. I would hurt rather than help your cause. Better to find someone else.''

''Perhaps I can help,'' came a voice from behind them, one that both of them recognized as Marthe, now Marthe Pryde, Star Captain Marthe Pryde. Joanna and Aidan both turned around, as did Ter Roshak, to see her standing a few steps away. She had apparently been observing them for some time.

Aidan did not know whether to run up and embrace her, or to maintain the same aloofness she seemed to reserve for him. But he did not have to ponder the matter for long. Marthe came forward with her hand extended, fingers splayed in position for the Jade Falcon handshake. Performing the ritual handshake meant more to Aidan than any embrace could have.

''Star Captain—,'' he started to say, but Marthe interrupted.

''I drop the formalities with all my warriors out in the field, and they may address me as Marthe. Sometimes it helps our performance as a unit. Given that we three shared some of our earlier days, it would be appropriate among us. Do you not agree, Joanna?''

''At this point, Marthe, I am not certain of anything I once held true. I will call you Marthe. At least away from warrior gatherings.''

''Fair enough. Now, what of my offer, Aidan? I can advise you well. I am of the House Pryde line, after all. What I am not able to do is sponsor you, however. The only way you can gain respectability is through the melee for the thirty-second open slot. As I am a holder of the Pryde Bloodname, I have already had my chance to nominate. Unfortunately for my candidate, she was killed in a training accident, and her opponent draws a bye in the round of the thirty-two. But I am free to advise you without interfering with other duties.''

''What can you offer him that others cannot?'' Joanna asked.

''Well questioned, Joanna. I can offer Aidan information about his opponents, for I know many of them. As a member of House Pryde, I have analyzed the accomplishments and potential of some candidates. And I can find out about others.''

"But why, Marthe?" Aidan said. "Why would you do this? You did not seem sentimental about the past the last time we met."

"I remember our days in the sibko better than you imagine. But no, my purpose here is not related to some unhealthy nostalgia. I studied your case before coming to Ironhold for the Grand Council, and I was present at every session. I requested to be an official observer at this Trial of Refusal. I have come to believe that Ter Roshak was right about you, that you are a fine warrior, one to be valued. As a praiseworthy warrior, you deserve your chance at a Bloodname. I do not know if you are the best who will compete for this House Pryde heritage, but you may be.''

"Will not others criticize you for lending support to a warrior who has only recently been condemned in council, which he challenged with a Trial of Refusal?''

"Perhaps, but I am allowed, particularly because my own nominee is gone. And remember, you won the Trial, perhaps earning respect in some quarters. At any rate, you must now get your BattleMech to a repair bay and ready it for the melee.''

Marthe turned and began to walk away, her stride showing a military precision. Suddenly Aidan broke into a run and went after her.

"Marthe, do you have some other reason for helping me?''

She looked at him with her cool, even gaze. "In a way, yes. I was shocked to learn that you had been a warrior these past few years, when all along I believed you had flushed out of training. After the shock, I was glad. There is much . . . well, unfinished business between us. I wanted to see you again, so I came to Ironhold. Perhaps it has to do with the sibko . . . I do not know. We will talk again tomorrow before the melee.''

Again she turned and resumed her brisk stride away from him. By now Joanna had come up alongside. "Things are not steady, Aidan. I am less sure of everything than I used to be. I do not like that.''

30

Before the Grand Melee, Marthe warned Aidan to be especially wary of one MechWarrior Nielo, who was a survivor of two earlier Bloodright trials. He had been a sponsored candidate in those, and in each one had lasted to the round in which eight warriors remained. He had lost sponsorship when the Bloodnamed warrior who had favored him discovered a younger, more adept warrior and transferred his sponsorship to her instead. It was common, even expected, in the Clan for Bloodnamed warriors to switch their sponsorships of warriors from one Trial of Bloodright to another.

Nielo would be piloting a *Viper*, a 'Mech lighter than Aidan's *Summoner*, but with excellent maneuverability. It had a greater jump capacity than Aidan's 'Mech, but its weaponry was fairly conventional. On Marthe's advice Aidan had reconfigured his *Summoner* back to its primary configuration. The only alteration he made was to replace the LRMs with SRMs, which would be more useful in the small area where the melee would take place.

"For the melee you need some variety, and the *Summoner*'s standard weapons configuration gives you that. No need to get fancy. In fact, what you must remember above all is to downplay your boldness, as Joanna has also advised you already. Caution works better in a melee."

"Are you sure of that, Marthe?"

Well, I have never participated in one, but the advice makes sense. It would be tempting to try too hard at the beginning, expend too much ammo, build up too much heat too early in the process. A warrior can lose the melee by what some in the merchant caste would call poor management. Therefore, caution. Defend yourself, but stay out of the way as much as you can.''

"That whole idea makes me uncomfortable."

"It would make me uncomfortable, too. But the strategy here is not to win skirmishes. You could fight and win a hundred skirmishes in the melee, only to lose the last one. The idea, Aidan, is to survive. The more you stay out of the way, the better off you are. You only have to fight the last battle and win it. Of course it would be difficult to go through the whole melee without having to fight some battles. You will have to make your judgments on the spot. In the beginning, go after the fights you can easily win. Use instinct, not calculation.''

Aidan surveyed the field of candidates as he listened to the House Leader's final briefing. The briefing was shorter than in the Trial of Bloodright contests, and the terseness was insulting.

More than a hundred warriors were gathered around the rim of the enormous Circle of Equals where the melee would take place. The Circle was used so that no candidate could hide out somewhere, resting up so that he would be fresh when he reentered the fray at a later stage.

Except for the heaviest of BattleMechs, which were not allowed in a Grand Melee, it looked as though every other kind of existing 'Mech available was represented among this field of candidates. Some of the 'Mechs were highly polished, while others showed numerous burn and chip marks, as if their pilots were boasting about their many hard-fought battles.

The House Pryde Leader, a thin young woman named Risa Pryde, ended her instructions. "Anyone who retreats back across the Circle of Equals line is automatically defeated. If you fall and land on the 'Mech's back, you are considered a 'kill.' If you land on the 'Mech's lower front torso, you may return to the melee. At the first cannon blast, you will all run into the Circle, proceeding to any position you choose. At the second cannon blast, the melee begins. May the spirit of Nicholas Kerensky guide you all.''

Aidan rested his hands on his controls and did not have long to wait for the signal. While others rushed into the circle, he merely strolled. Looking down at his secondary screen, which now displayed the moving BattleMechs, he saw that such sensors would be useless, at least for a while. With so many figures dodging around the terrain, it would be too difficult keeping track of them all. As Marthe had advised, he would conserve ammo by letting the others dispose of one another.

The second cannon blast came. To those observing, the enormous Circle of Equals seemed to erupt into chaos.

Aidan, in the middle of it, found it surprisingly easy to stroll past those in combat and travel a maze in which he was rarely bothered by another combatant. Clan warriors tended to be aggressive, which allowed the strategically unaggressive to amble, as Aidan was doing, through fierce conflict without much trouble. Any fighting he did do was desultory and brief. He was able to dispatch three 'Mechs with minimum expenditure of ammunition. It looked as though Marthe was right in her estimation that many of the combatants were not necessarily of the highest order of warrior.

Soon, as Marthe had also predicted, the Circle was littered with defeated 'Mechs, some of them standing pilotless, some of them metal ''corpses'' on the ground.

The ranks of contestants were thinning, and Aidan had not yet found Nielo or seen a single *Viper*. The only thing he saw was the continuing clamor. In his secret library was a book describing an old Terran myth called Hell. In Hell, sinners were placed in rings of punishment. Their movements were desperate and futile. The pandemonium of the Grand Melee made

Aidan think this Circle was like some warrior's ring of Hell.

In the end, it was Nielo who found Aidan. He landed in front of Aidan, having just performed a spectacular jump of several hundred meters from the edge of the Circle to where Aidan's *Summoner* was involved in his first really difficult engagement. An *Adder* had blind-sided his 'Mech, using its small pulse laser to chop away some torso armor.

Aidan did not know what was in the *Adder* pilot's mind. The 'Mech was only half the tonnage of his *Summoner*, and its firepower was pathetic, but it came at him with its ER PPC's firing. He stopped it short with a burst from his LB 10-X and would have finished it off if the *Viper* had not landed between them. With one kick, the *Viper* knocked the *Adder* over and turned toward the *Summoner*. Though *Aidan* was happy to see the bothersome *Adder* gone, he did not like to see it eliminated so perfunctorily, so insultingly.

Nielo had apparently also conserved his weapons, for he began to fire his medium pulse lasers at Aidan's *Summoner* even before the *Adder* had hit the ground. Aidan felt the impact of what the grid version of his 'Mech on the secondary screen showed as a long gash through the upper torso. He responded with some PPC bursts that came dangerously close to the *Viper*'s cockpit and made Nielo twist his 'Mech's torso side-ways, almost as a reflex action.

Aidan saw that the worst tactic at this moment would be to stand in place and trade fire with Nielo. He needed some distance from him, which he would create by engaging his jump jets and leaping. He quickly calculated that Nielo—whose 'Mech had a jump capacity at least a third greater than the *Summoner*'s—would quickly follow. And that, if Aidan responded rapidly enough, might be Nielo's downfall.

Locating his destination point as just inside the Circle to the rear of Nielo and his *Viper*, a place free of fighting, he initiated the jump. The *Summoner* lifted over the *Viper* in a low arc, so that Aidan could get off an intense barrage from his LB 10-X. Coming from above and at an angle, the barrage did little damage, but it prevented Nielo from turning his 'Mech and jumping to pursue. As Aidan landed, he prepared himself for Nielo's arrival.

The other warrior's response was too predictable. He copied Aidan's low-level arc, coming at him like a missile. The time he had bought worked in Aidan's favor. He had calculated that he needed to get the *Viper* with an SRM round before it could land. Zeroing in on the incoming BattleMech, Aidan fired before his opponent could reach the zenith of his 'Mech's low arc. As he had hoped, the missiles hit the *Viper* high. It seemed to founder in mid-air, then waver, then seemed to slide back before falling. Beneath it a *Kit Fox* was firing off missiles at an *Ice Ferret,* and the *Viper* fell into the line of fire. There was an explosion at cockpit level, and Aidan knew that Nielo, as well as his 'Mech, was finished. He had not wanted to kill a warrior whose fame had preceded him. Angry, he waded into the *Kit Fox* 's battle and demolished the 'Mech with a fierce fusillade. After it fell, Aidan also destroyed its *Ice Ferret* foe.

Checking his secondary screen, he saw that his ammo was getting dangerously low, although he still had missiles left.

But his blood was stirred now, and Aidan was ready to take on the rest of the field.

The only catch was that no one was left. Aidan was standing alone near the edge of the Circle of Equals, seeing damaged and destroyed BattleMechs scattered all around the wide area.

He had won, but Aidan did not understand his reaction. Why did he feel no sense of exhilaration?

31

At each ceremony preceding the succeeding contests in the Trial of Bloodright, Aidan could not mistake the hostility of the warriors competing against him. None spoke to him, though some muttered or growled insults under their breath. There was one muscular warrior who looked too big to fit into a normal 'Mech cockpit. His name was Megasa, and he was a Star Commander. The only time he spoke to Aidan, he said, "I hope to draw you somewhere in the competition. If so, I will end your life so that you can no longer stain the glory of Clan Jade Falcon." He walked away without waiting for a response, his thick legs giving him a rather comical gait, as if he had to make a special effort to keep one thigh from scraping away layers of skin from the other.

He asked Marthe about Megasa, but she seemed reluctant to respond. "I judge him to be the most dangerous competitor in this entire Trial of Bloodright. As far as the draw goes, he is in the other half from you. You can only meet him in the final battle. Let us hope some misfortune falls him before that time."

"On the contrary," Aidan said, "I hope to meet him."

Marthe smiled, reminding him of the way she was when they were young together in the sibko. He liked it.

"The more I see of you," she said, "the more I think you *should* win this Bloodname. Pryde would be an apt name for you. I do not exaggerate when I say you are the most prideful individual I have known.''

He shrugged. "Perhaps. But my desire to meet Megasa is more than that. If I defeat him, it will remove the taint these warriors believe I would lay on the Bloodname. Anyone else, and they will believe it is merely a matter of fortune, and not my skill. Or even the workings of fate.''

"Fate? You have beliefs about fate? That is not like you.''

"Not fate in the conventional sense. But sometimes I think there is a kind of fate that is guiding me, maybe all of us.''

"A kind of guidance system operating humans?''

"You might say that.''

"No, I would not say that. It sounds like nonsense to me. *And* we have tomorrow to discuss. Your opponent will be? Say the name, Aidan.''

"His name is Lopar, and he is a skilled BattleMech pilot.''

"Not just skilled. He is so good that at times he seems to be of a piece with his 'Mech, as though they constructed him to sit in its cockpit back at the factory. You could beat him in a head-to-head confrontation, but why bother? You want to make him, and any other opponent, fight you away from their natural element.''

As Marthe continued her briefing, Horse came into the small, bare room. While Marthe and Aidan conferred, he sat watching in one of the two remaining chairs. Across the way sat Joanna, nodding in agreement at several pieces of the advice Marthe gave. She had seemed to shudder when Horse walked into the room.

When Marthe was done, she left and Joanna took up Aidan's preparation by testing his physical responses. She tossed him a ball that he had to catch in one hand. He was quick, the ball invariably slapping into his palm. They also performed an intricate exercise with sticks, passing them back and forth in a pre-arranged but arhythmic order.

At a pause in the exercise, Horse caught Aidan's gaze. "Is it worth it, all this?" he asked. "You definitely need one of these stupid Bloodnames?"

"Yes, Horse, getting a Bloodname is worth it. It is the only way one can hope to have his genes selected for the gene pool."

"The gene pool, the Bloodname, they're just some jewelry to wear. You have already proven yourself as a warrior."

"Shut up, free—" A glance from Aidan told Joanna not to use the ugly word, so she finished it with,"—born. You are a member of Aidan's entourage. You have no right to belittle the Trial of Bloodright. It is an honorable tradition. You are jealous because you cannot participate in it."

Horse shook his head. "Not at all. Even if I were a trueborn, I would not want a Bloodname."

Joanna laughed abruptly. It was her cruel laugh, one that once had struck terror in the hearts and minds of cadets. "You are incompletely named, Horse. They should call you Horse's Tail. If you were trueborn, indeed! You can never know what it means to be trueborn, never know what it means to have a Bloodname, never—"

"And why have you not yet won a Bloodname? Aren't you good enough?"

It was lucky for Horse that Aidan stood between him and Joanna. From the way she started to come at Horse, even a skilled warrior like Horse would have been pushed back through the wall. Aidan stopped her before that could happen.

"You are my advisors, you two," he said. "I need your help, not your squabbling."

"You should get rid of that one, Aidan," Joanna growled. "The kind of advice he gives would put you in your grave."

"Not so, Joanna," Aidan said. "I need to see both sides of the matter. How can I respond instinctively if I am not a realist about everything?"

"I fail to see how his mutterings can assist you in any way. They denigrate the ideal of the Bloodname."

"And that is why Horse is helpful. His point of view lets me keep that ideal in perspective."

"I have no idea what you mean."

"I want this Bloodname so deeply, so thoroughly, that the perspective shows me its worth."

"Well, when it comes to competing for a Bloodname, remember that I have preceded you. I can say that no amount of philosophy ever drew an ounce of an opponent's blood."

Aidan knew how bitter Joanna was that she had not yet succeeded in winning a Bloodname in her house line, but Marthe returned to save him from further discussion.

At the odd look on her face, Aidan asked what was the matter.

Marthe did not answer immediately, as if trying to decide whether to reveal her thoughts. "An oath is being taken among all the competitors for the Bloodname," she said finally.

"I have heard of no such oath."

"That is because it concerns you. The oath condemns your participation in this Trial of Bloodright. Megasa is the one who started it. From what I have heard, the oath states that your opponents will try to kill you rather than just attempt to defeat you. Every competitor has taken the vow."

Aidan merely nodded, his lips pressed tightly together.

"Does this not concern you?" Marthe asked.

"Of course it does. But it comes as no great surprise. It is odd to be so hated, but I will find a way to use this. Anything can be used to advantage in combat."

"Withdraw, Aidan," Horse said quietly.

"No, he cannot," Joanna insisted.

"And I will not," Aidan said. "I failed in my first Trial here on Ironhold. If I fail again, at this Bloodright Trial, then I prefer to die."

A wave of sadness suddenly overcame Marthe. It might even have flickered briefly in her eyes, but the next moment she had her emotions once more totally under control. No one else in the room seemed to have noticed the lapse.

32

The Bloodright coin gave Aidan confidence. Something about the emblem of a jade falcon in flight on one side reminded him of the peregrine that he had raised and hunted with in his boyhood. He had named the peregrine Warhawk, after a mythological falcon in a story that sibparent Glynn so often told and after the massive BattleMech of the same name.

He could not recall precisely the falcon story Glynn had told with her typical dramatic flourishes. He mainly remembered that it ended with the falcon facing another of its kind high in the sky above a mountain peak. The Warhawk of the story had swooped down in a magnificent dive and managed to bite off the other falcon's head in mid-air. Thinking of it now, Aidan thought of how exaggerated were that tale and all the other ones with which Glynn had regaled the children of the sibko. But the stories had excited their imaginations and, as a result, had shaped their lives and values. Had Aidan not heard Glynn's story of Warhawk, he might never have wished to raise his own bird. Nor might he have felt such a fierce need to pursue his own destiny to this moment. It had all led up to this, where he stood fingering a coin showing a falcon like Warhawk as he awaited his chance to win the Bloodname he craved with every fiber of his being.

Although not always in agreement with Joanna, Aidan knew she was right in the argument with Horse about Bloodnames the night before. Being a warrior nourished his life, but winning the Bloodname would nourish his soul. The argument was moot now that the ritual prelude to the contest was about to begin. Joanna and Horse stood beside him as the three of them awaited the summoning by the House Leader.

Aidan wondered if Lopar, his slim opponent standing across the way, was experiencing the same excitement. If so, not a trace of it showed on his face, which displayed only hatred. The glare he gave Aidan was more than just the typical warrior pose, the ritual body language meant to intimidate an opponent. No, this was the real thing, hatred deep and pure.

So you hate, do you, Lopar? Aidan thought. Would you be surprised to know that I do not hate you in return? I would not waste it on a fool like you. Hate me well, then. It will bring you down, for I will be sure to find a way to exploit it.

Risa Pryde stood in the center of the vast chamber where the Bloodright ceremonies took place. She had already orchestrated the ritual for most of the thirty other combatants. Aidan and Lopar were next to last.

Watching the others, Aidan felt a thrill. Since his days in the sibko, he had dreamed of standing in just such a hall, awaiting the chance to win a Bloodname. He had never imagined it would happen like this, under such adverse circumstances, but how could he ever have foreseen that he would live posing as a freebirth, go through a Trial of Refusal to vindicate his trueborn status, and then enter the Bloodname contest with every one of his opponents having taken a secret vow to kill rather than merely defeat him? Even now, the other warriors in the Trial often glanced his way, their expressions ranging from distaste to disgust to utter gall. Well, he thought, I will as eagerly destroy any of you that I meet on any field, so we are even.

Finally Aidan and Lopar were summoned to the central dais, where stood Risa Pryde, surrounded by other members of House Pryde. Before withdrawing, Joanna and Horse each touched him briefly on the shoulder. Aidan walked briskly to the dais, remembering that Joanna had instructed him to show no hesitation at any point in the ceremony, no matter what happened. Marthe was near the end of one row of seated Pryde warriors, but she carefully avoided looking at him directly. None of the other Bloodnamed Prydes knew of her support for him, for Marthe believed she could do more by keeping her activities clandestine.

Risa Pryde wore the ceremonial robe of the Jade Falcon Clan, a striking cloak woven from brilliantly colored feathers. Before the melee she had seemed diminutive, but in full regalia, with the massive cloak sweeping down her back, she seemed taller, more impressive.

Nodding to the two contestants, she announced that she would be the Oathmaster and would represent House Pryde. "Do you concur in this, warriors?"

"Seyla," replied both Aidan and Lopar.

"What happens here, warriors, will bind us all until we shall fall." The words of the ceremony were similar in all the Clans, and Risa Pryde uttered them with deep feeling. Spreading her arms out, she said, "You represent the best of House Pryde and have so proven."

At this, many of the assembled warriors muttered among themselves, despite the rule forbidding anyone but the Oathmaster and the warrior contestants from making a sound. Aidan knew that it was the ritual reference to his being among the best of House Pryde that made them break the ritual silence.

Risa Pryde finished the introductory portion of the ceremony, explaining that the warriors would battle for the right and honor to claim the name of Pryde. Then she turned to Lopar. "You are Lopar and are twenty-five years old. Tell us why you are worthy to fight for the Bloodname of Pryde."

Lopar said proudly that he had earned his nomination by another Pryde warrior through his courage and heroism in several conflicts, including a defense of the Jade Falcon settlement on York in a territorial dispute.

Risa Pryde then turned to Aidan and asked him to verify his worthiness. The muttering began again, but the House Leader silenced the complaining warriors with a hard stare.

"I am not nominated, but come here as the winner over more than a hundred combatants in the Grand Melee. As a warrior of the Jade Falcon Clan, I have served well in several assignments. In the Glory Station battle defending the spawn of Kael Pershaw against predation by Clan Wolf, I turned the tide of battle. Against significant odds, I invaded the Clan Wolf camp and destroyed its communications center, thus effectively ending the conflict."

In coaching him for this speech, Joanna had insisted that Aidan not mention his masquerade as a freeborn, nor—as warriors frequently did—any of his achievements in the sibko.

A flash of consternation briefly lit Risa Pryde's eyes, as if she too felt shame at Aidan's participation in the Trial of Bloodright. But she completed the rest of her speech, which praised the qualifications of the two candidates, then asked them to present the coins that were the tokens of their legitimate right to compete. Aidan noted that she stumbled a bit over the word *legitimate*, but at least no further grumbles of protest came from the audience. A conelike device rose from the floor of the dais. It was called a gravity funnel, and was used to decide which warrior chose the weapons and which chose the venue.

The Oathmaster demanded a look at the coins, which she examined briefly to verify that the back of each was inscribed with the correct name.

Holding up both coins, she then announced, "These coins will pursue one another in the Well of Decision. This randomness imitates the conditions of battle, which no warrior can control. A worthy warrior must rise above the difficulties and defeat even superior enemies, overcome even apparently overwhelming obstacles. The Trial of Bloodright reflects this chaos of war. One of the bearers of these two coins will emerge as the hunter, who chooses the style of combat. The other will then decide the venue. You both understand this well?"

"Seyla," the two warriors affirmed.

The Oathmaster set each coin in a separate slot of the Well of Decision, a kind of gravity funnel, then pressed a button that sent them tumbling down into the funnel. Although the container was transparent, so rapidly did the coins whirl that it became impossible to distinguish one from the other.

To Aidan, the wait to see which coin would emerge first from the funnel's lower cylinder seemed endless. He and Joanna had decided that winning the role of hunter, and thus the choice of how the two would fight, was the outcome to be desired. Because Lopar was reputed to be a fine 'Mech pilot, Joanna thought it logical to choose some other style of fighting. Aidan had protested that he would rather fight in the style to which the other warrior was accustomed. He wanted no taint on any of his victories, he said. But Joanna was adamant, and Aidan finally gave in. Now, however, Aidan was not so sure. Looking across at the fierce-faced Lopar, he decided that, if luck deemed him the hunter, he would choose BattleMechs and beat Lopar at his own game.

When finally one coin emerged, then the other, the Oathmaster took care to remove them in correct order, the hunter coin in her right hand, the venue coin in her left.

"The hunter is Lopar," she said, holding out her hands, "and Aidan will choose the venue." It really did not matter one way or the other, Aidan thought, because he was sure Lopar would choose the same style. Perhaps the choice of venue was going to turn out to be the advantage. Then Lopar astonished Aidan and everybody else in the room.

"The hunter does not choose to permit this upstart to die honorably in a BattleMech. I will fight him in hand-to-hand combat. The only weapon will be a hunting knife. Minimal clothing. Victory will go to he who survives the combat with his life."

Death hunts were rare in the Jade Falcon Clan, but the rules of the Trial of Bloodright did sanction them. Many in the hall, their hatred still directed so forcefully at Aidan, seemed to approve of Lopar's scornful choice.

I had thought that I could exploit your hatred, Aidan thought, but now, Lopar, it will exploit you.

"So it is," said the Oathmaster, who then turned to Aidan. "What is your choice of venue? Where will you be hunted, Star Commander Aidan?"

"In Trial Field B, in the forest leading to the Trial of Position site. Tonight at midnight."

Some of the assembled warriors were obviously mystified. They could not know that the forest was where Aidan had slain a quintet of freeborn ambushers on the way to his first Trial of Position, which he was now so famous for having failed.

That was exactly why the forest was exactly the right place for Aidan to begin his formal quest for the great honor of a Bloodname. It was the place most fitting, for was this not where it had all begun? And should he fail, Joanna would see to it that this forest would become his body's final home.

33

Night noises surrounded him. Though another warrior might have found the sounds eerie or disturbing, to Aidan they were comforting. After Glory Station, what could be worse? Here at least were no strange lizards, no tree pumas. This forest was familiar to him, parts of it engraved in his memory from his two previous experiences in the place. The first time had been during his trueborn cadet training, when he had slain the four freeborns here. The second had been as a freeborn, when he had, ironically, saved some members of his unit from being killed.

From her investigation of the records, Marthe had learned that Lopar's scores in hand-to-hand combat drills were excellent, but Aidan had also scored high. Their scores, Marthe told him, were nearly identical.

"You start even," she had said. "Though your familiarity with the terrain might give you an edge."

"Not really," he told her. "If he is adept at hand-to-hand, the terrain will make no difference. If I have an advantage, it might be my general knowledge of Ironhold. For one thing, the forest will be impenetrably dark tonight because there will be no moon. I am used to the dark, and I like it. My experiences on Glory will also serve me in good stead. The Glory Station swamp and jungle may be the worst and deepest on any of the Clan worlds, and I certainly navigated them often enough. Nothing in any of Lopar's past assignments can match that."

But now all speculation was behind him. He felt for

the knife, which was sheathed in his belt. For clothing, he had chosen trousers and a shirt that were almost skin-tight, on the theory that the cloth would not rustle and give him away as he moved through the woods. On his feet were the softest leather sandals.

The night was pitch-black, and Aidan wished that Lopar had had the foresight to include IR goggles in the equipment specified for the battle. The dark was so complete that anyone moving about in this forest would inevitably run into unseen obstacles.

Perched on a low branch, listening for any sound that would reveal Lopar's location, Aidan had remained in place for a long while. When he heard no noise likely to have a human source, he began to wonder if Lopar might be doing the same thing—sitting still somewhere, waiting to catch Aidan if he should make some telltale sound.

How long could one of these Bloodright battles go on? If he and Lopar sat waiting like this at opposite ends of the forest, would some official eventually step in and judge both of them losers, allowing the warrior next in line to draw a bye?

No, that could not happen. The terms set forth by the hunter must hold. Lopar had not specified a time limit, but he had stated that the match was to the death. They could hold up the whole Trial of Bloodright by doing nothing the whole night long, but daylight must come eventually. The waiting game would end then. Aidan would also lose his best advantage, for his knowledge of the terrain meant even less in the light.

Trying to move as soundlessly as possible, he edged off the branch and jumped down into some soft grass, certain he had made no significant noise. He stayed near the tree, leaning against it momentarily as he listened, trying to distinguish among the cries, screams, whistles, shrieks, and other voices of the forest. He recognized the sad trill of the small but efficient bird of prey that was the Ironhold version of the nighthawk. He also made out other animal types moving through the forest, sometimes slowly, sometimes skittishly.

Nothing he heard sounded remotely like a Clan warrior on the prowl.

Aidan took a tentative step forward into a darkness so heavy it almost had weight. Though his eyes had adjusted to it by now, he still could not see his feet. Sometimes other dark shapes seemed to emerge from the blackness of the night, but he could not be sure which were trees and which were not. Most of the curving shapes hanging down were probably branches, but Ironhold had its share of poisonous snakes, some of which inhabited this forest.

He continued to edge forward cautiously, setting his feet down carefully with each step, hoping that if he contacted anything but the ground it would be harmless. After going only a short way, his outstretched hand touched a tree from which moisture dripped heavily. Or at least he thought it was moisture at first. Tasting it, Aidan knew it was neither water, nor dew, nor any kind of tree sap. It was blood. Reaching up with his hand, he fumbled against something warm and soft. His touch dislodged it, and it crashed to the ground with a loud thud. Again, touch and smell told him that the object was—or had been—some manner of forest animal, but he could not identify it in the dark.

From some distance away, he heard Lopar's exultant shout. "Now I know where you are, freebirth!"

Even with the insult, Aidan had the good sense to keep his own mouth shut. And I have a good idea where *you* are, he gloated silently.

Kael Pershaw was observing the battle on a monitor that viewed the forest through a thermal imager. The imager distorted some of the flora and fauna, but it made following the movements of Aidan and Lopar fairly easy.

Lopar's first actions had puzzled him mightily. The warrior seemed skilled at moving with stealth, yet he did not seem to be stalking Aidan. Instead, he tracked four different animals, killing each one by efficiently slitting its throat. Then he arranged their bodies precariously on low-hanging branches. It was not till much later when Aidan dislodged one of the dead forms that Pershaw understood Lopar's scheme. The warrior had no guarantee that Aidan would get under any particular branch, but it was only one of several traps the clever Lopar had set. Besides hunting and killing the animals, Lopar had also spent his first hours in the forest sharpening stakes and setting them into the ground. Then he located vines by touch, tying them between trees so that each vine ran at what was probably calculated to be at Aidan's neck level. During the several hours Lopar spent setting his traps, he seemed unconcerned about running into Aidan. Nor had he any need to worry, for Aidan had simply stayed in place the whole time.

Pershaw had requested permission to observe the Bloodname contest so that he could track Aidan's progress. Perhaps it would help him resolve his questions about the young man. When he had believed Aidan to be a freeborn, the warrior's rebellious ways had seemed part of his inferior nature. But ever since discovering that Aidan was actually a true, Pershaw had become confused about how to react to the young man. Then, when Lenore Shi-Lu had questioned Aidan's rights to be a warrior because he had failed his first Trial, Pershaw began to reconsider his own views. Considering the obstacles Aidan had encountered, his achievements had been extraordinary. And no matter the caste to which he had belonged, he had fought well and bravely.

But all that would mean nothing if Aidan did not work out Lopar's strategy. Otherwise he would be dead soon enough.

Aidan got away from the tree as fast as he could, heedless of whether Lopar could hear him running. Was that a breeze in the trees above him or was it Lopar up there, laughing? Suddenly he collided with one of the vines Lopar had stretched between two trees. Because Aidan had just taken a leap upward to avoid the dark shape of what might have been either a bush or a boar, the vine caught him at shoulder level instead of snapping across his neck. Ducking under the vine, he stumbled forward and fell. Though he scrambled quickly to his feet, he was disoriented.

Lopar had obviously done some survival training. So had Aidan, once. He struggled to remember anything at all he could use. He also cursed himself for having been too complacent. By lying in wait, he had given Lopar plenty of time to set his snares. Aidan had confidently assumed that the forest was his terrain, but Lopar had quickly adapted to it. Whatever advantage Aidan might have had, it was lost now. He was truly the hunted.

Somehow he had to turn that around.

Feeling ahead of him in the darkness, he went slower now, stepping cautiously. Discovering another of the vines stretched between trees, he cut it with his knife, then rolled it up loosely and slung it over his shoulder. A bit further on, he tripped on something and very nearly came down onto one of the sharpened stakes. Ripping it from the ground, he examined it by touch. Lopar's knife strokes had been smooth and even, for the wood came to a symmetrical point. He rammed the stake into his belt.

More alert now, Aidan was also using his sense of smell, which detected another of the slain animals. Carefully testing the branches of the tree in which it lay, he found that the body had been lodged between two branches. It was still warm, which meant the beast had not died long before. Pressing his back against the tree bark, Aidan listened for any sound that might be Lopar.

He heard nothing.

Leaving the stake at the base of the tree in order to find it again easily, he climbed stealthily up the tree, finding himself a place next to the animal. Feeling along the animal's fur, he located the spot where its heart would be. After cutting into the beast's hide, he felt for the heart through the ribs, then used the hunting knife to cut the organ away from its moorings. Working the heart out slowly and carefully, he finally lifted it from the rib cage. It was a small heart, a compact and strong muscle. Aidan held it close to his face and briefly touched its surface with his tongue. Its taste was somewhat salty, together with a sour flavor he could not identify. The blood smell was strong upon it.

Taking the looped vine off his shoulder, he placed it delicately on the animal, then put the heart carefully inside the loop so he could remove his shirt. He cut off a piece of the vine and used it to help fashion his shirt into a sack. With another section of vine, he made a kind of belt that he tied around the waistband of his trousers. After gently placing the animal heart into the improvised sack, he attached the whole thing to his belt. The rest of the vine he let drop soundlessly to the forest floor.

Then he crouched in the tree and yelled, "Lopar, I tire of these games. Are you a warrior or a coward who slinks around a forest leaving child-traps for his opponent? You called for combat that was hand-to-hand. Let us settle this matter once and for all."

He was counting on Lopar's being vexed at being called a coward. After shouting a few more insults to make sure Lopar was aware of his location, Aidan climbed quickly to a higher branch. The sack made the climb difficult, but not impossible. The thought crossed his mind that what he hoped to do to Lopar was poetry. Not the kind he sometimes read in his secret library, but a crude and cruel kind, a match for the kind of warrior Lopar was.

Finally Aidan heard a sound that was not one of the normal forest noises. It was the first time he had detected Lopar. Perhaps angered by the taunts, Lopar had become careless. The sound of his arrival was faint, the soft crunch of a shoed foot crushing vegetation.

Aidan took the sack from its improvised resting place and held it out in front of him. Lopar was now under the tree, he was sure of it. Taking the sack in one hand, he began to swing it slowly back and forth, increasing its arc slightly with each swing. When he had it swinging quickly, Aidan flung the sack away. When it landed a few steps away from the tree, it sounded, as he had hoped, much like the movement of a human foot through the brush. The weight of the heart plus the cloth brushing against the ground vegetation made a convincing rustling sound.

He sensed Lopar springing toward the noise. Guessing at his opponent's progress, Aidan leaped from the high branch, away from the tree, his legs out. His quick mental calculations paid off. He came down on top of Lopar, his right foot kicking the head of his foe, his left the shoulder.

Both warriors went down, and for a moment there was a confused struggle in the dark. Lopar ripped out with his hunting knife and delivered a glancing blow to Aidan's arm, making a shallow cut. Aidan, who had deliberately left his own knife in its belt sheath, concentrated on using his free hand to subdue Lopar. Managing to get both hands on the man's knife arm, he pushed it away. Maintaining his hold on the arm, Aidan shoved it against a nearby tree.

Still gripping the knife tightly, Lopar reached up with his other hand to grab a clump of Aidan's hair, which he pulled roughly. The pain brought tears to Aidan's eyes, but he did not let go his grip on Lopar's arm. After ramming the arm against the tree bark again, he felt something land at his feet. It had to be the knife. Releasing Lopar's arm, he broke the man's hold of his hair by jabbing upward with his closed-fingered hand into the side of his foe's arm. When he dug the fingers into Lopar's arm, it was with enough force to draw blood and make the warrior let go of his hair.

Though both warriors were skilled in martial arts, the training was useless in the pitch dark of a forest where one could not aim at his target. Aidan had reduced the fight to the level of a brawl, which, as a former freeborn warrior, he knew something about.

From what Aidan could hear and sense, Lopar was scrabbling around on the ground looking for his knife.

"Take your time, Lopar," he said. "I will let you

find it. I would not kill you while you are weapon-less.''

That stopped Lopar. ''What kind of freebirth scum are you? You do not even fight like a trueborn warrior. Weapon or no weapon, I would kill you immediately.''

''I know that. I have reasons to want this battle judged on the merits of its participants and not on our luck. Get your knife.''

Aidan drew his knife and held it loosely in front of him. Moving sideways, he felt around with his foot in the area where he thought the sack containing the animal heart might have fallen. He found it easily, mentally noting its location.

Lopar stopped his fumbling around, and Aidan knew he had retrieved the knife. This would be interesting, he thought. With no light and only their vague dark shapes to go by, they would have to guess at each other's next moves. It would be more like animal instinct. An animal did not need to calculate, did not need to speculate on its enemy's tactics. It just attacked, clawed, bit, crushed. If it could have held a knife in its paws, it would not parry and thrust, it would shove the blade forward as many times as necessary. It would not worry about the other animal's knife.

''Are you ready, freebirth?''

''I am not a freeborn.''

''Go ahead and prove it.''

''I will.''

Lopar lunged, but Aidan was ready for him. Like an animal, he moved to his left, then thrust the knife out in front of him. It made contact with something, with some part of Lopar's body. The man groaned. As Lopar slid past, Aidan struck again, this time connecting in what was obviously a glancing blow.

He moved away, toward where he had detected the sack. The dark form that was Lopar did not stop to reset himself, but instead turned and sprang, knife blade forward. It hit Aidan in the shoulder, but he reacted quickly. He moved backward with the thrust of the knife, and the blade did not enter deeply. His own knife-swing at Lopar was also ineffective, except that it made Lopar veer away.

Reaching down, Aidan picked up the sack. He felt by its weight that it still contained the animal heart. Good. As Lopar's dark form came toward him again, Aidan swung the sack at what he thought was the man's head. It landed firmly against the side of Lopar's skull, knocking him off his feet. As the other warrior fell, Aidan tried to stab him in the area he guessed to be the stomach. But even as Lopar was slipping to the ground, he managed unexpectedly to seize Aidan's knife arm. He gave the arm a savage twist, and the knife flew out of Aidan's hand. It bounced off the side of a nearby tree, vanishing forever into the darkness. He knew Lopar would not grant him the same privilege of searching for his weapon.

Aidan tried to back away from Lopar, who was now on the ground, but his opponent grabbed his ankles and pulled them forward. His feet flying out from under him, Aidan fell onto his back. For the first time, he cursed the dark setting he had chosen. Just when he needed to know precisely where Lopar was, he could not see a damn thing.

From the noises just beyond his feet, which Lopar had now released, Aidan surmised that his adversary was struggling to stand up. He rolled sideways and felt Lopar land on the ground beside him in a miscalculated move. Lopar's error gave Aidan a chance to get halfway up and swing the sack again. It made ineffectual contact, but from the sound of Lopar letting his breath out, Aidan guessed that it had grazed the man's face.

He knew there was no point staying in this position and trading blows with Lopar, especially when his blows were from a wet sack, while Lopar's were made with the knife Aidan's generosity had permitted him. As Aidan made one last glancing blow with the sack, he felt it come apart, letting the heart fall to the ground. The only good thing about the maneuver was that it gave him time to get to his feet and scramble to the tree with the dead animal caught in its branches.

Sensing Lopar coming up behind him, Aidan felt around for the stake and vine he had left there. He found the vine first. Turning quickly, he whipped it out at Lopar. It flicked across the other man's face, making him yelp with pain, temporarily stopping him in his tracks. Feeling around some more, Aidan found the sharpened stake leaning against the tree where he had left it. Grabbing the shaft, he wielded it like a long knife, directing it at the center of the dark form leaping toward him.

The force of his thrust with the stick was enough. The point, so carefully honed by its victim, penetrated Lopar's midsection, drawing a groan that momentarily drowned out the myriad noises of the forest. Aidan got out of the way, and Lopar fell against the tree trunk. Hearing his foe choke, Aidan sensed that he was coughing up blood. The stickiness on Aidan's bare arm was probably blood from the wound itself.

With Lopar so close to him, Aidan knew he could not relax for an instant, even though every nerve in his body felt strained to the limit. His enemy still had his knife.

As he expected, Lopar weakly jabbed the knife at him, but Aidan merely twisted the man's wrist, then heard the knife fall.

"Lopar, you asked for a fight to the death."

"That is true."

"I do not wish to kill you, and your wound may not be mortal."

"That is also true, freebirth."

"Admit I am not a freeborn."

"Never."

"You may ask the judges to release you from the hunter requirements of a fight to the death."

"Never."

"Well, then, I must kill you, even though it is not my wish."

Taking the vine in both hands, Aidan wrapped it around Lopar's neck and squeezed it tightly until Lopar went limp. Then he did something that was as brutally primitive as it was insulting to his victim and

to all the other Jade Falcon warriors who had vowed to kill him. Retrieving the heart of the dead animal from the ground, Aidan took it and stuffed it into Lopar's mouth.

Carefully, almost reverently, he removed the dead animal from its place among the branches of the tree and dragged it away. At the edge of the forest, he buried it in a shallow grave, dug with Lopar's hunting knife.

=== 34 ===

Someone eavesdropping on the next strategy conference between Aidan and his entourage might have wondered if he had stumbled into one of the Bloodright contests instead. The group argued furiously and for some time, but in the end Aidan won his point.

"If I am to become a Bloodnamed warrior," he said, "I must do it my way. Caution may have gotten me through the Grand Melee, but it nearly finished me in the fight with Lopar. I appreciate all you have done for me, but we must plan aggressively if I am to finish this."

Though Marthe had been his most heated opponent, she finally capitulated the point. "It is true that you can only win with the abilities you have, Aidan. And your greatest may be tenacity."

When Aidan had gone, Marthe smiled at Joanna, who resisted the urge to return it. "You were right, Marthe," she said. "He needed to be pushed to find his own way. I admire your cleverness in accomplishing the goal."

Marthe laughed softly. "After the Trial of Refusal, I sensed that something had gone out of him. Call it the fighting spirit—for want of a better term. We had to help him recover it. And that we have done. Even Horse did his part."

"I merely followed your instructions, Star Captain."

Joanna was taken aback. "You mean this . . . this MechWarrior's insults were part of the plan, too?"

Marthe shrugged and Horse would say no more on the matter to Joanna.

On the parade ground, Megasa strode proudly past Aidan. He waited until he had actually gone by to say to a member of his entourage, loudly enough for Aidan to hear, "If I fight that one, it will be an easy battle. If he hides, I will find him by his stench. If he turns and fights, I will home the missiles in on his stink."

Aidan whirled angrily, but when he spoke, his voice was cool, detached. "Perhaps you wish to fight here and now, Megasa. Forget Bloodright, forget Bloodnames?"

Megasa laughed. "I have no wish to beat you so easily."

"You would not last long against me in hand-to-hand combat."

"Are you sure? You will find no big sticks or animal hearts on this parade ground."

"Then I will smother you. With my stench."

The joke relieved the tension, and Megasa's companions led him away. Aidan had longed to blast Megasa off a battlefield, but he would save it for the Trial combat. He would live to gloat over the fallen Megasa.

Kael Pershaw watched the next round of Bloodright battles from the command center, where elaborate holotank images of some of the individual contests were projected. He joined Joanna and the other members of Aidan's entourage, but took care to stand well away from MechWarrior Horse, whom he despised more than most freeborns. There was a continual flare of defiance in Horse's eyes that made trueborns particularly uncomfortable around him.

In the coin ceremony for the next contest, Aidan's coin had emerged second from the gravity funnel. As the hunter, he chose conventional BattleMechs. As venue, his adversary, a Star Captain named Jenna, had chosen a mountain range in the far north of Ironhold. At first the holotank mountains were small and the BattleMechs like the tiny toy versions with which sibko children play in their holotanks. As the two fighting machines tracked one another, however, each trying to find some terrain most favorable to his skills, the holo projections grew larger. In the vast area below the spectators, it was not long before they were viewing a pair of 'Mechs approximately one-third their normal size engaged in a hard-fought contest on rugged terrain.

At this point Jenna's strategy became obvious. Knowing that Aidan would be piloting a seventy-ton *Summoner,* she had chosen a lighter 'Mech, a fifty-five ton, jump-capable *Stormcrow* that she could use more effectively in mountainous terrain. Kael Pershaw was not sure, however, whether the *Stormcrow* would be successful in the long run. The ability to move about the mountain faster than the *Summoner* would, he thought, be enough to prolong the battle but not to win it. Still, he admired the audaciousness of the choice.

Aidan's aggressiveness would be a help rather than a hindrance in the fight with Star Captain Jenna. At one point, he could have remained in an easily defended cliffside, shooting at Jenna across a wide crevasse, the two of them exchanging LRM volleys that did about equal damage to their 'Mechs. Most other warriors would have taken that approach. What Aidan did was jump his *Summoner* from the cliff to a precarious icy perch above and off to one side of Jenna's *Stormcrow.* From here he fired his LRMs straight down, not so much at Jenna's 'Mech but at the junction between the cliff face and the ledge where she stood. As the LRM warheads battered the rock, the ground beneath the feet of Jenna's 'Mech began to show cracks. Aidan fired again. The *Stormcrow* seemed to sway with the ledge beneath it, then the cracks opened further and the ledge collapsed into the crevasse, taking with it both *Stormcrow* and its brave pilot.

The end came so suddenly that Kael Pershaw almost did not follow it. When the *Stormcrow* suddenly disappeared, he silently uttered words of praise for Aidan and words of regret for Star Captain Jenna.

"You have fought three major battles," Horse said, "the Grand Melee and the two first rounds of the Bloodright. All three of your opponents are dead. Is a Bloodname worth all this, well, *blood?*"

"You know it is, Horse."

Horse said nothing. He had never truly understood his friend.

Marthe saw that what might be termed the psychological advantage was shifting to Aidan's favor. In the next battle, his opponent, perceiving that Aidan had twice survived in unusual terrain, had chosen as venue one of the many Trial fields on Ironhold. Marthe leaned against a rail to watch the holo projection of the battle. She could not stand with the rest of Aidan's entourage without revealing her true role in Aidan's Bloodname quest. Joanna and Horse viewed the battle from a section of seats in the next tier up. Arms folded, Kael Pershaw stood on the same level as Marthe, but directly across from her.

Aidan's foe, a Star Commander Grayling, had come onto the field in a *Timber Wolf*, a 'Mech especially popular with Clan Wolf but uncommon among Jade Falcon warriors. With the double LRM-20 racks mounted on its shoulders, the *Timber Wolf* looked like a beast of burden, carrying heavy loads on bowed shoulders.

The two 'Mechs kept their distance at first, firing long-range missiles at one another in a way that suggested this battle might be a prolonged one. The missiles did considerable damage, distributed evenly between both sides. Armor lay spread around both 'Mechs.

Then the *Timber Wolf* started to close in on the *Summoner*. Lumbering forward, using its large lasers now, the 'Mech was sketching lines of damage across the surface of Aidan's 'Mech.

Aidan had studied Grayling's codex, however, and knew that the man almost invariably fought by the book. To counter the *Timber Wolf*'s plodding slowness, he started his 'Mech toward it, gradually breaking into a run straight at his foe. Then he fired off a volley of LRMs directly in front of him, letting the smoke and dust thrown off by the explosion envelop his 'Mech. Aidan was gambling that Grayling was concentrating on the visual spectrum display of the primary view screen. In the instant it would take for his opponent to track the *Summoner* on the secondary screen, Aidan maneuvered it to one side, suddenly emerging from the thinning cloud of smoke to come at the *Timber Wolf* from a different angle.

Without slowing down, Aidan came at the *Timber Wolf*, relentlessly unloading his entire supply of short-range missiles. According to the plan Aidan and his team had devised, the goal was to take out the LRM packs on each of the *Wolf*'s shoulders.

And the strategy worked. First one blew up, then the other, followed almost immediately by the *Timber Wolf* itself. The observers (including Aidan, viewing from his cockpit) were relieved to see Star Captain Grayling shoot out the 'Mech in his ejection seat just before the 'Mech exploded.

"That was lucky," Kael Pershaw said as he passed Joanna at the command center door. Joanna made no reply, but she definitely agreed.

Megasa had also reached round four, but he and Aidan were not scheduled to fight one another. Not yet.

Many warriors had gathered on the various tiers to view the combats involving Aidan and Megasa. Megasa, in his *Mad Dog,* quickly vanquished an opponent in an *Executioner.* Indeed, the fight was over so soon that he was able to come to the command center in time to watch Aidan's contest.

Aidan's coin had made him hunter, while his opponent chose as venue an island in the middle of a lake. Aidan was not so concerned how or where the contest would be fought. It was more that he was so exhausted from the previous contests that he wanted to polish this one off quickly. If he was going to fight in the final Bloodright battle, he wanted to be ready for it. Joanna supplied the strategy for an island battle, basing it on a fight in which she had participated several years before.

For this fight, Aidan's *Summoner* was configured entirely with long-range missiles, plus a narc beacon. Marthe wondered if it might not be wise to keep some of the other armament or at least add some medium lasers, but both Joanna and Aidan wanted to go for everything.

"What if he gets in close?"

"I will risk it," Aidan said.

"He will risk it," Joanna said.

"Yeah, risk," Horse coarsely agreed.

Aidan's foe, a MechWarrior named Machiko, would be in a *Hellbringer*. That would not affect Aidan's strategy, which had been devised to operate against whatever type 'Mech entered the field against him.

Joanna studied the terrain, which was relatively flat for an island. She decided that Machiko had chosen it to prevent Aidan from being able to carry out any elaborate maneuvers. If Aidan kept his distance, however, the strategy for this battle was viable.

As soon as he saw the signal to begin, Aidan executed a ground-skimming jump right at the *Hellbringer*. Machiko meanwhile took the opportunity to chip away at the *Summoner*'s armor with her medium laser and a PPC.

As soon as he was close enough, Aidan fired his narc missile beacon launcher at the *Hellbringer*. The specialized missile struck the other 'Mech and attached itself. His mission successful, Aidan jumped back to his original point near the shore of the island. He was conscious of the water lapping gently at his heels as he fired volley after volley at the *Hellbringer*, each missile homing in on the song that the narc beacon sang to it.

As Aidan had hoped, the battle was soon over. Machiko's *Hellbringer* was so shredded by the missiles that it was not long before it was rendered completely helpless.

Watching from the command center Megasa did not hide his disgust. When the miniature figure of Machiko ejected from her 'Mech, her form seemed to come close to him, and he leaned over the railing as though to catch the holographic projection in his hand.

"It is now up to me to remove this stench from our Clan," he said loudly as he turned to leave the command center.

"Do you believe Aidan can beat him?" Horse asked Joanna.

"In truth?"

"Yes."

"In truth, I did not think he would get this far."

Three days later, Aidan took a long time going to sleep after the prebattle briefing by his entourage. He lay in his bunk, endlessly fingering and moving the codex bracelet on his wrist. Wishing he could read the future in the past, he finally drifted off into a fitful sleep.

≡ 35 ≡

All the ritual words had been spoken by the Oath-master and the two participants. The coins had gone down the gravity funnel and come out again. Megasa was to be the hunter, meaning Aidan had choice of venue.

Awaiting Megasa's words, Aidan once again felt the sheer hatred emanating from the Jade Falcon warriors packed into the hall. How could so many despise him so? Inside, he was no different from the days before he had made his claim to seek a Bloodname, but sometimes he could not help but wonder if his fellow Jade Falcons might be justified in their enmity against him. Had he truly nullified his right to a Bloodname by accepting that second Trial and by posing as a free-born?

Fortunately for Aidan, these moments of self-doubt never lasted long. He was a Clan warrior, trueborn and deserving. If he had not proven that by getting this far in the Trial of Bloodright, what had he proven?

Megasa turned to face the audience. "I realize that it is unorthodox for me to speak now of any matter except my choices as hunter," he boomed in a voice that easily reached the last row of the assembly, "but there is an issue of importance to this final Bloodname contest that must be emphasized. Important not only for myself, but for all Clan Jade Falcon. This warrior has dishonored us, and I will not permit him to further tarnish the glory of our Clan."

The words drew a roar of approval from the crowd,

while they made Aidan wonder if the Oathmaster could not simply scrap all the ritual and let him and Megasa slug it out here and now.

"The Pryde Bloodname is an honorable one," Megasa boomed on. "Even when we have not yet won the right to bear the Pryde name, those of us who share the bloodline venerate our heritage. Generations of our Bloodnamed warriors have fought and often died gloriously in battle. They did not die so that our line could be tainted by a warrior who, in spite of his true birth, is more freeborn than true. On the planet Hector, several fine warriors in my Star were killed in a fierce battle with the Hell's Horses Clan. To avenge their death, we wiped out the entire Cluster to which those Hell's Horses warriors belonged. That is what it means to be a Jade Falcon warrior.

"Why else would the Bloodnames of our Clan be so widely respected? Why else would the other Clans so often attempt to seize the Jade Falcon gene legacies? It is because we, of all the Clans, produce the finest warriors. We cannot condone anything that brings us shame instead of esteem. Let us not allow this warrior to disgrace us any longer."

With a nod of his head, Megasa finished his speech and turned back to the Oathmaster. Even though public displays were forbidden during the Bloodright ritual, a clamorous cheer went up in the vast audience. Risa Pryde's hand immediately shot up to quiet it, but Megasa had made his point and the warriors of Clan Jade Falcon had seconded it. Aidan was the enemy. He must be defeated. For an instant, Aidan almost believed it himself.

But he had not come this far to be demoralized by a speech just as the final Bloodright battle was about to begin. Aidan vowed that he would impose the ultimate cruelty upon Megasa. Once he had defeated the other man, he would let Megasa live, cursing him with the shame of being bested by the very warrior he had condemned so savagely.

It was no surprise that Megasa, a famed BattleMech pilot, chose a battle between 'Mechs as the style of combat. He and the Oathmaster turned toward Aidan to hear his choice of venue.

Aidan struggled to keep his voice toneless, not wanting to further incite the audience. ''My choice of venue is Rhea.''

A mixed reaction had greeted those words. Some warriors showed their anger, while others were visibly impressed. Rhea was Ironhold's moon. Because the combatants would fight in one-sixth gravity, Marthe calculated that this factor would diminish Megasa's combat skills enough to bring Aidan as close to even as possible with this adept warrior. Though still the underdog, he would have a fighting chance.

At Risa Pryde's behest, the warriors were allowed an hour to acclimate to Rhea's gravity. Aidan knew that Megasa had some previous low-gravity combat experience, and he also knew that the other warrior's tech had reconfigured his *Mad Dog* to accommodate the moon's low gravity and lack of atmosphere.

Nomad had similarly readjusted the weapons and control systems of Aidan's *Summoner,* but he had done it by referring to instructions from manuals. Nomad had no experience in preparing 'Mechs for low-gravity operations.

That did not trouble Nomad, however. ''It should be like walking on pillows,'' he told Aidan. ''Or flying in a dream. Just remember that the conditions are not any more natural for your foe, and you will do well.''

''Strange advice from a tech, Nomad.''

''In service to Star Captain Joanna, I have learned to add psychology to my skills. Serving her is something like fighting in a severe environment. Just like the contest you face now.''

''You are not supposed to speak in such a way about your superior officer, especially in front of another officer.''

''Well, yes, but I am difficult to punish. Ask Star Captain Joanna.''

Nomad, whom Aidan had known since his cadet days, had grown old. Even more so since his injuries on Glory. Yet even though he held his arm at an odd angle to his body, his mechanical skills did not seem impaired when working on the *Summoner*.

When the hour of acclimation was nearly over, Aidan was finding the low-gravity conditions amenable, despite his unfamiliarity with them. He liked the light, easy way the *Summoner* could now move across the rugged terrain. He liked the fact that every jump felt almost like it might launch the 'Mech into space unless he held the maneuver down. He liked knowing that weapons fire would travel farther because less energy was lost resisting atmosphere. He liked the way the 'Mech sailed over the pits and gullies that dotted the moon's surface, even without the help of jump jets.

Risa Pryde, her voice sounding harsh over the commlink, announced that time was up. The contest would now begin.

Aidan was ready. Strapped into his command couch, he began marching his *Summoner* toward the horizon, knowing that Megasa was heading toward him from the other side.

When Megasa's *Mad Dog* came into sight, it was firing the large pulse lasers on both arms. The pulses came fast and true, several hitting before Aidan was able to get his *Summoner* into cover. Briefly he watched the pulses that missed him, speeding on their way to eventual dissipation but looking like they could go on forever.

Before Megasa could adjust his aim, Aidan went on the attack, firing off a rack of LRMs. Immediately he realized that his targeting system had not been fully adjusted for the change in ballistic characteristics dictated by low gravity. The missiles impacted twenty meters away from the *Mad Dog*, and before Aidan could get off a second shot, Megasa had moved his 'Mech into a field of rubble and boulders. Although the other man's 'Mech was not jump-capable, the big steps it took turned into low-arc leaps.

Megasa fired with each step. Aidan could sense his 'Mech's torso armor flying off, sailing long distances before settling onto the ground among small dust clouds. A missile he had not even seen until the last instant hit his *Summoner* high on the torso, near the shoulder. The recoil from the impact startled Aidan, and his 'Mech was nearly knocked off its feet as it stumbled backward and turned 180 degrees, giving Megasa a clear shot at its back.

Planetside, in the command center, the large audience was struggling to get a good view of the holographic version of the battle on the moon. When Megasa's missile hit and spun Aidan's *Summoner* around, followed by a peppering of laser pulse shots to the 'Mech's back, the pro-Megasa audience laughed out loud. Marthe shrank back slightly from the railing, appalled as much by her fellow warriors' vindictiveness as she was by Aidan's plight.

When someone suddenly laid a hand on her shoulder, she whirled around, ready to fight anyone who dared touch her. She recognized Kael Pershaw from his participation in the Grand Council session.

"May we talk, Star Captain?" he asked.

"I do not wish to leave here. Perhaps after the battle?"

"What I have to say can be said here. Everyone is concentrating on the battle anyway."

Marthe turned her own attention back to the projection. Aidan's *Summoner* had turned around and was now firing wildly, alternating between its LB 10-X and its PPC.

No, Aidan, she thought, *you are using up your ammo too fast. You cannot go for the kill this early with a master warrior like Megasa.*

"I have been watching you," Kael Pershaw said. "Your body leans toward the battle when Star Commander Aidan is doing the fighting. I know you came from the same sibko. You are helping him, are you not?"

"I suppose I am free to admit that now, yes. No violation of Clan law or custom is involved."

"Then why keep it secret? Are you ashamed to help a warrior who previously fought as a freebirth?

Ashamed to support a warrior against whom nearly everyone else is arrayed?''

"I feel no shame. My clandestine participation was political, not strategic. I do not agree with the charges against Star Commander Aidan, and I believe he deserves this chance, that is all.''

"It may interest you to know, Star Captain, that I agree with you.''

That was perhaps the only thing Kael Pershaw might have said that could draw Marthe's attention away from the battle scene. By now Megasa had retreated a bit, using the mountainous terrain to escape from Aidan's heavy fire, rendering much of it useless. The expended fire made a pretty picture as it rose off Rhea's surface like new rays of moonlight.

"You support his cause. I thought, as his commanding officer, that you despised him.''

"I did, and perhaps still do. But ever since he defeated Lopar in the first round of this Trial of Bloodright, I have come to admire his skill. That is all there is to it, and I wanted someone on his side to know it. But Star Captain Joanna will not listen, and I cannot converse with the freebirth MechWarrior, so I am telling you.''

A roar from the crowd whisked Marthe's attention back to the holographic scene. Megasa had come out from the rock formation, sending off two missile salvos. With the massive dust cloud stirred up by the failed missiles, for a moment it looked as though the shots had actually destroyed Aidan and his *Summoner*. The next moment Marthe was relieved to see the 'Mech walk steadily out of the cloud of debris. When she turned back to Kael Pershaw, he was gone.

She had no time to wonder about that for the battle scene was compelling. What she saw made her gasp in shock, perhaps the strongest reaction she had shown to anything since her sibko days. Aidan's *Summoner* was on the run, heading toward the *Mad Dog* at too great a speed, the fire from his weapons preceding him. The speed at which he was moving created an illusion that he might run into his own fire and explode his own BattleMech. It was not the illusion that concerned Marthe, however. She had warned Aidan about moving too fast in the moon's low gravity.

On Rhea a BattleMech could travel six times faster than in normal gravity, but such low gravity affected the structural integrity of a running 'Mech. Anything could happen, from the freezing of myomer muscle clumps to fractures on any surface area.

What Marthe feared finally happened. As the *Summoner* ran along, its left leg came down hard on the moon's surface. The leg, built to support a seventy-ton 'Mech running at eighty-six kilometers per hour, was a mechanical marvel of supports and shock absorbers. But Aidan was testing its limits and surpassing them threefold. It was no surprise when the 'Mech's leg snapped off at the knee.

As the lower leg fell away like a gantry at a rocket launch, dust enveloped the 'Mech's foot. The *Summoner* continued forward, the Mech's momentum making it look as though it had hopped several steps more. Then it began to topple like an exploded building. It fell sideways, then abruptly disappeared.

Aidan sensed the fall even before he knew his 'Mech's leg had snapped off. He tried to control his fall by moving the left leg inward, but because it was now a "phantom" leg, nothing happened.

The 'Mech came to the edge of a wide hole and teetered there for a moment. Then the right foot slipped forward, sending the *Summoner* plunging into the deep, wide pit.

The 'Mech bounced once off the wall of the pit, which turned it sideways for the rest of the fall. It came to rest at the bottom of the pit, the impact knocking Aidan unconscious.

The holographic projection did not recreate the pit. Aidan's *Summoner* merely disappeared from view the way things did on flatscreen video.

Marthe watched Megasa's 'Mech come to a stop and seem to stare at the pit before ambling to the edge. She wondered whether the judges had already decided

on the match's outcome. If Megasa wished, he could claim victory now, then permit rescue teams to get Aidan out of his 'Mech. But Marthe knew that Megasa, like all the other Bloodright participants, had vowed to kill Aidan, and she knew that was on his mind now. He had plenty of ammunition left. All he needed to do was fire it into the pit. Aidan could not eject. In Rhea's vacuum, he would die immediately. His only hope was the one thing that could not happen—that Megasa would give him his life.

Joanna was now beside her, having pushed several warriors aside to approach the rail. "He did it again," she said.

"Did what?" Marthe said morosely.

"Over-reached. That has been his history. In battles, Trials, in personality conflicts. He would have qualified in his first Trial but for that flaw."

Marthe did not wish to talk of this now. She especially resented Joanna's cold, clinical tone.

Megasa was standing at the edge of the pit, his 'Mech's torso leaning over the hole so that its pilot could look down into it.

When he came to, Aidan was groggy. Looking up, he saw the *Mad Dog* bending over the pit. And there was Megasa at the viewport, obviously checking on Aidan visually, not trusting his sensors to give the accurate picture he wanted of Aidan's pathetic circumstances.

Shaking off his daze, Aidan checked his weapons systems on the secondary screen. It showed that the few missiles left were useless because of the angles of the launch mount. And with the PPC destroyed, his only operable weapon was the LB 10-X. According to the onscreen data, however, its ammo feed had jammed. Besides, only one cluster round was chambered in the weapon. A glorified shotgun shell to be used against a raging elephant.

Seeing Megasa wave from his cockpit, Aidan saw no point in firing his weapon. He was already dead. He wanted to shut his eyes and simply accept his fate.

But no, even now, something in him could not give

up. He had never been able to give up. In cadet maneuvers, he had persisted in trying every maneuver or
strategy even when it went against the training given
the sibko. At his first Trial, he had nearly won with
unorthodox tactics. The same kind of performance had
won his second Trial. His experiences as a warrior
reinforced the tenacity that must have been with him
from the moment he dropped from the canister. As
with all his victories, it had been his ability to perse-
vere that had also won the victory at Glory Station.

He did not give up then. He would not give up now.

Quickly lining up his shot, aiming it for the part of the
Mad Dog's upper torso that was visible over the pit, he
fired. He planned the cluster of shots as a final defiance
against Megasa and, for that matter, all the other Jade
Falcons who so despised him. They would, of course,
never know that. But he knew and that was enough.

He watched all the essentially ineffectual hits dotting the
Mad Dog's upper torso in a patternless way. He even saw
the dust raised by a hit against the surface of the cockpit.

At first, however, he did not see that the cockpit hit
had created a hairline fracture. The first sign of the hit
was the stream of vapor escaping in a thin line that
quickly expanded. It was then that Aidan saw the fracture, which widened even as he watched. The last sign
was the face of Megasa coming forward, eyes wide,
skin paling, mouth opening.

In a sudden rush of decompression, the cockpit exploded
outward. Megasa apparently flew out with it, but Aidan did
not see him. Some of the debris, maybe some of Megasa,
settled down onto the *Summoner* buried in the pit.

Perhaps it was shock, perhaps he was still dazed
from the fall. Whatever the cause, Aidan fell into un-
consciousness before he could react further to the
events of the last few moments. As the world around
him went dark and void, all he knew was that he had
just won the Trial of Bloodright. Aidan had won his
Bloodname.

Epilogue

A few years after Aidan won his Bloodname, his daughter Diana, of whose existence he was still ignorant, qualified in her Trial of Position and became a warrior.

Had she defeated more than one 'Mech at the Trial, she would have begun her career as a Clan warrior with the rank of Star Commander. She had won respectably against only one 'Mech, however, and so it was MechWarrior Diana who climbed down the side of her *Hellbringer* at the end of her Trial. The 'Mech's surface was still so hot that accidentally touching it burned the palm of her hand.

Though proud and happy, Diana had no grandiose notions about her warrior status because she could never compete for a Bloodname. She merely wanted the privilege of being part of her Clan's invasion of the Inner Sphere, which had just begun. She was, in fact, eager to join her unit.

The Bloodname issue that had so obsessed her father would not drive her life. She was, after all, the product of a union between Aidan and his former sibkin Peri. Though the daughter of the two trueborns, her natural birth made her a freeborn and forever ineligible to win a Bloodname. Diana did not really mind that. She did not even mind that the trues showed so much contempt for her kind. Perhaps she had simply grown so accustomed to it that it seemed merely a fact of life. Like her father, she had fought many a truebirth who taunted her, but that was more an acceptance of the necessity to fight back as a freeborn legacy.

Standing alongside the massive foot of her *Hellbringer*, Diana gave it a salute. You got me this far, she told the 'Mech silently. Now I will do right by you.

In all the time she had dreamed of being a warrior, Diana had never imagined encountering her father. She saw no reason why he would want to see or know her. What trueborn would seek to acknowledge a freeborn child? Trueborns, of course, rarely met either geneparent.

Diana had known only her mother, but like a trueborn, she had wanted nothing more from life than to be a Clan warrior. Now that her wish had become reality, she looked forward to a fulfilling future in service to the Clan. Envisioning that future did not yet include any fantasies of knowing her father.

As she walked away from her 'Mech, she clenched and unclenched her right hand, testing the burn that still stung painfully.

Peri, now an important scientist, sent her blessing, but did not come to see her daughter off on the day her unit began its long journey across the stars that would take them to join the invasion of the Inner Sphere.

While Diana was beginning her days as a warrior, another was ending his life in Clan service. He was Ter Roshak by name, and had lived out the years of his vindication as though they were years of disgrace instead. He was welcome in none of the places where he wanted welcome, no longer had a single friend among warriors, had no position in the ranks. He was an old warrior now, sixty-one years of age and considered useless to the Clan.

Well, not completely useless. He was part of an infantry unit composed of warriors judged too old to pilot a 'Mech or engage in combat except as cannon fodder to accomplish some larger military end. That infantry unit was on a planet somewhere deep in the Inner Sphere, a place that for so long had been only a dream in the hearts of the Clansmen whose ancestors had exiled themselves generations before. The inva-

LAUBENSTEIN ·91·

sion the Clans had been preparing for all those generations had begun, but Ter Roshak did not even know the name of this world or how the battle was going.

All the members of his unit had been issued uniforms, boots, a gun, and a knife, then sent on this march on foot toward the enemy. Ter Roshak was no fool, he knew what was happening. This trek was exactly why all the old warriors of this unit had joined.

As they drew nearer the front, Ter Roshak saw 'Mechs spread across a wide, hilly clearing. With the Clan 'Mechs in temporary retreat, the commanders needed to buy some time. To do that, Ter Roshak's unit was to march directly into the enemy, firing at them with outdated, old weapons, equipment that was expendable if dropped in the field.

They were all going to die, but their deaths would buy other Clan warriors time to regroup, reload, and recharge. Their commanding officer had ordered Ter Roshak's unit to stay alive as long as they could, and to keep on shooting the whole time. If they ran out of ammo, they were to use knives. If they lost their knives, then they must go after the nearest enemy with their bare hands. If their hands were broken, they must kick the enemy with their feet. If their feet were shot off, they must crawl to the enemy warriors and try in some other way to kill them. If they could not crawl, then they must fire into the nearest brush. If they could not move, then they must simply wait to die. If they could not die, then there must be something wrong with their attitude.

Ter Roshak marched forward, feeling more elation than he had for a long time. He had not known such excitement since the days when he and his 'Mech had ridden alongside Ramon Mattlov. Ramon Mattlov would be proud of him now. Firing his weapon here, in this battle, Ter Roshak would cleanse the dishonor that had stained his existence for so long. With each squeeze of the trigger, his heart and spirit lightened a bit more.

He knew he would die soon.

That knowledge gave him joy, and relief.

GLOSSARY

During the fall of the Star League, General Nicholas Kerensky, commander of the Regular Star League Army, led his forces out of the Inner Sphere in what is known as the Exodus. After settling beyond the Periphery, the Star League Army itself collapsed. Out of the ashes of the civilization Kerensky's forces tried to create rose the Clans.

Clan military unit designations are used throughout this book. The structure of each unit is as follows:

Point	1 'Mech or 5 infantry Elementals
Star	5 'Mechs or 25 Elementals
Binary	2 Stars
Trinary	3 Stars
Cluster	4 Binaries
Galaxy	3-5 Clusters
Nova	1 'Mech Star and 1 infantry Star
Supernova	1 'Mech Binary and 2 infantry Stars

AUTOCANNON

A rapid-firing, auto-loading weapon, the autocannon fires high-speed streams of high-explosive, armor-piercing shells.

BATCHALL

The *batchall* is the ritual by which Clan warriors issue combat challenges. Defenders may request that the attacker risk something of worth comparable to what the defender is risking in the contest.

BATTLEMECHS

BattleMechs are the most powerful war machines ever built. Ten to twelve meters tall and equipped with potent weapons, they pack enough firepower to flatten anything but another 'Mech.

BLOODING

Blooding is another name for the Trial of Position that determines if a candidate will qualify as a Clan warrior. The candidate must first demonstrate physical prowess in personal combat by defeating at least one of three successive opponents. If he defeats one, he begins his service as a MechWarrior. If he defeats two, or all three, he is immediately ranked as an officer in his Clan. If he fails to defeat any of his opponents, he is relegated to a lower caste.

BLOODNAME

Bloodname refers to the surname of each of the 800 Warriors who stood with Nicholas Kerensky during the Exodus Civil War. These 800 are the foundation of the Clans' elaborate breeding program. The right to use one of these surnames has been the ambition of every Clan warrior since the system was established. Only 25 warriors are allowed to use any one surname at one time. When one of the 25 Bloodnamed warriors dies, a trial is held to determine who will assume that Bloodname. A contender must prove his Bloodname lineage, then win a series of duels with other competitors.

Bloodnames are determined matrilineally, at least after the original generation. Because a warrior can inherit only from his or her female parent, he or she can have a claim to only one Bloodname.

BLOODRIGHT

A specific Bloodname lineage is called a Bloodright. Twenty-five Bloodrights are attached to each Bloodname. A Bloodright is not a lineage as we define the term, because the warriors who successively hold a Bloodright might be related only through their original ancestor. As with Bloodnames, certain Bloodrights are considered more prestigious than others.

CANISTER

Clan slang for the eugenics program of the warrior caste. It can also refer specifically to the artificial wombs.

CASTE

Clan society is rigidly divided into five castes: warrior, scientist, merchant, technician, and laborer. Each caste has many subcastes based on specialties within a professional field. The warrior caste increases its numbers and controls genetic heritage by a systematic eugenics program using genetic material of prestigious, successful current and past warriors (see **Sibko**). Other castes maintain a quality gene pool by strategic marriages within each caste.

CODEX

Each warrior's codex is his or her individual identification. It includes the names of the original Bloodnamed warriors from which a warrior is descended. It also includes his generation number, Blood House, and codex ID, an alphanumeric code noting the unique aspects of that person's DNA.

DROPSHIP

Because JumpShips must generally avoid entering the heart of a solar system, they must "park" at a considerable distance from the system's inhabited worlds. DropShips were developed for interplanetary travel. As the name implies, a DropShip is attached to hardpoints on the JumpShip's drive core, later to be dropped from the parent vessel after in-system entry.

Though incapable of FTL travel, DropShips are highly maneuverable, well-armed, and sufficiently aerodynamic to take off from and land on a planetary surface. The journey from the jump point to the inhabited worlds of a system usually requires a normal-space journey of several days or weeks, depending on the type of star.

ELEMENTAL

The elite battlesuited infantry of the Clans. These men and women are physical giants, bred specifically to handle Clan-developed battle armor.

FREEBORN

An individual conceived and born by natural means is freeborn. Because the Clans value their eugenics program so highly, a freebirth is automatically assumed to have little potential.

KHAN

Each Clan elects two Khans. One serves as the Clan's senior military commander and bureaucratic administrator. The second Khan's position is less well-defined. He or she is second-in-command, and carries out duties assigned by the first Khan. In times of great internal or external threat, or when a coordinated effort is required of all Clans, an ilKhan is chosen to serve as the supreme ruler of the Clans.

JUMPSHIP

Interstellar travel is accomplished via JumpShips, first developed in the twenty-second century. The ship is named for its ability to "jump" instantaneously from one point to another across distances of up to 30 light years per jump.

JumpShips never land on planets, and only rarely travel into the inner areas of a star system. Interplanetary travel is carried out by DropShips, vessels that attach themselves to the JumpShip until arrival at the jump point.

LASER

An acronym for "Light Amplification through Stimulated Emission of Radiation." When used as a weapon, a laser damages its target by concentrating extreme heat on a small area. BattleMech lasers are designated as small, medium, and large. Lasers are also available as shoulder-fired weapons operating from a portable backpack power unit. Certain range-finders and targeting equipment employ low-level lasers also.

LOREMASTER

The Loremaster is the keeper of Clan laws and history. The position is honorable and politically powerful. The Loremaster plays a key role in inquiries and trials, where he is often assigned the role of Advocate or Interrogator.

LRM

This is an abbreviation for Long-Range Missile, an indirect-fire missile with a high-explosive warhead.

OATHMASTER

The Oathmaster is the honor guard for any official Clan ceremony. The position is similar to that of an Inner Sphere sergeant-at-arms, but it carries a greater degree of respect. The Oathmaster administers all oaths, and the Loremaster records them. The position of Oathmaster is usually held by the oldest Bloodnamed Warrior in a Clan (if he or she desires the honor), and is one of the few positions not decided by combat.

PERIPHERY

Beyond the borders of the Inner Sphere lies the Periphery, the vast domain of known and unknown worlds stretching endlessly into interstellar night. Once populated by colonies from Terra, these were devastated technologically, politically, and economically by the fall of the Star League. At present, the Periphery is the refuge of piratical Bandit Kings, privateers, and outcasts from the Inner Sphere.

PPC

This abbreviation stands for particle projection cannon, a magnetic accelerator firing high-energy proton or ion bolts, causing damage both through impact and high temperature. PPCs are among the most effective weapons available to BattleMechs.

REMEMBRANCE, THE

The Remembrance is an ongoing heroic saga detailing Clan history beginning with the Exodus from the Inner Sphere to current time. *The Remembrance* is continually expanded to include contemporary events. Each Clan has a slightly different version reflecting their own opinions and experiences.

SEYLA

This word is the ritual response voiced in unison by those witnessing solemn Clan ceremonies, rituals, and other important gatherings. No one is sure of the origin or exact meaning of the word, but it is uttered only with the greatest reverence and awe.

SIBKO

A group of children from the warrior caste eugenics program who have the same male and female gene-parents and are raised together as a sibko. As they mature, they are constantly tested. In the course of testing, many members of the sibko will fail, or flush out, and be transferred to the lower castes. A sibko consists of approximately 20 members, but usually only four or five remain at the time of the final test to become warriors, the Trial of Position.

SRM

This is the abbreviation for short-range missiles, direct trajectory missiles with high-explosive or armor-piercing explosive warheads. They have a range of less than one kilometer, and are accurate only at ranges of less than 300 meters. They are more powerful, however, than LRMs.

STAR LEAGUE

The Star League was formed in 2571 in an attempt to peacefully ally the major star systems inhabited by the human race after it had taken to the stars. The League prospered for almost 200 years, until civil war broke out in 2751. The League was eventually destroyed when the ruling body, known as the High Council, disbanded in the midst of a struggle for power. Each of the royal House rulers then declared himself First Lord of the Star League, and within months, war engulfed the Inner Sphere. This conflict has continued to the present day, almost three centuries later. These centuries of continuous war are now known simply as the Succession Wars.

SUCCESSOR LORDS

Each of the five Successor States is ruled by a family descended from one of the original Council Lords of the old Star League. All five royal House Lords claim the title of First Lord, and they have been at each other's throats since the beginning of the Succession Wars in 2786. Their battleground is the vast Inner Sphere, which is composed of all the star systems once occupied by Star League's member-states.

SURKAI

The *surkai* is the Right of Forgiveness. The Clans honor uniformity in thought and belief above all other tenets of their society. When warriors disagree, when a Clan disagrees with the Clan Council, or when a member of one caste offends a member of another caste, *surkai* is expected. It is a matter of pride that the offending party freely admit his wrongdoing and request punishment.

SURKAIREDE

The Rede of Forgiveness, or *surkairede,* is the honor-bound agreement between the majority and any dissenters. According to the *surkairede,* once a dissenter accepts punishment for having disagreed with the majority, he should be allowed to resume his role in society without suffering any further disgrace for having spoken out.

TRIAL OF BLOODRIGHT

A series of one-on-one, single-elimination contests is used to determine who wins the right to use a Bloodname. Each current Bloodnamed warrior in that Bloodname's House nominates one candidate. The head of the House nominates additional candidates to fill thirty-one slots. The thirty-second slot is fought for by those who qualify for the Bloodname but who were not nominated. The nature of the competition is determined by "coining." Each combatant places his personal medallion, a *dogids,* into the "Well of Decision." An Oathmaster or Loremaster releases the coins simultaneously, so that only chance determines which coin falls first to the bottom of the well. The warrior whose coin lands on top chooses the manner of the combat ('Mech versus 'Mech, barehanded, 'Mech versus Elemental, and so forth). The other warrior chooses the venue of the contest. Though these Bloodname duels need not be to the death, the fierce combat and the intensity of the combatants often leave the losing candidate mortally wounded or dead.

TRIAL OF POSITION

The Trial of Position determines whether a candidate will qualify as a warrior in the Clans. To qualify, he must defeat at least one of three successive opponents. If he defeats two, or all three, he is immediately ranked as an officer in his Clan. If he fails to defeat any of his opponents, he is relegated to a lower caste.

TRIAL OF POSSESSION

This trial resolves conflicts in which two or more Clans claim the right to the same thing, be it territory, a warrior's genes, or even supremacy in a difference of opinion. This trial uses the formal challenge of the attacker and the response of defending forces, and favors those commanders from the attacking Clan skillful enough to bid minimal forces.

TRIAL OF REFUSAL

The Clan councils and the Grand Council vote on issues and laws that affect the community. Unlike Inner Sphere legislation, however, any decision can be challenged and reversed by a Trial of Refusal. This trial allows the losing side to demand the issue be settled by combat.

The forces used in the Trial of Refusal are determined on a pro-rated basis. For example, if the contested vote carried by a three-to-one margin, the attacking forces can field a force three times the size of the force challenging the decision. Bidding often results in a smaller attacking force, however.

TRUEBORN/TRUEBIRTH

A trueborn is a product of the warrior caste's eugenics program.

Type: Adder
Mass: 35 tons
Chassis: Endo Steel
Power Plant: 210 XL
Cruising Speed: 64.8 kph
Maximum Speed: 97.2 kph
Jump Jets: None
    Jump Capacity: None
Armor: Ferro-Fibrous
Armament:
    1 Flamer
    16.25 tons of pod space available

ADDER

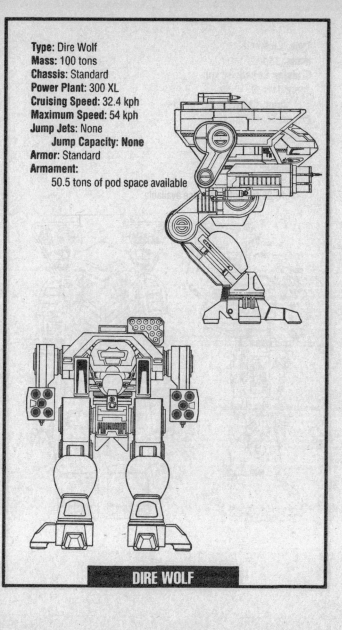

Type: Dire Wolf
Mass: 100 tons
Chassis: Standard
Power Plant: 300 XL
Cruising Speed: 32.4 kph
Maximum Speed: 54 kph
Jump Jets: None
    Jump Capacity: None
Armor: Standard
Armament:
    50.5 tons of pod space available

DIRE WOLF

Type: Elemental
Mass: 1 ton
Cruising Speed: 32 kph
Jump Jets: 3
  Jump Capacity: 90 meters
Armor: Ferro-Fibrous
Armament:
  1 SRM 2
  1 Small Laser

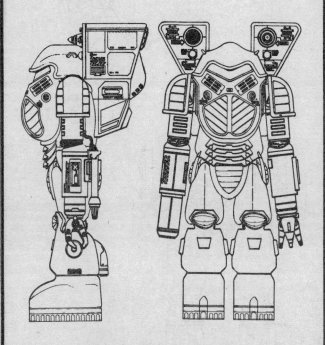

ELEMENTAL

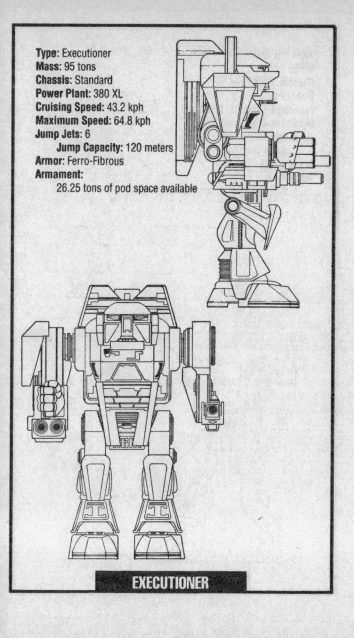

Type: Executioner
Mass: 95 tons
Chassis: Standard
Power Plant: 380 XL
Cruising Speed: 43.2 kph
Maximum Speed: 64.8 kph
Jump Jets: 6
    Jump Capacity: 120 meters
Armor: Ferro-Fibrous
Armament:
    26.25 tons of pod space available

EXECUTIONER

Type: Fire Moth
Mass: 20 tons
Chassis: Endo Steel
Power Plant: 200 XL
Cruising Speed: 108 kph
Maximum Speed: 162 kph
Jump Jets: None
    Jump Capacity: None
Armor: Ferro-Fibrous
Armament:
    6.75 tons of pod space available

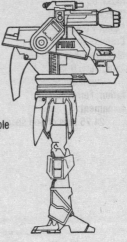

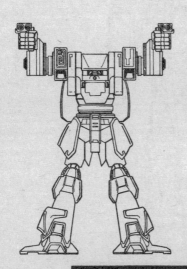

FIRE MOTH

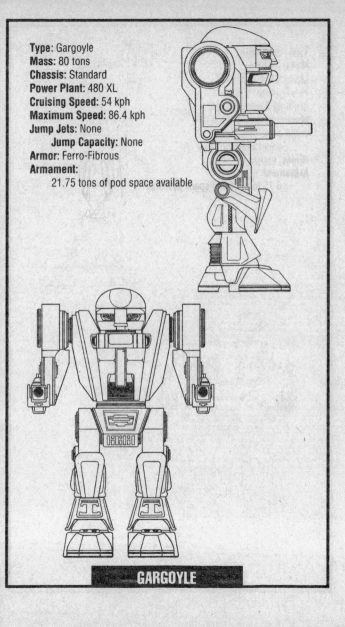

Type: Gargoyle
Mass: 80 tons
Chassis: Standard
Power Plant: 480 XL
Cruising Speed: 54 kph
Maximum Speed: 86.4 kph
Jump Jets: None
　　Jump Capacity: None
Armor: Ferro-Fibrous
Armament:
　　21.75 tons of pod space available

GARGOYLE

Type: Hellbringer
Mass: 65 tons
Chassis: Standard
Power Plant: 325 XL
Cruising Speed: 54 kph
Maximum Speed: 86.4 kph
Jump Jets: None
  Jump Capacity: None
Armor: Standard
Armament:
   28.75 tons of pod space available

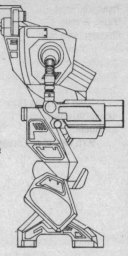

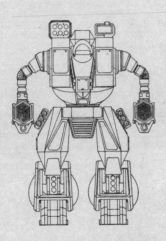

HELLBRINGER

Type: Ice Ferret
Mass: 45 tons
Chassis: Endo Steel
Power Plant: 360 XL
Cruising Speed: 86.4 kph
Maximum Speed: 129.6 kph
Jump Jets: None
      Jump Capacity: None
Armor: Ferro-Fibrous
Armament:
      9.75 tons of pod space available

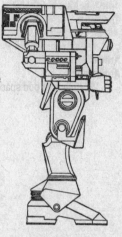

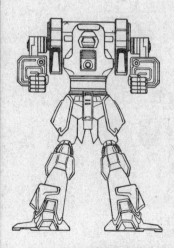

ICE FERRET

Type: Kit Fox
Mass: 30 tons
Chassis: Endo Steel
Power Plant: 180 XL
Cruising Speed: 64.8 kph
Maximum Speed: 97.2 kph
Jump Jets: None
Jump Capacity: None
Armor: Ferro-Fibrous
Armament:
16 tons of pod space available

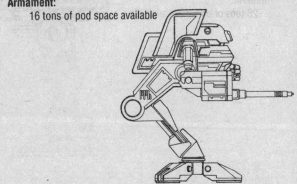

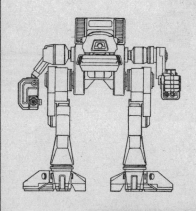

KIT FOX

Type: Mad Dog
Mass: 60 tons
Chassis: Standard
Power Plant: 300 XL
Cruising Speed: 54 kph
Maximum Speed: 86.4 kph
Jump Jets: None
    Jump Capacity: None
Armor: Ferro-Fibrous
Armament:
    28 tons of pod space available

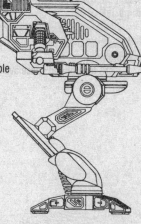

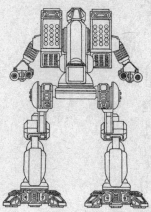

MAD DOG

Type: Mist Lynx
Mass: 25 tons
Chassis: Endo Steel
Power Plant: 175 XL
Cruising Speed: 75.6 kph
Maximum Speed: 118.8 kph
Jump Jets: 6
    Jump Capacity: 180 meters
Armor: Ferro-Fibrous
Armament:
    8.75 tons of pod space available

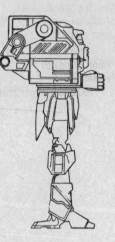

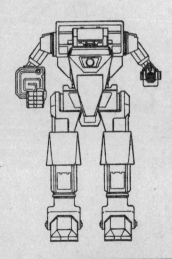

MIST LYNX

Type: Nova
Mass: 50 tons
Chassis: Standard
Power Plant: 250 XL
Cruising Speed: 54 kph
Maximum Speed: 86.4 kph
Jump Jets: 5
    Jump Capacity: 150 meters
Armor: Standard
Armament:
    16.25 tons of pod space available

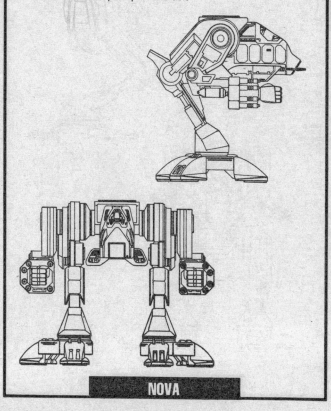

NOVA

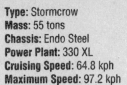

Type: Stormcrow
Mass: 55 tons
Chassis: Endo Steel
Power Plant: 330 XL
Cruising Speed: 64.8 kph
Maximum Speed: 97.2 kph
Jump Jets: None
    Jump Capacity: None
Armor: Ferro-Fibrous
Armament:
    23 tons of pod space available

STORMCROW

Type: Summoner
Mass: 70 tons
Chassis: Standard
Power Plant: 350 XL
Cruising Speed: 54 kph
Maximum Speed: 86.4 kph
Jump Jets: 5
    Jump Capacity: 150 meters
Armor: Ferro-Fibrous
Armament:
    22.75 tons of pod space available

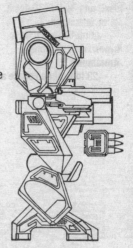

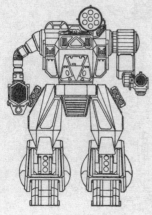

SUMMONER

Type: Timber Wolf
Mass: 75 tons
Chassis: Endo Steel
Power Plant: 375 XL
Cruising Speed: 54 kph
Maximum Speed: 86.4 kph
Jump Jets: None
    Jump Capacity: None
Armor: Ferro-Fibrous
Armament:
    28 tons of pod space available

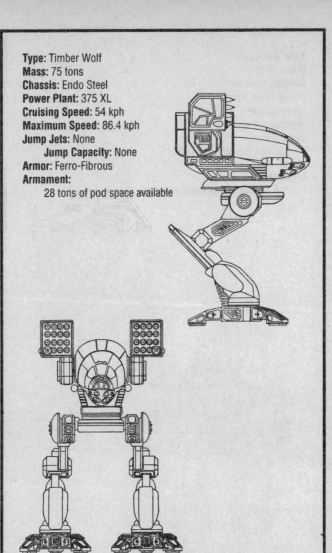

TIMBER WOLF

Type: Viper
Mass: 40 tons
Chassis: Endo Steel
Power Plant: 320 XL
Cruising Speed: 86.4 kph
Maximum Speed: 129.6 kph
Jump Jets: 8
    Jump Capacity: 240 meters
Armor: Ferro-Fibrous
Armament:
    8.75 tons of pod space available

VIPER

Type: Warhawk
Mass: 85 tons
Chassis: Standard
Power Plant: 340 XL
Cruising Speed: 43.2 kph
Maximum Speed: 64.8 kph
Jump Jets: None
    Jump Capacity: None
Armor: Ferro-Fibrous
Armament:
    32.5 tons of pod space available

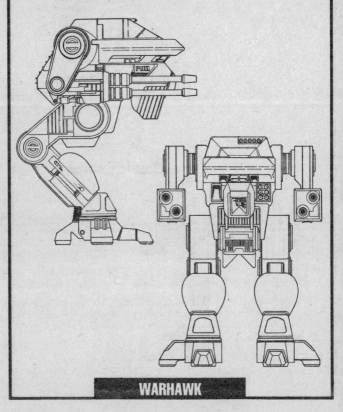

WARHAWK